ABOUT THE AU

C000135604

Born with an obsession for the written word, ̶g̶a̶t̶e̶d̶ ̶h̶e̶r̶ youth armed with pen, paper and an overactive imagination, characters whispering to her from the shadows.

Rowena weaves romantic tales of flawed heroes who fall hard and love deeply, and strong, passionate heroines courageous enough to take a risk.

She lives on her farm with her husband, doing her best writing against the backdrop of Victoria's breathtaking South Gippsland hills, surrounded by cows, sheep, and one crazy dog.

For more information about RowenaSpark and her books visit www.rowenaspark.com and facebook.com/RowenaSparkAuthor

ALSO BY ROWENA SPARK

STAND ALONE ROMANCE

Her Whole Heart

SCARS OF CREDENCE SERIES

Credence

Prudence (Release 2020)

Reticence (Release 2021)

Stealing BRYNN

ROWENA SPARK

LIME TIGER ENTERPRISES

COPYRIGHT

STEALING BRYNN
By Rowena Spark

Please note: This is a work of fiction. Characters, places and incidents are fictitious. Any resemblance to people, places or real situation are purely coincidental.

First published 2020
© Leanne Poulter All rights reserved.

No part of this book can be reproduced in any form, or by any means, graphic, electronic, mechanical, including photocopying, recording, taping or by any storage retrieval system persons or entity without written permission from the author, except in the case of brief quotations embodied in book reviews or critical articles related to the subject matter.
The author has made every effort to contact copyright holders for material used in this book.
Any persons or organisation that may may have been overlooked should contact the author.

NATIONAL LIBRARY OF AUSTRALIA
A catalogue record of this book is available from: www.trove.nla.gov.au

ISBN (print): 978-0-6489089-2-0
ISBN (eBook): 978-0-6489089-3-7
Editor: Sharyn Constantine
Cover Design: White Clover Creative
Cover Images: Shutterstock: Dark Moon Pictures/Puppy 4
Interior Design: White Clover Creative
Print typesetting and eBook production: Adobe Indesign

CHAPTER 1

KADE

I lean my elbows on the wooden handrails around my veranda and watch the last of the night burn down with the fiery oranges and pinks of dawn. My favourite part of the day. I imagine if I listen hard enough, I can hear a faint sound that vibrates over the world at the very moment night becomes day. I shiver when the temperature drops a couple of degrees as the sun chases away the remnant stale air of the old night.

Rebirth. New hope. I need this time each day to centre myself and reconnect with the earth. Chase away the thoughts and demons that crawl through my head every night and remind me that everything I care about turns to poison. Relentless voices in my mind telling me I'm not enough.

I draw a lungful of air in an attempt to erase the thought, clean my coffee mug and put it away with the rest of them. The set of six matching mugs mock me in their ordered white lines. The only time I use a second mug is when Mum comes to visit. Nobody else has set foot on my land in the years since I moved in just three months after my eighteenth birthday.

I love the farm. There's something about it that makes me feel like I truly belong somewhere, and watching my cows fatten and my crops flourish is a soul deep nourishment. I slip on my torn, stained jeans, consider the weather and forgo the shirt, feeling the breeze tickle my skin as I work. I hitch up the post driver to my tractor, the faithful diesel chugging and growling in wait. It's a perfect day to fence a new paddock.

***

"You're quiet." Mum murmurs, running her hand down my spine.

I drag my hand over my face and blink up at her, watching her lips thin. This is why I love Mum. Just a glance and she understands. I don't have to try to explain the often overwhelming storm of turbulent emotions just beneath my skin. They're feelings I don't recognise in other people, as if they have managed to trap them all away deep inside and not have to feel the heaviness of sadness or the sting of hurt. Or if Mum is truly right, nobody else has them in the first place, at least not the way I do.

"You have to talk, Kade. You need to open your mouth and use that voice of yours. Nobody can read minds, and you're not doing yourself any favors hiding in the shadows."

I shuffle in the seat, shifting my gaze to the cup of tea she set before me.

"You know that's not me. That's what you had Daryl for, to do all the social things I won't." I snap.

My jaw clamps on his name. Daryl. My little brother and golden child, blonde haired, blue eyed heir to the Walker Empire.

Mum's breath sinks her shoulders as she lowers beside me on the couch.

With a silent glance, I apologise for my tone and she accepts with a gentle pat of my knee. The light from the window glints off her favourite ring and I touch the green stone, running my fingers over it the way I always do. Father hates that she refuses to take it off. Although he constantly showers her with diamonds, all she ever wears is her wedding band, and this intricately designed green sapphire.

"You need to start somewhere, Kade. You can't shut yourself away from the world on that farm of yours just because you're afraid of the pain. At some point you'll need to learn how to stop reacting so aggressively and driving people away. Sometimes, no matter how debilitating the hurt might be, it's worth it."

Her eyes shimmer and I know she's immersed in her own secret pain. One we used to share before she stopped talking about it.

Or I did. I can't remember any more. The more I felt rejected, the less I spoke, so maybe I was the one who let the topic of our shared past slip away.

I'm not like Daryl at all. Social gatherings make me uncomfortable; the trite conversations leave my feet itching with the urge to escape. What my head thinks rarely falls off my tongue the same way. Whatever I say when I step from my comfort zone carries the sharp defensive tone almost always mistaken for aggression. I open my mouth and watch faces recoil in horror or disgust, strangers forming their conclusions before I can take another breath. Sometimes I'm even grateful to Father for excluding me from the family responsibilities, making excuses for my absences where he deems appropriate. These days, my lack of presence isn't often remarked upon since anyone who's anyone knows I'm the black sheep of the family. They all have different stories of my violence, or my unlawful behaviour, but they don't understand that sometimes the only law some men respect is the one with hard knuckles.

But I can never seem to shake that persistent, niggling awareness that reminds me that everyone I dare to love turns their back on me. At first I thought I'd imagined the prickle of detachment emanating from Father, but it was only when my little brother came along that I finally realised the truth of it. Father would glare at me, reprimand me for the slightest faults, and he'd save every one of his smiles for Daryl. No matter the lengths I'd go to to win his affection, it only served to heighten his resentment towards me.

Father wasn't the first to find me lacking, and he wasn't the last.

They all know the story of the copper's son whose jaw I fractured, but none of them seemed to remember the underage girl I pulled sobbing from his car and returned safely home before I was taken away in handcuffs. I should have told the cops what really happened, but Bella made me swear I wouldn't tell.

Even as a younger man, I kept my word. I think Mum suspected there was more to the story, but she just looked at me like she always does, with that expression of pain that twists my gut, and kept her mouth closed.

I lift my face to her and find her eyes still on mine. She's elegant and cultured, as is expected of the wife of Antony Walker, but sometimes I catch a glimpse of the carefree and wild woman I know she used to be. She hides it well, yet often, when she's alone, she unlocks the box inside her and sets it free for a few stolen moments.

"I'll try, Mum. I love you."

She answers with a kiss to my temple.

***

I don't know what possesses me to torture myself in the frosty company of the prejudiced townsfolk, but I drive into town anyway. Parking behind the small cluster of shops, I walk to the cafe, hands shoved in jeans, head bent to the ground to avoid the stares. There's judgement in every sideways glance, some who already know the texture of my knuckles, and others who made up their minds about me from the juicy tidbits of gossip they hear. Regardless, they're either wrong or guilty, but it doesn't stop the sting.

"Usual, Kade?" The gentle voice sends the knot to my throat, even with my signature scowl firmly in place.

Sometimes I think Mrs. Curtis and Bella are the only people besides Mum in this miserable town brave enough to make up their own minds about me. They watch me sometimes with a sadness that makes it seem like they talk about me when I'm not around, but neither of them say anything to me. And Bella; the girl I saved? Mrs Curtis' daughter grew into a lovely girl. And she's Brynn's best friend.

Brynn. We used to be inseparable, Brynn, Daryl and me. As kids there wasn't a free moment Brynn wasn't in our house, or we were at her's. Funny how time changes things. These days, there's nothing but bitterness and resentment between Daryl and me, and Brynn may as well be a stranger to me. She doesn't even spare me a glance anymore.

Bella carries my order to where I'm sprawled in a booth to wait.

"Here y'are Kade. Mum says it's on the house if you stop scaring away the customers with that growly face." Bella holds the takeaway mug just out of reach, eyebrow quirked.

My lips twitch, my scowl softening as I shoot a look at Mrs. Curtis who stands facing me with arms crossed and wide smile. When I reach out, Bella moves my coffee further away, tut-tutting.

I feel my mouth curve, rubbing the nape of my neck as I scrutinise Bella.

"You women play dirty. You know I'm not human until I have my coffee." Slowly I relent, showing my teeth and flicking my obvious reluctance between the pair.

Mrs. Curtis chuckles and turns her attention to a customer while Bella relinquishes my reward. She sinks into the chair opposite me, regret making her eyes shimmer.

I glare at her and keep my mouth shut.

"Why do you insist on hiding under this arsehole exterior as if you prefer the town's prejudice, Kade?" She sighs, and I shrug, dropping my eyes to the table.

"People believe what they like, Bell. I can't change that." Futility crawls in my throat, and I bid goodbye by dropping a twenty on the table.

I lean against the tree trunk, sipping my drink and taking in the quiet streets of Corymbia. Lined with the ancient intertwining limbs of the flowering gums the area is famous for, it's a place I can't seem to want to leave, even though it would be best for everyone if I did. I'm bound to it as if it were an artery, and no matter what the townsfolk think of me, I know I will die here.

It's Wednesday afternoon and nothing much happens in this sleepy Australian town nestled in the foothills of Victoria's Gippsland region. Nothing happening except…my spine straightens.

Brynn's old faded blue sedan pulls into her usual parking spot with one brake light out, and my hands curl into fists. She should have had that fixed weeks ago. That old primal urge to keep her safe pushes against my skin, and it's all I can do not to make the call to arrange a mechanic for her. But it's not my place. It used to be. I used to be the one she ran to when she needed help. Then one day she simply stopped reaching out to me, and in the years since, I never once stopped missing it. The intrinsic need to be the reason she feels safe enough to smile is an ache that won't die.

I stand straighter, lungs bursting with anticipation as she steps out of her car.

It wouldn't be too hard to overlook her beaten up car considering all the similar beaten up cars and battered farm utes around her, but once she appears, it's as if the air itself shifts and gravitates towards her. Brynn is breathtaking. No longer the kid who used to tackle me with fire and fury when I'd tug her ponytail, she's now a woman with delicate curves that make my fingers burn. She wears jeans like a second skin, molded to the swell of her hips and the graceful dip of her waist. Her short top lifts up enough to give me a tantalising flash of bare skin when she pats her hair; thick, dark brown tresses she still ties back in a ponytail. And I still want to tug it. I still burn to watch her eyes ignite as her spirit fights defiantly, because that seems to be what's missing from her these days.

Eyes of deep violet scan the streets, and as usual, they pass right through me. I swallow my disappointment as I watch on, see her delicate features, exotic and perfect like an angel, searching for something.

Me?

If I remind her, will she remember the day when she was ten and I was sixteen, when she danced with me in the storm, soaked to the skin and covered in mud like she was born from the earth itself? Will she remember the way she held me and laughed like she'd never known such happiness? Did she even know that it was the same instant she crashed into my heart?

She's standing there, all alone. Brynn should never be alone. She should have someone at her side, feeling the warmth of her skin, giving her a reason to laugh and setting her spirit free. Pulse thumping through my veins, I push off the tree and walk towards her. She's looking the other way when I cross the street, and I swipe my damp palms over my jeans, eyes zeroed in on her.

When I'm two parked cars away, she turns her head and smiles, and my feet refuse to move me forward any further. It's an expression I breathe for, the upward curl of those delicate lips, the way her chin lifts in pleasure. I can almost feel her excited exhalation from where I stand. Her face is transformed by an adoration that should send me crazy with joy, but instead drives a dagger deep in my heart and gives a sharp twist.

She's not looking at me. She hasn't even noticed me, even though I'm the closest person to her. There's a man crossing the road, a wholesome smile lighting his features, and that special expression on her face is just for him. My jaw clamps on the pain that threatens to escape.

Brynn closes her car door, scooting around her bonnet to intercept him. Still, she doesn't see me.

"Hello, Brynn." I hear him say in his educated tone.

She falls into step beside him, and my fists ball as I watch them walk away. They make a beautiful pair, even if it pains me to admit it. They are a perfect contrast. Ebony and ivory, his deep voice and her birdsong notes weaving together in a kind of harmony I'll never be a part of.

I ache to chase him down, explain with my fists that he needs to leave her alone, but I can't. I bleed helplessness, because even though she isn't supposed to, Brynn gives too much of her heart to him. I see it in the tilt of her head and the way her shoulders curve towards him as they talk, and wish I wasn't so tuned in to her.

For too many years I've listened to the gossip, about how endearing it is that two children could make a promise of forever to each other, and keep it, cultivating it into the kind of romance that you only ever read about in fairytales. I can't shut out the image of the two of them, hand in hand, sharing looks. Those memories haunt me as I lie in bed each night, feeling like there's no way out of the mess I'm in.

Because she's supposed to be mine, but she thinks she's in love with my brother.

CHAPTER 2

BRYNN

I sit on Bella's bed, silently watching as she expertly applies make up and shimmies into a short black dress. She's the blonde bombshell with pure intentions everyone loves to hate, but there's nothing you *can* hate about Bella. She's all heart and insight and ever since she shared her chocolate biscuits with me in kindergarten, we've been inseparable. Probably would be for life. She tells it the way she sees it, and she understands that I'm strong willed, and not hostile and stubborn like my parents insist I am. We have each other's back, Bella and me, and neither of us will leave the other behind.

She dresses up to feel good when she dances, not to trawl for attention. That's another thing I love about her. I've no fear she'll ditch me when the pretty boys start closing in. Like me, she's not about to leap into a meaningless romp with some big-mouthed jock to pass the time. She's waiting for something *real*.

Not that I have a choice in the matter. My parents refuse to lift their ridiculous curfew, even though I'm over eighteen. I've hovered on the precipice of rebellion for years, but the respect drummed into me since birth always won out in the end. It frustrates me that I'm a perpetual child in their eyes, forever the scamp who loves farm work and doesn't mind being covered in mud, instead of seeing me as a young woman who finds genuine satisfaction in physical labour.

When they made the decision to invite shareholders in on their farm to expand their production, I assumed they'd relax a little. With the extra money they were able to pocket from their success, I thought they'd learn to live a little, but the only thing it did change was the behaviour they expected of me. No longer was it adorable when I fell asleep in the barn. That was no longer acceptable from the daughter of a now notable family. And I certainly wasn't at liberty to attend school parties where I might get drunk and embarrass them.

"Oh my god, Bell, you look divine," I breathe as Bella spins in front of me.

Her smile sinks into a frown.

"Oh, why can't you come too? Just once, Bry? You never get to have any fun."

I roll my eyes.

"Apparently I'm supposed to be locked in the highest tower with my maidenhood protected until my prince decides it's time to fetch me."

Bella wrinkles her nose.

"Seriously, Brynn. You're twenty. You're officially an adult, and you're still not allowed out. It's ridiculous. You know I love your parents, Bry, but if you don't start coming out and having a bit of fun, you'll be a fifty-year-old spinster who's never been to a party!"

My lungs deflate noisily.

Bella slips her arm over my shoulder, her voice dropping.

"Listen, Bry, why don't you tell them you're staying the night with me? You can wear something of mine, you can go to the party and shower again before you go home in the morning? They'll never know."

"Famous last words right there! You may as well have said 'what could possibly go wrong?'!" I snag the white linen pillow and toss it at Bella.

"Daryl will be there…" her sings coyly.

My body locks.

"Are you sure? How do you know?"

"Oh, I *might* have heard Alice invite him, and I *may* have still been eavesdropping when he agreed…" She baits me with a wicked grin

Throwing myself backwards onto the queen bed, I groan.

"Alice? No! Daryl can't be interested in Alice! What else did he say? Bella? He said more, didn't he?"

Bella twists a wisp of ash blonde hair into place and pins it. She turns then, eyes of brown coloured with sympathy.

"You know what men are like, Brynn. He told Alice he'd go if she'd meet him in the spare bedroom. I'm sorry, Bry."

A lump lodges in my throat. I heard the boys all through school talk about sampling the goods before finding one to settle down with. I know Daryl is different, knowing him all my life I'm certain of that, but Bella's admission brings a ball of queasy uncertainty to my stomach. I mean, Daryl and I aren't even 'official'. I guess that means he's single and free to sow his wild oats, and it seems that whenever I spot him lately, Alice isn't far behind. I get the awful impression that he might be interested in her. Unless I convince him otherwise.

Bella lowers to the bed, gripping my thigh.

"Come on, Bry. Mum will cover for us. You can come to the party, take Alice's place in the bedroom, and kiss the ever loving sense out of him! One kiss from you and he'll be hooked, I just know it!"

A wicked shiver of rebellion silences my whining. Because there's one thing I love more than my parents, and that's Daryl Walker. Blonde haired, blue eyed golden child of Evie and Antony Walker, Daryl is destined for great things. He's being primed to take over the Walker Empire worth billions and he's promised me I will be his wife.

"They can't find out, right?"

Bella flicks a non existent speck off her dress. "Bry, your parents won't even know there's ever been a party in this town. So are you coming?"

Guilt washes over me when I picture the heavy disappointment on my father's face, but it's dwarfed by the shinier image of Daryl with love in his eyes. Bella's smile widens, ripping open her wardrobe and pulling out a tight red thing.

"I'm not wearing that!" I gasp. Red would clash with my dark hair and violet eyes.

"Nope. I'm wearing the red. You need *this* dress." She yanks out a hanger with a flourish of black fabric and a sly grin.

"This is the perfect dress to show off your curves and stop Daryl in his tracks."

***

"I feel sick, Bella." I whisper.

The sound of loud voices and wild laughter is something I'd never experienced before. It unsettles me, like an eerie, school yard bathed in darkness. Somehow, by removing the light of day from a gathering, it becomes exciting and forbidden. And a little bit sinister. Silhouettes hover on the edge of the shadows and I find my ears automatically honing into the night to listen for people lurking in the dark. Bella threads her fingers through mine, pulling me to a stop.

"Bry, you don't have to be nervous. You're not doing anything stupid. We can just dance if you like. You don't even need to speak to a single person if you don't want. We'll just dance until we're too tired to dance any more, then we'll go home."

"Really?" I wet my mouth with my tongue as Bella nods. I love this girl.

"You look absolutely breathtaking Bry. By far the hottest thing here. Even if you don't get to kiss Daryl, once he sees you, he'll be blown away."

Biting my lower lip, I relent with a small nod, following my friend into the flood of lights and bass thundering beneath my feet.

There are so many bodies it almost overwhelms me. The smells of sweat and perfume collide with the clutter of voices and laughter and I find myself on the verge of drowning in sensory overload, but I tune into the comforting beat that fills the night and focus on it. It anchors me, soothing me until I don't feel quite so claustrophobic, my heart rate calming to the hypnotic rhythm of the music. It's one thing to be closed in your room to dance, but here the dance space is endless, the music weaves around, drawing every willing soul into its demanding beat.

Someone bumps into my shoulder, but I barely feel it as Bella pulls me through the ocean of faces. Most I don't recognise, probably because everyone looks so different now that school's finished and everyone's out of uniform. Every head turns towards me as I pass, like nobody expects me to be here.

That's right. Square old Brynn made it to a party, folks!

The thought makes me giddy and my cheeks tighten in a giggle.

My skin prickles with awareness. The air shudders, and the overwhelming sense that someone is watching me quivers beneath my skin. I frown into the shadows, sure I would find the source, but all I see is darkness. I scan the crowd.

Then, like destiny, I spot him. Daryl. He's talking to Alice, but as if he feels some cosmic pull, he glances up.

He straightens, frowns, runs his gaze over me. Over the short hem that shows off the length of my legs, the tight fabric that clings like a second skin to the swell of my hips, the way it pulls in at the waist, slowly widening at my chest. The dress is stretched tight over my ample breasts, offering him a tantalising glimpse of creamy cleavage encased in black lace.

And I feast on Daryl. Tight jeans, a sapphire blue collared shirt that hints at the toned body beneath.

Daryl is looking at me like he wants to devour me. Excitement shimmies at the base of my neck.

Bella shoves a cup in my hand, yanking my attention back to her.

"It's water, Bry, and now he's noticed you, make him chase you."

I take a grateful swallow that washes away the sudden dryness.

"Now, Brynn girl. Let's dance."

All my teeth show as I sneak one more glance at Daryl before Bella drags me to the centre of all those writhing bodies.

***

"Oh my god, tell me again why I have not done this before? Can this night get any better?"

Bella throws her pretty blonde head back and laughs.

"It's much more fun with you here with me. Come on. I need another drink."

We catch our breath as the water cools us.

"Oh, Bry, look!"

I turn just in time to see Daryl's unmistakable blonde head disappearing through the crowd towards the house.

Bella's fingers bite into my arm urgently.

"It's now or never, girl. You gonna kiss the hell out of your man or not?"

Time slows as I stare at the empty space Daryl occupied moments ago.

Do I really want to do this? Panic washes over me, the knot in my stomach so uncomfortable I press my belly to soothe it.

"I'm going to regret this. Promise me if it gets awkward you'll tell everyone I was drunk?"

Bella nods and shoots a reassuring grin.

"Plastered. But you'll be fine. I'll be here."

CHAPTER 3

KADE

*A*nother party. I feel eyes on me, but I ignore them, melting into the shadows beneath the trees. I find Daryl easily, Alice by his side as if they are a couple. Alice is planning on getting her business degree but even without the schooling she has a head for it. I've watched them growing closer by the day and with it, the hope of Daryl choosing Alice over Brynn is clutched tight in my chest.

She's a better match for you than Brynn.

I settle against the rough trunk of the gum tree. I only come here for Daryl, but if he ever knew, or saw me here…

The air shifts. The back of my neck prickles, and I scan the darkness.

She's here!

Her parents don't allow her out. Brynn shouldn't be here, but I know she is. I can feel her, and I search the night with anticipation.

My breath hisses and my chest constricts when she finally appears, tentative and uncertain as a rabbit. I push off the tree trunk, my blood pounding in my head. Brynn is stunning. Those curves, the hint of thigh beneath the hem of her dress brings a growl to my throat. The thought of other eyes ogling her makes my blood boil, the fear that someone might lay their hands on her twists that knife deep inside my gut. I'm coiled so tight I've already taken steps towards her when Bella appears at her side, and my shoulders loosen up a little. Bella will watch over her.

I slide my gaze over the length of her, taking my time to worship every dip and line, wishing it were my hands in their place. My head spins with her beauty, and her curves drive me to the brink of insanity. Everything in my body screams to be next to her, so instant that I wonder if it's meant to be tonight that I find the courage to talk to her. It's just her and Bella there, on the edge of the party, and I wouldn't even need to fight to get her alone. I shove my fists in my jeans pockets and move towards her, but just before the dull lights touch my face I freeze.

I wasn't invited to this party. Nobody knows I'm here except the handful of girls who seek me out each time and don't care that I won't talk. Even if I arrived on the arm of one of them, I still wouldn't be welcome. I recognise faces in the crowd I've exchanged words with, some who've staggered beneath the justice I dealt out. They don't want me here, and I can't have such a pivotal moment with Brynn disturbed by their hatred.

I retreat into the shadows, watching.

My eyes don't stray from Brynn. I detect the moment she decides she wants to dance by the softening of her spine and the smile that blooms to life and replaces her tension. Brynn needs to dance. It's the one time that she allows herself to feed the spark inside, feel it burst to life again for a stolen moment, even if she isn't truly aware of it.

My heart surges with pleasure, the powerful wave of something primal within calling out to her. Instantly, her head jerks in my direction, a vaguely puzzled expression on her face. It's an expression that fills me with hope, renews my faith and resonates in every fibre of my soul.

Oh, yes, this is it! Now I know she feels me, she will no longer find me invisible. Her subconscious will seek me out as mine does her and its only a matter of time before she's in my arms where she belongs.

Her eyes stab into the night around me, even though I know she can't see me. I watch her expression soften as she glances through the crowd, as if she knows she won't find what she's seeking, but not yet ready to give up.

Then they lock on something, and when I see who it is, my heart turns to ice.

No! Oh god please, no!

Even from this far away I recognise the heat in Daryl's eyes, the flare that erupts in pale blue as he slides his gaze over her with new found hunger, because he's never seen her dressed up and looking so beautiful before. The same expression is on her face, and my bones weld with the bitter inevitability of Daryl and Brynn.

Alice is forgotten.

No matter how I rub my chest, the ache doesn't ease. It only builds as I watch helplessly while their connection intensifies wordlessly across the crowded lawn.

The air burns my lungs, and everything throbs with blinding pain.

Bella jams a cup in her hands, and Brynn's eyes drag back to her friend. I sag bonelessly against the tree trunk, grateful for Bella's interruption. When they begin to dance I struggle to inhale strength back into my limbs.

It seems for a while that all is as it should be. Brynn and Bella take a break, snagging bottles of water from the table, laughing and talking.

When Daryl's head disappears into the crowd, I hold my breath, but he doesn't approach Brynn. He walks by unnoticed, and I begin to think that the moment they shared earlier was a cruel ruse created by my imagination.

That is, of course, until Bella digs an elbow into Brynn's side and Brynn's head whips towards him. Her whole body stiffens with intent and my mouth dries out. The determination in her profile rocks me, the tip of her tongue running over lips in search of courage. Eyes glinting with the primal urge that was meant to be on me. Crippling agony explodes in my chest, and I clutch at the tree for support, the grunt escaping me that of a broken man.

I'm utterly hollow as I watch the woman who owns my heart follow the man she loves into the house, and all that I can hope for is that Daryl will refuse her.

CHAPTER 4

BRYNN

*M*y heart pounds in my chest as I round the corner. Nobody is around, its so eerily quiet considering the hundreds of people jammed together just a few yards away. I steady my breath.

Spare bedroom. Which one is that?

I frown as I wander down the dim, carpeted hallway. I don't even know whose house this is, and the only pictures hanging on the walls are jungle scenes instead of kids. I'm drawn to the image of a cow, magnificent curved horns so wide and thick I imagine that merely keeping balance would be its greatest challenge. The comical scene flashes through my mind and I stifle a giggle, hearing my father's warning: *Now, Brynn, do you think that's an appropriate topic to entertain?*

Since he's not here, I allow myself a quiet chuckle, so enthralled by my inner thoughts I almost miss spotting the door halfway down slightly ajar. The only one not closed. The spare bedroom? Reaching the door, I pause, suddenly nervous.

He's waiting for Alice. What if he thinks I'm her? What if its the wrong door?

"Hey?" I whisper, startling at the sound of my own voice, "Hey, its Brynn."

A hand snakes through the darkness, clutching my hand softly.

I don't expect the bolt of electricity to heat my blood at the simple touch, and I gasp. The warm grip falls away at the same moment, and my skin chills at its sudden absence. Did he feel that, too? My pulse skips.

Just a kiss.

Sucking in a shuddering breath, I crack the door. It's so dark inside I can't even make out furniture. Tentatively, I step inside.

He's here. I hear him breathing, deeply, carefully.

Oh my god. I feel like a child suddenly and unsure of what to do, I shift my weight, swallowing loudly.

From the darkness, his voice rumbles, low and dark, deep and hungry.

"Brynn, I need to kiss you."

Tingles shoot through my bloodstream. They're merely words, but within them, a forbidden fruit ripens.

Oh, yes!

The absence of sight makes me hyper-aware of his lips, so warm and soft, as they graze over my mouth gently. So feather light, way too light. I find myself leaning in.

I need more. The strong scent of woody testosterone assaults my nostrils and sends a wave of desire through me.

Whatever this is he's making me feel, I like it!

Such a careful, thoughtful kiss, so tender it almost hurts.

More. Quivering in delight, my hands come to rest against the wall of muscle of his chest. I feel every sculptured ridge moving and flexing with life. Beneath my fingers his body shudders with the same sparks that fire haphazardly in my own. This kiss. This one simple, chaste kiss manages to suck the life out of the old Brynn, and replaces her with a wilder version, one that needs to feed to sate this ravenous hunger that builds with such force it threatens to consume her. I'm a starving lioness trembling before my first kill, uncertain and aching with need.

The animal inside me is awake.

The heat that burns through his clothes, his breath heavy against my lips, drives me wild with a lust no longer dormant.

Large, rough hands slide over my cheeks, taking the lead. His thumb reverently caressing while the pressure pulls me ever closer.

His tongue darts out, sliding sensuously over the seam of my lips and my heart almost pounds right out of my chest. He's seeking permission, holding back, tangible with promise.

I wait, uncertain. The next time I feel his tongue flick out, I open with a groan.

It's all the invitation he needs. His hands dig into my hips, holding my body hard against him, his soft mouth instantly hardens. Hungry and rough with desire. I hear his sharp intake of breath at my surrender, note the harsh waver in his lungs, the way his muscles ripple and flex. His scent changes, deepens, drowning me in his heavenly ambrosia. He smells like…like *mine*. His body quivers.

Hell, yeah.

Once unleashed, he's a starving beast, wicked and sinful, his own groan vibrating through my mouth with the force of his need. I revel in how utterly desirable this makes me feel, like I'm a precious gem and he's the one chosen to worship me. And worship me he does. With every touch, every breath, all my thoughts drift away. My body becomes a feral thing beyond control, fingers exploring the hard planes of his chest, his hips, then up to dig into the hard valley of his spine to bring him closer.

His tongue plunges in with a struggling inhale I feel on my cheeks, filling my mouth with his dominating need, until his mouth is all that matters.

With each expert stroke of his tongue and precise pressure of his lips he leads me closer to the fire, that raging inferno he's created that I ache to lose myself in.

Body wound like a spring, my moan coats his tongue. He pulls away suddenly, leaving me to whimper with disappointment, but only to press those incredible lips against my neck. Shivers congregate beneath my skin where his mouth touches.

The iron hands on my hips tighten, slamming them against his own, the hot length straining against his jeans burning into my belly.

It's suddenly so real, this bulk of a man enveloping me, his jagged breaths sawing against my neck, the intensity of his need short-circuiting my mind.

"Oh, god." I gasp, trying to make my hands push him away. They betray me, dragging nails up his spine instead, delighting when he shudders.

He moves lower, his palm swallowing my breast, kneading with confidence, with ownership. I moan when he drags a finger over a nipple, feeling it deep in my core. *How can my breast make me feel so much down there?*

I've gone too far! Knowing I should stop before it goes any further, open my mouth to end it just as the dress resigns and his tongue swirls with embers over my nipple.

"We should-"

He bites down gently at that moment, taking me to a higher plain of pleasure that throbs between my thighs.

"Ohhhhh!" My moans tense my core and my pulse races so fast I feel my heart might fail. But it's my legs that give instead, my body giving itself over to the pleasure this man inflicts. I'm vaguely aware of Daryl picking me up and laying me gently on the bed. Only barely register when he covers my body with his, beginning a new journey with his lips back at my mouth, working his way down with nipping, licking torture.

"Oh, please." I don't recognise that voice, more mewls of pleasure than actual words.

A blazing heat drags up my legs, between my thighs, as he tortures slowly, inching his strong fingers higher. My body is a thing of quivering, panting hunger, nails digging into his thick hair as he kisses over the fabric of my dress. My growl tells him that the dress needs to go, and I feel him chuckle. He kisses me again, knowing it's frustrating me.

His palm slides upwards, my hips bucking when he contacts my centre beneath the lacy fabric barrier. I jerk upwards, pressing into his hand, needing…something.

His other hand hooks over the waistband of my underwear and drags it down, pausing briefly before they slide too far.

"Tell me to stop, Brynn." Daryl's voice is course, broken, barely leashed.

I quiver at the force of his desire. Always the epitome of control and sensible predictability, I never thought he could be like this. Had I known before that Daryl could let go like this, become so wild and exciting my body melts beneath his touch, I would not have waited so long. And in every touch of his lips and fingertips, he brands me with the depth of his love for me.

I can feel it. He's starving. For me. Blood pounds in my head, desire roaring through my body as I struggle to catch my breath. Daryl's breath drags and pants. He's so worked up I feel his flesh catch fire. Or is that mine? It's one and the same now.

The last thread of self control evaporates with his next words.

"Let me show you how good you can feel, Brynn."

My breath explodes, clattering around me.

Show me how good I can feel? Oh Lord, nothing on this earth can feel like this, and he's making promises I couldn't resist even if I wanted to.

"Don't…don't stop." I pant.

He slides a finger through my slippery folds, tearing a sharp cry of pleasure from my lips at the delicious intrusion. My hips strain towards him, desperate to put an end to this gentle punishment and feel the power of his hard grip. I need him to show me, teach me. Take me. Own me.

"Is that 'Don't. Stop' or is it 'don't stop?'" His breaths rasp, but I detect a smug amusement in his rumbling timbre.

"Quit teasing" I gasp desperately "and put your money where your mouth is."

"I think you got that the wrong way around."

There's a smirk in his tone, but I lose my ability to speak when he dips his head, swiping his tongue through my folds.

A starburst stabs through me and I buck and cry out as rapture consumes me.

"You taste so sweet, Brynn, sweeter than I ever dreamed."

Nonsensical words trip from my tongue as he ravages me, dipping, licking, sucking, while I buck and writhe with a primal need bigger than both of us. I spiral towards something, and he senses it, slips a finger deep inside me.

Oh, that feels good! He bites down gently, the sharp sting of his teeth splitting atoms throughout my nervous system.

"Oh, Jesus, oh Jesus, Jeeesuss!"

My body gathers, quavers then shatters, convulsing around his thick finger, soaking him with the force of my orgasm, my spine arching harder against his face.

"Fuck that was beautiful, Brynn."

He brings me down gently, slowing the swirls of his tongue, sliding his finger out.

"You're so slick for me, baby." He gasps, climbing over my sated body, stealing a kiss.

I moan with wonder when he probes me with a daring tongue and I taste myself. He was down there, between my legs, and by giving me a taste, he's showing me his ownership. He's claiming me.

"I need you baby, I have to *feel* you." The wild desperation in his voice makes me groan.

His hunger for me is stronger than him, and that sends embers spiking through me.

Running my hands down the hard lines of his back, I grip the firm globes of his backside as his jeans fall away. He grabs my hand and presses it against his erection. It's so hot and hard, yet smooth as satin. And huge. I struggle to wrap my hand around his girth exploring his size while he growls into my neck. My breath explodes, heart racing, flesh on fire, and for the first time, scared.

"You won't fit." My voice is thin and tight.

"Brynn, baby, It'll be fine. I promise. Let me make you feel good."

Those words again, the promise to make me feel good. He made good on his promise last time, awakening me to pleasures before unknown. I shiver. I breathe him in, my man in the dark, commanding my pleasure, so big, wide and masculine, covering my body completely with his, making me feel safe.

Making me feel like this is where I belong.

"Relax, Brynn, I'll never hurt you." Soothing velvet words making my body do just that. He doesn't ask this time. He takes the lead, sending me crazy with lust. I swallow thickly. Rucking the hem of my dress, bunching it in his giant fists until it peels off my body, sliding his palms over my bare skin.

Finally.

I ache for this, the sensation of skin against skin. I arch towards him. My gasp catches as I feel something hot and hard at my entrance. He senses my hesitation, pausing, running those burning hands over my belly until he feels me relax, then he slips an arm under my knee and presses steadily forward.

My inhales quake with awe as he breaches me. I feel the wide tip of him slide excruciatingly slowly into my slick entrance, and I can't hold back my moans, low and long as he stretches and burns his way inside my body. On the threshold between pleasure and pain he holds me as inch by inch he sinks deeper. His breath hisses with excruciating restraint, his teeth grind with the effort to go slow.

He pulls back a little before pressing deeper, that exquisite burn driving every other thought from my mind but him.

"Aaaaahhh!" My breathless sigh of ecstasy slips out.

"Christ I love those noises you make, Brynn. You're so damn sexy you make me crazy." The restraint he clutches at weakens, teeters and threatens to fall away. I hear the grind of his teeth as he pushes halfway in, sliding deliciously deeper into my snug wet heat.

"You're so damn tight, Brynn, tight as a-"

I grunt and flinch when sharp pain like the nick of a blade spreads inside me, coinciding with a harsh and colourful curse from the dark.

He freezes, panting with barely leashed need. He swallows.

"Shit, Brynn, I didn't know-"

"I'm fine." I snap as the stinging subsides, grateful he can't see my face heat up or the tears that spring to my eyes from the pain. He waits with commendable patience, caging his desires with harsh exhales and rigid spine until the sting dissipates. I marvel at how he fills me, how somehow, there is another human being inside my body. It's the most intimate sensation, having invited a body inside your own. I clench my muscles curiously, moaning in wonder. He's embedded so deep that when I do, I feel it in my spine. I marvel at the way I can make out every inch of him, the vein pulsing along his shaft, the swell of his tip. I contract around him again in awe, and his groan strangles. Grinning in the darkness, I do it again and he responds with an agonised growl.

"I'm barely holding on, baby. Do that again and I'll lose it."

His admission steals my breath.

What would it feel like, to have him lose control? Do I really have that effect on him?

I know what I want.

I sink my nails into his shoulders, wrap my legs around his hips, and clench. Hard. I grip his length so tight I think I'll hurt him, but he snarls as the last of his control evaporates, draws my legs over his shoulders and bites his fingers into my shoulder. My blood hums its excitement. Then he dives in, all restraint lost. So hard, so deep, so long, I scream in pleasure with the power of it. There's no pain, just that glorious stretching burn and incredible friction. He draws back again and slams into me so hard I imagine him pressing through into my heart. I cling to him, intoxicated by his breath panting in my face, the scent of him, and his powerful body at the mercy of its own desire for me. He plunges in ever deeper with animal grunts and growls that make my mind malfunction. His pelvis slaps against me, his thick shaft hitting against a spot far inside that makes me coil and tense as the waves build around me. The hand on my shoulder hauls me hard into him, pleasure spiking. Our bodies, slick with sweat, tangled, reaching, writhing against each other in a perfect dance of dark desire.

"Christ, Brynn, come with me, baby."

When he lifts me off the bed for deeper penetration, the waves of release crash down hard. I scream with blinding release, drag my nails, bite down on his shoulder. I feel him thicken and twitch as he comes inside my convulsing tight channel with a primal, animalistic roar that tears at his throat.

In the darkness, he drags his nose down my neck, breathing me into his lungs.

He kisses me, languidly, like he's searing it to memory. When the bed lifts in the darkness, my stomach bottoms out. Daryl is leaving.

"Just in case someone walks in." He whispers, helping me into my dress. It's difficult with my body aching and spent, but between his gentle laughter and careful wiggling we manage. When our clothes are donned, he climbs back on the bed, rolling my back against his hard chest and tucking an arm over my waist.

"Hmmmm." I murmur, and he laughs softly, tickling my neck with his breath.

"You are exquisite, Brynn. Perfection." His voice vibrates through my back as I fall into the arms of sleep. Before I drift completely away, I think I hear him whisper.

"You're mine now, Brynn. Now I've had a taste, I can't let you go."

CHAPTER 5

BRYNN

*M*y eyes slam open at Bella's voice.

"Bry! Wake up!"

Puzzled, it takes me a while to gather my bearings. I'm in someone's bedroom, curled up on their bed. My memory returns with the blinding light Bella snaps on. I slept with Daryl. I only meant to kiss him, but I slept with him, and it was incredible. I blink, dazed, as I scan the room for him. Bella frowns in concern, but she's alone. I'm alone. He's gone.

My stomach sinks. So much for never letting me go.

Only the pleasant ache between my legs reminds me it really happened.

I frown, unable to explain why I came for a kiss but instead surrendered my virginity any more than I can understand why Daryl promised he wouldn't let me go only to have disappeared when the lights came on.

***

I fold into Daryl's convertible when he pulls up with a grin.

"Hey, Brynn" He greets me with lips firm against mine.

Sometimes, even after four months, I still find it hard to believe that we're finally official. The day after that party, he appeared on my parent's doorstep and asked if I would like to be exclusive with him. I almost laughed when he pledged to go slow with me, assuring me that he wanted to do everything right, as if he was admitting that his passionate loss of control was something he didn't bargain on. But he was so serious that I accepted with as much grace as I could considering my heart was leaping from my chest.

"Where to tonight?" I ask. It's always some exclusive restaurant, the newest show or some red carpet after-party Daryl's contacts sneak us into. Not only do I get to rub shoulders with A-listers, but it helps for Daryl to be seen at these events as he prepares to take over Walker empire. I carry a bag of clothes so I can change at a moment's notice.

"I thought you could choose tonight." Blue eyes twinkle in amusement.

I drop my mouth dramatically, playing along with subtle sass. "Oh, I'm honoured! What are my options?"

Daryl leans closer, tucking a loose strand of hair tenderly behind my ear. "Nothing. Anything. We can go for dinner, or to a show. Even dancing if you like."

His expression dulls a little with the mention of dancing. He knows I love it but it bores the life out of him. I've backed off dancing so much with Bella lately, too, because Daryl needs to be everywhere I am and it takes the fun out of it when I see him huddled in a corner smothering a yawn.

Where do I want to go?

"Okay, I know a place, but we need to make a stop first."

We stop to grab some dinner, then I call out directions and try to ignore the way Daryl's jaw tics with irritation when I mix up left and right and he has to backtrack twice. Eventually we make it to our destination with Chinese noodles still warm in their boxes.

"Come on." I laugh excitedly. It's been years since I came up here, but it's just how I remember, towering gums peering down on a narrow pathway. I don't wait for Daryl, bouncing up the path as the daylight dims.

Turning the last corner, my grin widens even further. A boulder slumps right against the edge of the drop, the weather worn shape carved into a perfectly serviceable bench. Shifting my weight impatiently, I squeal when Daryl emerges.

"This is…nice." He attempts a grin.

"It *is* nice. Just you wait till the sun sets. It's incredible." Right now it's already stunning, mountains and valleys decorated with a thick carpet of gum trees, rosellas and galahs gliding and calling above us. I could stare at this all day.

I smother a chuckle as I watch Daryl arrange himself carefully on the rock, inspecting it first for critters and dirt. His forehead creases as he swipes at the small pile of dead leaves before dusting off his hands. Inspecting the smudge of dirt it left, Daryl tentatively selects his perch. As soon as he's settled, I launch against him, lifting his arm over my shoulders.

"Now what?" He clears his throat.

"Now we watch, Daryl. Just look at it. We could be the only two people in the world right now for all the trees."

He swallows loudly, scanning the undergrowth nervously as though he expects some wild beast to lunge from the bushes and attack him. I smother a chuckle. He's clearly ill at ease without the security of four walls and a suit.

Me? I love the fresh air and the magic that waits on the edge of dawn and dusk. A thought strikes.

"Do you think we'll live in this town forever, Daryl? I mean, after we're married?"

"Goodness no. We'll move closer to the city after the business has finished transitioning. I think it's clever to be as close as I can to my clients, and for you, my sweet morning lark, so we can stay out later while still getting to bed at a decent hour. All the shops will be close by and you can have a wardrobe full of satin shirts and those sexy skirts."

I know the ones he means. Its not the first time he's mentally dressed me in knee length skirts, red satin shirt tucked in and black high heels. It's certainly not my taste, and would suit a woman with a more lithe figure, but if it means that much, maybe one day I'll do it for him.

I gaze wistfully over the darkening hills. I love the trees, the birds and the crisp country air. I've been reared on open spaces and green grass. I guess there was a part of me that assumed that since Antony can conduct his business from Corymbia, Daryl and I would, too. It's a sobering thought, and an alien chill embeds in my spine at the thought of a tiny apartment that awaits us in the concrete, neon jungle of the city.

Daryl's phone alerts him to an incoming message. The shrill tone is alien nestled among nature, and irritation twinges as he checks the screen.

Alice.

"What does Alice want?" I rein in the heavy tone, but I still sound jealous.

"We're friends, Brynn. That's all we are."

My sigh hits the air. Alice with hair that's never out of place, who always looks immaculate. I grind my teeth. Daryl responds with the phone angled so I can see his response in the dark. Berating myself silently I try to imagine Daryl cheating on me and can't. He just wouldn't. And being open about his texts is meant to soothe my doubts, but all it does is irritate me more, because it shows me that there is no way he'd give up his friendship with her, even if it appeases his future wife.

He tucks his phone away and lands a smile on me that makes me forgive him. I scrape the strands of hair shaken loose behind my ears, and shovel a chopstick full of noodles in. I swallow down both my mouthful and the intrusion of Alice, determined to have an enjoyable night.

I giggle when a noodle escapes and lands on my chin. Daryl shakes his head as he digs a napkin from the bag, leaning over to wipe it off, but I pull back.

"No Daryl, not with that…"

He frowns before his expression smooths in understanding. My breathing deepens.

"I'm not going to eat it off you, Brynn." He rolls his eyes and wipes the scrap off my face.

He can't understand my determination to use chopsticks. If you were meant to eat Chinese food with forks, they'd include them. I smother my disappointment as the stars tap in. Since the party he's kissed me a few times, but never with the same intensity as that night, and not once has he shown me the hunger that I tasted and now crave.

CHAPTER 6

KADE

*M*um is frantic, and I wonder again why she won't just leave the lot up to the event planners.

"Here, Mum, let me help." I offer, taking an armful of white linen tablecloths from her.

We share an easy silence as one by one the tables are covered, until we're standing together surveying our work. Mum digs me in the ribs, and I smile.

"There it is, my son. I thought you'd forgotten how to smile."

"There's not much to be happy about." I murmur, and her hand comes to rest on my arm.

Creases that never used to be there, cobweb over the back of her hand, the once smooth skin now shiny and segmented. Mum's getting older, and one day she'll leave me too. I anticipate the grief, dreading it, fearing it, because she's the only person on this godforsaken planet who finds me worthy.

I turn to her, my thoughts on the tip of my tongue, when a chill touches my neck and I clamp my mouth.

"What are you doing here, boy? Your presence isn't required until this evening, remember?"

The frosty eyes of my father, the same shade as Daryl's, condemn me. I remember well. The guests arrive at seven, so I'm to make a cameo appearance between nine and half past. Then I'm to go home. I'm not welcome here. My muscles pop with the need to defend myself, and my blood simmers. I think of Mum and lock my jaw against a retort.

"Antony, dear, he's helping me." Mum reasons, and blue eyes melt a fraction when they land on her.

"Fine, but you'll make sure he doesn't make trouble tonight, won't you?" He instructs.

"I'm right here, Father." I growl, and instantly regret it.

He slides his gaze over me with a curl of his lip as if I were detestable.

"Indeed." He sneers.

I bristle, but the largest emotion inside isn't injustice, it's his utter refusal to give me a chance to love him, to offer any hope that maybe he could find a breadcrumb of love for me.

"In that case, Kade, you know what's expected. Make believe we're a happy family, say the right things, then leave without causing a scene. And I'm warning you, don't upset Daryl by interfering with his relationship with Brynn."

His smile widens when I flinch, eyes dancing in cruel victory as he leaves us.

Mum's fingers bite into my arm.

"Kade, don't let him get to you. Just have faith that everything will unfold as it should."

I huff a derisive laugh. Unfold as it should? Was it supposed to be anguish and calamity? In my mind, Brynn was supposed to have understood years ago when I held her soaking body beneath the summer rain. She was meant to let me walk beside her and share our thoughts and secrets. She was supposed to look at me the way she looks at Daryl.

Since the party, something changed between them that makes my stomach turn. Daryl was always interested in her, but that night, his eyes lit on her as if he finally recognised the woman she'd become. And Brynn...so much more passionate than Daryl could ever be, the desire in her too powerful for him to bear.

I could take it. I'm strong enough to take the intensity of her because I was designed and made to carry it, just as she was crafted from the earth to carry my heart. Together we could burn for eternity, but apart...

I can feel myself dying a little more sometimes, and that spark that used to live and play in Brynn is all but snuffed out by the stuffy conformity of what she imagines is where she belongs.

No. Destiny is certainly not unfolding as it should. Destiny needs assistance at times, and the familiar twinge of guilt is like an ice shard in my soul.

"Don't lose hope, Kade." She murmurs, but I look away.

You can't lose something you no longer have.

***

I despise wearing the monkey suit as if I were just another act in my father's circus. I'm not his puppet. I do this for Mum. Unlike my father, Mum loves both of her sons and I know it hurts her that the only words Daryl and I have exchanged in the last few years are full of anger and bitterness. Our relationship, once the strongest force on the planet is now a broken, toxic thing, and I have no idea what changed.

I wait, still and alone in the drawing room, watching the clock, perched on the arm of one of the expensive leather chairs that fill their home. Their home. Not mine. Never mine. Mum's and Daryl's and his.

Laughter and trite words filter down the hallway as guests begin to arrive in glamorous apparel and giant gemstones. I roll my eyes. High heels clatter and the sound of glasses touching indicates the party is well underway, but I still need to wait another hour before my act begins. I lean my head back, listening to the voices gather and merge into that odd rumble that I always associate with too many people. I spent the day wiring up a new fence with the sun on my back and sweat on my forehead, and the background chatter has the effect of white noise on my exhaustion, inviting me to relax, tempting my eyes closed.

I wake with a start and climb to my feet with a heavy sigh. It's time for my performance.

When I step into the harsh glare of the ballroom, the first thing I see is my father glaring over his wristwatch. It's okay for him to judge, but he wasn't up with the dawn working his arse off. He curls his lip in disgust and returns to his conversation. I walk through the centre of the room and feel a hundred eyes reach their own verdict. I wear my scowl as armor, shoulders wide and chin up as I make for the bar.

Young Danny works here often enough to have an apple juice ready, and I curl my fingers around the glass, grateful to have something to occupy my hands as I scan the room.

I felt Brynn the moment I stepped in the room. She's the echo of my heartbeat that trips in my chest and compels me towards her. I find her without trying, and I bleed at the sight. Perfect face desecrated with color that mutes her natural beauty, black dress that, while graceful and elegant, may as well be prison garb. The style may be different to everybody else, but the function is just the same; trying to convince them that she belongs in this shallow charade with them. She doesn't. I see her tight shoulders and stiff steps and mourn the free spirit she's trying so hard to kill. Even her hair rebels, fighting out of her regimented bun with a loose tendril escaping over her cheek.

She doesn't glance my way, her focus fixed on Daryl as he moves around the room with her on his arm. He wears a look of contentment, oblivious to the strain on Brynn's face. She's weary from too many faces and the ache of her forced smiles, yet she's determined to love it like Daryl does. Like Alice does. But it won't be long before she seeks the refuge of the night, needing the sweet summer air in her lungs as much as I do. I finish my drink and flick up two fingers. Danny slides two juices at me and I make for the door, hoping I've hit my quota with my father.

CHAPTER 7

BRYNN

I'm not one for parties, but when it's a necessary networking tool in the family business, I suck it up and slip on my favourite black dress. If I'm going to be bored, I might as well feel pretty. The massive dining area could accommodate five hundred guests, but tonight it's reserved for the one hundred most influential business potentials in the industry. One hundred and one, if you count Alice.

When we step into the room, my hand hooked over Daryl's crooked arm, he immediately seeks her out with a smile and wave that makes my fingers dig. Daryl frowns as he pulls me to a stop, pressing his lips into my hair to placate me.

"She's a *friend*, Brynn, and I refuse to lose someone like her because she makes you uncomfortable. I love you, I'm going to *marry* you like I promised, but my friendship with her is important too. Besides, she's an asset to the company and assures me she can get a few more investors on board tonight."

I sigh between clenched teeth. He's right, of course. Alice is genuinely passionate about Walker Enterprises in a way I will never be. I'm not designed to live and breathe for shareholders like she is. She smiles elegantly at Barnaby Coates, the biggest investor, but also the creepiest, and I shudder. I don't think I could stomach standing where she is, Barnaby's oily interest sliding all over her. I taste the slow chill of that realisation. Bouncing my eyes between Alice and Daryl, it's apparent they belong here, and I feel suddenly out of place.

As Barnaby disengages with a stiff bow, I catch Alice's victorious smile find Daryl across the room and my mouth dries. I wonder again if there's something more between them.

Filling my lungs I attempt to eject the thought from my head. I've known him for way too long to doubt his sincerity that they're merely friends, but the feeling lingers that it was Alice that Daryl was searching for the night of the party only months ago. Not me.

She's stunning, as always. Not a hair out of place, make up perfect, and the way she moves around the room is all class. Not like me. Beside her I feel frumpy and unkempt. As Barnaby is absorbed back into the crowd, I make my way over. She watches my approach with a glimmer of uncertainty and I feel myself bristle.

"Alice, thank you for coming. It means a lot to my future husband."

I see it. The barest flinch as I stake my claim.

"My pleasure, Brynn. You know I'll do whatever is required to ensure the success of the company you and Daryl will run."

My eyes narrow, but there's no malice to be found.

When I don't respond, her mask slips a little and her voice lowers.

"Listen, Brynn, Daryl is a good friend, and he's been kind enough to offer his future company to put my business degree to use. I'm no threat to you, is what I'm trying to say, and he loves *you*. It would mean a lot to me if we could get along."

I'm stunned into silence, because instead of the competitiveness or snark I expect, all I detect is a gentle, honest sadness. With a blink of her pretty eyes, Alice's mask is back in place and she's turning her charming smile to the next investor.

When the cool evening air hits my face, I can't help the sigh of pleasure that escapes. I can't fathom how they can all stand to be locked in that stuffy room with stale oxygen and so much shop talk. I fill my lungs again and again, purging the room from them. Resting my palms on the balcony railings, I stare into the moonlit rose garden and chew on Alice's words.

She loves Daryl. She might deny it with her words, but that flinch when I reminded her Daryl would marry me tells a different story.

"Realising you don't belong in there?" The deep voice rumbles from the dark.

Spinning with a yelp, I seek the source in the dark with adrenaline surging through my veins. The end of the balcony is shrouded by the night, hidden away from the intrusive glare of the dining room lights.

A single footstep sounds, the silhouette separating from the darkness enough for the shadows to hide his features, but illuminate his eyes, silver as a wolf. They never move from mine.

I know those eyes. I've seen that liquid metal too many times not to recognise them. Daryl's brother.

"Kade! You scared me. I thought everyone was inside."

"Everyone who belongs in that circus is. It would appear you and I are the odd ones out."

I glare through the dark, annoyed and off balance by the way he's manged to reach into my thoughts and pluck out my doubts like that. It stings to hear the words, and I bite.

"Oh, I belong in there, unlike *you*. I just needed some air. What are you doing here, sniffing around? Were you even invited?"

The soft chuckle reaches through the night and runs its fingers down my spine, warming my skin. The feeling lingers, unsettling me. He doesn't move from the shadows.

"I assure you I *was* invited. It would cause controversy if Father wasn't able to keep up the happy family farce by a token appearance by his least favourite son. I find it disconcerting that my little brother failed to mention it to you. Alice extended the invitation."

Bitterness fills my chest. *Of course she did.*

Kade moves from the shadows, and I'm inexplicably drawn to the sight. He's taller than Daryl's six foot frame, and much broader. His tailored suit is stretched tight over his strong shoulders, hugging the ripple of abdominals and drawing my gaze even further down.

Kade speaks with his fists. As children, he'd been the annoying older brother who'd stand silently to the side of all our games, but as we grew, Kade picked fights, and his hard fighter's body is testament to the trouble he's been in. As a teenager, when I would visit Daryl, I'd be often met by the red and blue lights seeking Kade. It was a shame, though, because despite the cold, contemptuous attitude, and unpredictable intentions, Kade Walker was a breathtaking specimen of testosterone. Both the Walker boys are handsome, but so different its hard to tell they're brothers. Daryl is the blonde haired, blue eyed god. He's the type every girl wants to marry. But if Daryl was a god, his brother was the devil. Dark of hair and of soul, the lines of Kade's features and the strength in his mouth promised wicked things. He was always the bad boy the girls swooned after, but there's something in the invisible presence of him that captures and holds. It's his voice, crushed velvet and rumbling. It is the scowl he wears. It's the ghosts that live inside him. He's trouble.

The intensity of his gaze makes him unforgettable. I feel the familiar shiver tickle my spine, and force my attention to his large hands. In each is a glass. One is empty, the other full. I arch an eyebrow at him, and the corner of his mouth curls in amusement. He defeats the darkness with a confidant step forward, the broken light catching on his face.

"This one's for you. The ice has melted, but I expected you to have escaped earlier than you did."

I glare at the glass.

"Shows how wrong you are about me. I don't drink."

Kade is so close now I can smell his aftershave. My head sp<del>in</del>
and in my confusion, I feel the glass press into my palm.

"I know, Brynn. It's apple juice."

I can smell it on his breath, the sweet apple scent finding its way into my lungs. My thoughts fracture when he steps so close I can feel the heat of his body. I focus on the glass, trying to settle the sudden spike in my pulse, when his chuckle plumes against my forehead.

"You needn't be so suspicious, Brynn. I didn't poison your drink. Here, I'll prove it."

When his hand engulfs mine, the sparks that ignite in my bloodstream draw a gasp from me. I flick my eyes to his and the depths in those silver eyes stops my heart. He watches me, lifting my glass to his lips with my hand captured against it, the contrast of the cool glass and the scorching heat of his hand leaving me light headed. Unable to look away, I watch the liquid slip into his mouth, swallowing loudly as his own throat bobs.

"There," he smirks as if he knows where my thoughts are. "Perfectly safe."

"What are you doing, Kade?" I choke, mouth open to catch my breath.

"I'm reminding you, Brynn. I'm showing you that the carnival going on inside is not where you're meant to be."

I'm so caught up in the scent of him and the timbre of his voice that it takes a while to process his words. When it finally registers, I retreat a step, desperate for space between us. I draw a shaky breath, settling the turbulence beneath my skin as best I can. Kade tilts his head to one

s if he's listening to some meaningful conversation that passes
tly between us that gives him full access to my thoughts. His eyes
int. I get the distinct impression he's just peeled me open, taking in
the raw parts of me I don't share with anyone. I force the feeling away,
clenching my teeth with the need to keep him away.

"You don't say a word to me for years, then suddenly have an
overwhelming urge to tell me I don't belong here? If you're such an
expert on my best interests, where do I belong, if not by my future
husband's side?"

Silver embers catch fire as his spine stiffens.

"Oh, I assure you that you do belong by your future husband's side,
Brynn. But it won't be with Daryl. Just look at them all inside that room,
every one of them playing a part. I can guarantee you, there's not a single
person in there who is honest about themselves. My father's company
has been working with these clowns for generations, yet they have
no idea what lives in the heart of any of them. For example, Richard
Alvin and his wife always wear the same outfit to every event, because
they hate these parades as much as we do. Every other day they live in
jeans and prefer a barbecue to hors' d'oeuvres. And Barnaby Coates
over there? He likes to dress in women's clothing and watch romantic
movies."

I choke on my mirth, swallow a breath and press my fingers to my
mouth, recalling my thoughts as I watched him with Alice.

"Does the thought offend you?" Kade asks lightly, his tone belying his
own amusement.

I cough down my laughter, clear my throat.

"Offend? Not at all. I was just realising that Barnaby wasn't ogling Alice back there as I assumed, he was probably imagining himself in her outfit."

Kade's laughter rises and mixes like honey with mine. Both of us, too caught up in our mental imagery to realise the din from the dining room suddenly grew louder.

"What are you doing, Kade?" Daryl's glacial snarl shocks me to silence.

Kade's laughter sours as he turns to his brother.

"I'm having a meaningful conversation with Brynn, Little Brother. I'm socialising. Isn't that what I'm here for? Flash a smile and pretend that the amazing Mr Antony Walker is such a noble creature for allowing his troubled son to be present? Paint a picture of togetherness to impress the money walking around in there. I'm ticking that box for you, Daryl. I'm simply taking pleasure in conversation that isn't shallow drivel before I sell my soul in there."

"Keep away from Brynn." Daryl growls, wrapping his arm possessively around my waist.

Kade slides a glower over him, clenching the muscles in his jaw.

"No."

There's something bone deep and heavy that quivers to life with the determination of that one word. It's so unexpected and…familiar…that I quake with it. Alarm yanks my gaze to Kade's, and those piercing eyes zero in on me as if he was waiting for it. He delves inside, strokes the corners of my thoughts, curls his presence through my lungs. Reaches further, deeper…

I break the contact, seeking Daryl's response. There's destruction in his glare, his teeth welded in loathing, but when I sneak another look at Kade, his attention is still on me.

His features have softened in some epiphany, lips parted and nostrils flaring.

Bewildered, I shake free of Daryl's arm and escape to the safety of the party.

***

"Care to tell me what that was all about?" Daryl asks as soon as the car door closes.

I know what he means. The event was a success, business relationships strengthened and Kade's cameo performance drew sympathetic smiles from investors, even as it grated on me.

"I just went outside for some air, Daryl. I didn't know he was there. Then we started talking. I wasn't aware I was supposed to avoid him completely. We just had a completely harmless, simple conversation."

"And what did you discuss?" He growls jealously, and I freeze.

I don't particularly want to draw his attention to my failings when it comes to these events, but I won't lie to him, either.

"He said schmoozing doesn't come naturally to me, and backed it up by pointing out that I was the only person who felt compelled to step out for some quiet."

The tension leaches from Daryl's shoulders and he manages a sympathetic smile.

"Brynn, dear, Kade's specialty is tapping into every one of your doubts and waving them in front of your face. I know it's not your thing, but that doesn't matter to me. It's handy for these functions to be able to share ideas and discussions with my wife about the business, but enough of that will come in time to do what is expected of us. Right now, I'm delighted that you attend them with me. Did you notice how most of the people there were men who'd left their wives at home? Please don't worry about it."

I blow out a lungful of air, reaching up to stroke the side of his face.

"Daryl, how is it that you always know what to say to calm me down. I've been so worried about it lately. There's some huge changes coming up for you, and I'm so excited for you, but I don't want a single thing I do to come between us. You've always been there for me, and I want to be the same pillar of strength for you."

In a rare display of emotion, Daryl pulls the car to a stop and presses his lips to my temple.

"But you have, Brynn. You always seem to just *know* when I need you most. We've already shared a lifetime together. You've seen and accepted every one of my failings, my mistakes and still find it inside you to love me back."

"But Alice?" The question tumbles out before I can stop it.

Daryl sighs, curving his back against the car seat as if he wants to put space between us.

"This again, Brynn?" His eyes narrow, and I'm reminded of the way his father looks at Kade sometimes.

His jaw ticks and he pulls back onto the road. I'm hollow, the lack of reassurance from Daryl, sends little hooks of unease into my stomach.

CHAPTER 8

BRYNN

*T*he world knew Daryl and I would marry, but I still didn't wear his ring. As expected, Daryl planned it out perfectly. Before a string quartet at the opening of a ritzy new restaurant, Daryl dropped to his knee and asked with shaking voice if I would be his wife, even though he knew my answer.

"I know we've already been discussing it and making plans, but I wanted to make it official. I've been promising this for years, and I thought it high time to fulfil that promise."

A sudden chill shivers along my back as I stare down at the ring. The diamond is huge and catches the light, even in the faintly lit room. Its not what I would have chosen, but it suits Daryl's tastes perfectly.

"We'll have it re-sized before the wedding. I've spoken to Father and he's already making arrangements for a day in two month's time." He smiles.

The waiter takes our order and pours Daryl a wine before refilling my water.

I stare at him with an unexpected sense of detachment. When I was ten, Daryl promised he'd marry me, and I've anticipated this moment for over eleven years. Now it's really happening and I should be ecstatic. Instead it's anticlimactic. He proposed like it was a business deal. There was no shimmering passion in his eyes as he declared that he loved me, as if the thought of being without me wasn't unbearable. It was clinical. But that's just Daryl being Daryl, I guess.

His hand clasps mine, and I give it a squeeze. Perhaps I'm just being ungrateful, considering I've had years to build unrealistic expectations about this moment.

"We really should start looking for a place soon" he says, his blue eyes shining on my mouth.

Then suddenly his fork clatters to his plate and his expression hardens.

Hair rises on the nape of my neck as I detect a presence behind me, and I turn slowly.

A man approaches us beneath the dull light, shadows seemingly attaching themselves to him as he stalks like a predator towards us. Broad shoulders, menacing height, he's the bigger, darker version of Daryl.

"Shit." Daryl growls and snatches up his phone. The screen lights up and is filled with missed calls and texts.

"Shit."

He drags the napkin over his mouth and is standing when the figure approaches.

"Little Brother." The deep voice winds through my ears.

"Kade." Daryl responds suspiciously.

I don't look up when he stops beside me, but I can feel the heat radiating from his body.

"Your phone's on silent, Daryl. You know how Father doesn't like it when he can't summon you on a whim."

"I was busy-"

"Save it for our *dear* father, Little Brother. It's so urgent he's sent his favourite minion to fetch you. I'll finish up here."

The chill of his tone irritates me.

"Don't order Daryl about like that. We're just about to have dinner. Can't he have a meal without interruption?."

Eyes of liquid metal swirl over me, eyebrow crawling up as he languidly takes me in. I lock my jaw and glare a challenge.

"Daryl will eat when Father says he can eat, princess, and no sooner. Don't fool yourself into imagining he's a man of independent thought."

Daryl scrolls through a message on his phone, flicking an alarmed glance between Kade and me.

"Brynn, darling, I have to go now. I don't know how long this will take, so I'll order you a taxi."

Kade crosses his arms over his thick chest.

"Oh, come now, Little Brother, the meals have just arrived. It would be rude to waste them. I'll eat with your companion and make sure she gets home safely afterwards."

"I don't want her near you at all, Kade. Not. Going. To. Happen." Daryl's fists clench.

I narrow my eyes on the both of them.

"Just stop. Both of you. I am capable of calling a taxi myself, thank you, Daryl, and I get to decide if I want to eat my meal or get take out, Kade. Not you."

Kade's eyes flash, and Daryl stabs an anxious look at his watch.

I land a kiss on his lips and take my seat.

"It's okay, Daryl. You need to go. I'll call you tomorrow."

"Sweetheart… be careful, okay? And Kade…just *don't*." Daryl growls, pushing past his brother.

"Just don't." Kade smirks as he lowers himself into the chair opposite me. He lifts the fork, poking the sliver of pork belly with distaste. The waiter appears beside him.

"Something wrong with your meal, sir?"

"No, thank you, but I've changed my mind. Put it all on the tab, and add a scotch fillet, medium rare with a side of vegetables."

"Very good, sir."

I'm startled by the kind tone in his voice for the waiter, but it morphs into the oddest tenderness the moment his eyes burn on me.

"Eat." He invites.

But he's soured what should have been one of the best nights of my life, so I cross my arms and glare at him.

"Defiant little thing, aren't you? I can hear your belly rumbling, but I do believe you'd starve yourself to get your point across."

He smirks, watching with interest to see what I'll do. Either way he wins. Either I obey him, or wait on him.

I select the option that would show less respect and raise a forkful of salmon.

Victory blazes as he watches it disappear behind my lips. It's unsettling having him silently watch me eat, focused on my mouth as I chew.

"So you're a hired thug for your father now? Putting all that aggression and violence to use I see."

Kade stiffens, his expression suddenly glacial. I know it's a low blow. The scars on his face are a permanent reminder of all the battles he's fought that ended with him hauled away in handcuffs. He's always been in trouble. The times I'd walk in to his home and see him standing defiant and wild with knuckles split and mouth grim, and Daryl and I would watch the door, knowing the cops would arrive soon.

"So you *have* been keeping tabs on me." He wings a brow.

"No, but everybody likes to gossip about the local bad guy. Do you act out because you have no friends? Is that it? Poor, troubled Kade isn't really a criminal, he's just misunderstood and needs a hug." Sarcasm drips from my tongue.

His knuckles whiten on the table and I flick to his face. Emotions I can't name crash over him and realisation punches me in the gut. He might appear cold and cruel, but his barely veiled emotions hover just below the surface. He's trying to rein them in, expression wild and raw, and I feel it inside me like an empathy carved in my bones. With a tilt of his head, he slips on his mask of nonchalance.

"You slay me, *pakvora*. A worthy opponent, finally. It's just a pity it will be wasted on my little brother."

I stiffen.

"What is *pakvora*?" I demand, a forkful of salmon hovering between my plate and mouth.

I catch his frown before he smooths it out, lifting those broad shoulders at me.

"It is you." He smiles, and I roll my eyes at his intentional evasiveness.

"You're enjoying this, aren't you? You know it riles me up and you get off on it." I accuse.

He answers with a wolfish grin I feel all the way to my toes. My lungs flounder when he leans forward, resting his chiselled jaw on one hand.

"Go on, *pakvora*, make my day and tell me you hate that I offer you a challenge that feeds your spark, how that urge to spread the wings you were born with isn't growing the longer you're with me. Lie to me, Brynn."

The low rumble of his voice soaks into me, and I'm grateful when his meal arrives and interrupts. He thanks the waiter, never shifting his attention from me. Carving a sliver of steak, Kade pauses before it reaches his mouth.

"Tell me, Brynn. Why do you want to marry my brother? What does a wild hawk want with a penned chicken?"

His stare intrudes too much until I'm left feeling like he knows the answers before I do.

"What do you know of me, Kade? I'm no wild hawk. You may not think too much of Daryl, but we were always meant to be together and you need to accept it."

He rolls his eyes. "It's not *real*, *pakvora*. It was never written in the stars. It's nothing more than a childish promise that should have remained in your childhood where it belongs. Deep down you know it. I *know* you do. You ask yourself where the passion is, the hunger you crave, the flames you want to be consumed by. What makes you hold on to that dream instead of chasing the reality?"

My breath catches. In my mind, a hawk launches into flight, soaring over the treetops with freedom in its heart.

"I have lost you, *pakvora*." He smiles softly and I blink the image away.

"I love Daryl, Kade. I love being with him. He takes care of me -"

"You do not need to be taken care of, Brynn. You need to be free."

"What do you know of my needs, Kade?" I hiss. "You're a stranger to me."

He tilts his head, a shock of untamed dark hair spilling over one eye.

"But I'm not, am I?" He murmurs, slipping the steak between his lips, his strong jaw working as his stare burrows into me.

My thoughts soften in confusion. The faint scent of exotic spice and dawn takes root in my lungs, and I instinctively pull in a deeper breath of the oddly familiar fragrance as I chew my lip. He's so damned sure of himself he intrigues me and I find I'm instinctively chasing the epiphany he's taunting me with. When I realise I've taken his bait, I glare defiantly.

"If you're not a stranger, who are you?" I bite.

"I'm a troubled, misunderstood man who just needs a hug."

I huff a laugh. "I see you removed the criminal label off yourself. Reformed so quickly?"

He smiles then, wide and genuine. A dimple pops on his cheek and my focus locks on to it. Then I reach for my water and Kade catches sight of the ring. His smile freezes and breaks.

"You're engaged?" He rasps.

He's rattled. Truly shaken. I lift my chin.

"Before you interrupted us, Kade. We made it official. I'm going to be your sister-in-law."

His huge fist tightens around his cutlery and his tone is straight from hell.

"You will *not* marry Daryl, Brynn. You can't…"

Something about his response makes me uneasy. I feel his anger, watch wild expressions dance over his features. Other emotions mix in, tumbling about inside.

Panic?

His grip shoots around my fingers, his warm hand sending sharp tingles through my veins. With a startled cry I try to escape his clasp, but he traps my hand.

"This has gone too far, Brynn. Stop this now. Too many people have been hurt already. Please."

Real fear seizes me, and I drag my hand free. Feral eyes plead with me as I stumble to my feet and manage to dodge his reaching hand. He stands with me, the look on his face so raw I clutch at a pain in my chest that feels foreign and familiar all at once. Logic fragments and I uselessly seek council among the shards.

"Kade? I…I don't understand."

At my whisper his throat bobs, and right before he buries it all away, I catch sight of the lost and frightened child behind it all.

I make my way to the door and out into the street, my mind whirling, and climb into the taxi.

CHAPTER 9

KADE

She got away. Again. Too weak from the shock, I wasn't able to hold on to her and she slipped from my grasp. It's a cruel pattern that never stops tearing at my heart.

All the things I needed to say to her became trapped in my throat, and what did manage to squeeze through my lips caused her to bristle and fight me instead of warm to me the way she should have.

I noticed how she reacted to me, saw how she stubbornly fought it as if she'd forgotten how to trust her instincts. She fought me. And for a fleeting second, that old spark she's learned to stifle in Daryl's presence came to life. Right now, I'll take any victory at all.

I drag the napkin over my mouth and toss it on the plate. Mum told me to have faith, but all that's given me is front row tickets to the blossoming, deepening relationship between Brynn and Daryl that holds me on a fragile blade between breaking and rebelling. Now it's gotten out of hand, and the sour taste of deception burns my throat with the need to intervene.

I've spent the best part of eleven years watching from the sidelines as Daryl steals my podium. I let him have it, coiled with angst as I impatiently waited it out, but I can't stand by any more. When all weapons are bloody and the battle is done, Brynn *must* choose me.

I drag my hand through hair that refuses to be tamed, and lean back, willing my pulse to calm. I need to speak to Daryl, and I can't do it with this adrenaline coursing through me. I glare at the two plates, neither meal finished. It's appropriate, really. When it comes to me and Brynn, it's not nearly over. We're fate interrupted, and I need us back on track. She's always been mine but somehow, along the way destiny became confused.

I grunt at the food I can no longer bear to eat, empty a handful of notes on the table, and seek night's reprieve.

The chill of the air does nothing to calm the beast that stirs below my skin, and my knuckles itch. I slide my key in the lock, still surprised that Father hasn't changed them on me, knowing after tonight he probably will. The lights are all out. I prowl down the hallway, slamming open Daryl's door amid the seething growls of betrayal scorching my lips.

"What the fuck do you intend to do now, Little Brother? Do you really intend to see this ridiculous scheme through? Do you even care that you're hurting Brynn?"

His face is lit with fear by the night light beside his bed as he scrambles from beneath the covers. My rage falters when I spot it, the soft glow still giving him comfort all these years on. It shines like a beacon over everything I no longer know about him.

"What can I do to make you stop this, Daryl?" I hiss.

"Stop what, Kade? Nothing I do has anything to do with you, so you've no right to step into something you don't understand. And not that it's any of your business, but I'm not hurting Brynn. Nothing can ever cause me to hurt my future wife."

Future wife. He's making it perfectly clear he has no intention of stopping now. My fist lands on his cheekbone with all the force of my white hot rage and he crumples to the floor with a cry of pain.

Shit. I've done it now.

I struck my own brother. I stagger away with a grunt of horror, curbing my need to keep swinging and swinging until the pain leaves me.

"What the fuck was that for?" Daryl cradles his eye, knees pulled up protectively against his chest.

"You *know* what it's for, Daryl and there's something else you need to know, too. I've let you have your fun up until now, but since you insist on playing dirty, you can expect me to be everywhere you are, playing my own dirty game. This is one battle I won't let you win, so cut the shit before it hurts more than just the three of us!"

Daryl stares blankly up at me, fingering the darkening bruise on his face, and the remorse streams in like poison in my veins. I raised a fist to Daryl. I hurt my little brother.

I lock my knees so I don't drop to the floor and beg him for forgiveness.

He's gone too far for that. Instead, I snarl down at him and watch him flinch as I flex my fists in a silent threat before turning my back on him.

I storm down the hallway, another bridge collapsing in flames behind me, and toss my house key on the hardwood floor. I won't feel the sting of rejection from Father if I reject him first, because I know he won't tolerate me threatening his golden haired protégé.

Guilt collides with relief as my shoes crunch on the stone driveway. I already have my assurance that this wedding won't happen, but I was hoping I'd save Daryl the humiliation, and not have to resort to speaking to Father again. But after tonight, I know he's fixing to win whatever fucked-up game he's playing and it's time to act.

My stomach churns, and it feels so damned wrong, but I pull out my phone before I lose my nerve completely.

CHAPTER 10

BRYNN

"W hat happened?" I gasp.

"Kade" Daryl seethes, his glare emphasising his swollen, closed eye. My heart bottoms out.

"Your brother *attacked* you?"

He doesn't need to clarify. I remember feeling overwhelmed by Kade's emotions last night. What pushed him so far he felt the need to use his fists on Daryl?

"Why?" I ask.

Daryl flicks his attention to the floor, shrugging with confusion.

"Is it because we're engaged?" I press.

Daryl startles.

"Why do you say that?" He demands in a tight voice.

"Perhaps because when he saw your ring last night he…became upset. Said I couldn't marry you. What's that all about, Daryl?"

"He's insane, Brynn. I told you he's demented, now you've seen it for yourself. Just flipped out and attacked me for no reason. He's dangerous, Brynn. You need to keep away from him."

***

"I love you, Brynn." Daryl whispers as his lips drag across my forehead. After a lovely meal on the waterfront, we're in Daryl's car, my feet curled under me and head resting in the crook of his neck while we talk.

"Show me." I whisper, running the tip of my tongue over his ear lobe.

He shivers. I hear his heart beat faster. I swallow in anticipation. Nothing but the gentleman since the night of the party, and I've given up trying to bring that subject up.

His lips burn, but they don't shift. He sighs heavily, pulling away.

"I can't, Brynn. I want to, so bad, but we need to wait until we're married."

"Are we in the sixteenth century, Daryl? We're going to be married. We're engaged, for crying out loud, and It's not as if we haven't-"

"But we can't. Just…trust me, Brynn. I need to do this right."

Daryl blows out a harsh breath, cutting me off. He flexes his fist, turning his blown out pupils to me. The flash of heat in his darkened eyes considers my proposal briefly before they harden in determination.

I mentally roll my eyes, biting the inside of my cheek as I bury the waves of desire once more.

"No one will know... Just like the-" I mutter weakly, already knowing my point is moot.

 Right on cue he barks out an oath and slams the wheel. "Yes they will." He growls and points into the darkness.

Kade leans against a tree, one foot against the trunk, hands tucked into the pockets of his jeans. Although it's close to midnight, he wears a cowboy hat dipped over his eyes so low I wonder if he even sees us.

I watch his white teeth glow in the darkness as he nods. I'm out of the car before I register, storming to a stop before Kade.

"What the hell are you doing, Kade? Don't they have curfew in prison?"

He grins, clutching his chest dramatically and I see the torn skin of his knuckles from Daryl's face.

"Oh, you wound me, *pakvora*. You will be pleased to know I am on a noble mission this lovely night. I'm your chaperone, here to guard your chastity."

I snort incredulously.

"I don't need a chaperone. In fact, I don't want you here at all. Do everyone a favour and leave."

His eyes widen and I glimpse the shimmer of silver beneath the rim of his hat.

"But I was enjoying the show! It was a good one tonight, a bit of steam, but not too much. It's got to hurt that he's still knocking you back."

Horrified and burning with shame, my palm snaps against his cheek. I gasp as heat flashes in his glare.

"Look at this, Little Brother. She's a real wildcat and definitely more than you can handle. Why don't you give her what she needs?"

Daryl growls in his throat, takes a step towards Kade and pulls up short.

Kade's lips peel back in a sneer.

"Scared of me, Little Brother?"

"What do you want, Kade?" I snap.

Kade straightens. "Ah, now *that's* an interesting question, don't you think, Little Brother?"

"Kade!" Daryl exhales sharply.

"I'm just making conversation, Little Brother, but take a closer look at your fiancee, here. Just by speaking with me she's a breathless mess. I'll bet she doesn't react to *you* like that!"

I choke on a curse. My lungs strain and my blood thrums.

I hiss as I aim another slap at him, but he catches my wrist before I see him move. He yanks me against his chest so hard I feel the thunder of his heart and his body burning against mine.

"Don't touch her, you piece of shit!" Daryl threatens behind me, but makes no move to step in. My free hand flies up to break away from Kade, but it collides with the hard ridges of his abs instead, and I'm immobilised by the ripple of them every time he breathes. I feel everything, and his face is so close to mine, his wild and unapologetic hunger filling my view.

He lifts my wrist to his mouth and presses his lips lightly there, the violent explosions that detonate in my veins curling the corner of his mouth up.

"You will not marry my brother, *pakvora*." He murmurs only for me as he steps aside and melts back into the darkness.

***

My world begins to crumble quickly after that night. Every time Daryl and I are together over the next few weeks, silver eyes seem to be lurking somewhere in the shadows. The atmosphere becomes so tense between us that on the Friday afternoon, I cancel our dinner plans and seek the solitude of McAllister farm instead. With my obsession with Daryl and the added madness of the wedding plans, I've barely spent time with Mum and Dad.

"How are the wedding plans progressing?" Mum slides my plate of roast lamb at me with sparkling eyes.

"I suppose they're going okay. Antony is pretty adamant that it follow certain guidelines, so Daryl and I are leaving him to organise it. I don't care as long as we're married in the end." I shrug.

Mum's brow crinkles.

"Don't you think it's a little strange to be so nonchalant over getting married? When I married your father, I was so excited that there was nothing in this world that could stop me from involving myself in every aspect of it. Time drags so slowly when you're crazy with anticipation, and every color choice and flower selection brought me closer to my forever with him."

My lips thin.

"I guess this is different. We've known forever that we would be married, so we've had plenty of time to get used to the idea. I guess…maybe I'm having a hard time preparing myself for the changes. I mean, once we're married Daryl wants us to move closer to the city, and I never gave that much thought until now. I love our farm, and there's a chunk of my heart that hopes Daryl will one day buy us some land, too, even though I know he won't. I know marriage means compromise, and it makes sense that we'd move closer to his work…But I figure if I need to walk for hours through some paddocks, I can always come back here."

Dad clears his throat and Mum frowns at the table, and a shiver chills my spine. The silence stretches and neither will meet my eyes. Dad pokes at his potatoes but seems to have suddenly lost his appetite.

"I *can* come back here to visit, can't I?" My voice thins.

Dad gently rests his cutlery beside his plate and explains hesitantly.

"Uh, we were going to wait until after the wedding to tell you, but your mother and I have decided to sell the farm, downsize and maybe travel a little."

My heart freezes. McAllister Farm has been in the family for generations, and I lost count of the times Dad claimed the only way he'd leave the farm was in a wooden box. Emotion hardens Mum's face and rims her eyes red. Dad grows old as I watch. When his throat bobs, I realise it's not a choice.

"What happened, Dad?" I choke, and he grips the napkin in a fist.

His heavy sigh empties his chest, and suddenly, my proud, strong farmer father is an empty husk of a man.

"You remember when we made all the improvements years ago? We only did so by opening the farm up to investors who collect dividends from our profits. It's enabled us to optimise the production, and line our pockets substantially. Last month, our largest investor pulled out, and we've had trouble finding another to replace it. We have a couple of weeks to source another, but it's not very promising. If we can't, the only option we have is to sell, pay out the remaining investors and find a place in town."

My eyes dart around the kitchen. I grew up here. I slept beneath the hay in the barn behind the house. There's a chunk missing from the oak tree behind me from where Dad attempted to teach me to drive. This is my home. Every one of my memories and secrets is embedded in the plaster walls, hidden beneath the layers of grass in the paddocks. Echoes of my soul in every nook and cranny on the farm. I feel free here, and I can't lose that.

My mind is a turbulent collision of thoughts and emotions, but something floats to the surface and niggles at me. Daryl is set to take over Walker Enterprises, a company worth billions of dollars, and the farm financials can confirm McAllister Farm would be a damned good investment. Then Mum and Dad can stay as long as they like, and I will have a place to breathe when the city gets too much.

Before I head upstairs to bed, I kiss Dad gently on the temple.

"Just hold out for a while, Dad. I think I have an idea."

I can't promise anything. Antony's still in control of the company, but it doesn't mean Daryl can't have a say in it. In less than a month, Daryl and I will starting a new life as husband and wife. After that, the transitioning will begin for Antony to step back and Daryl to step up. Surely he can be free to make an investment at that point. My stomach turns gently with the doubt that Daryl will stand up to his father, even for me. Or maybe that curdling feeling came when I thought of growing old with Daryl.

***

I open the door to Bella, her hands clasping an overnight bag and a tub of ice cream. I collapse in her arms, sobbing.

"Brynn, sweetie. I'm here for as long as it takes to figure this out. Now tell me what's wrong."

Between my bleeding heart and heavy hiccups I explain about Kade's behaviour, and his promise that I not wed Daryl.

Her mouth gapes as I continue, the scoop hovers and ice cream melts, forgotten, as she listens.

"...And now the major investor in McAllister farm has withdrawn. If Mum and Dad can't find another one within the next few weeks, they will have to sell the farm!"

Bella blinks, unable to summon comforting words.

"I don't know what it is with Daryl since Kade attacked him. He's been really agitated and he won't tell me why. He assures me he wants to marry me, but he's so distant at times that I'm beginning to have doubts."

"I don't know what to do about your parents, Bry, I mean, who has that kind of money? But I'm sure Walker Empire has a tiny account to cover it if it came to it. It's only three weeks out from the wedding, the banks might hold off. And as for Daryl, I'm sure this is just nerves. He's a good guy, Bry, and he'd be beside himself if he knew you were worried about him."

"You're right, Bell. Maybe this is part of the pre-wedding jitters people keep talking about. I have a meeting on Monday with Antony, I assume it has to do with a pre-nup or something, and then it's a waiting game."

Somewhat pacified, Bella and I spend the weekend watching old movies in our pyjamas.

CHAPTER 11

KADE

I try and reach Brynn, but the church is so thick with people it seems the more I push through, the further away from her I get. I catch glimpses of her, but she never looks my way. The church becomes a steep mountain, and I can barely make out the figures of Brynn and Daryl at the peak. The sheer cliff face is broken glass that slices through my fingers and shreds my feet, but it can't stop me from chasing her. Night and day circle past as I climb, and I'm so cold without her that my bones ache. Finally, I make it to the top. On shredded hands and knees I crawl to her, a finger length from touching her when the chilling voice comes from above.

"I now pronounce you husband and wife."

Daryl aims his sneering victory my way as he winds his arms around her. He kisses her the way I was fated to. It's impossible to breathe, and I'm aware of a burning pain in my chest. Still on my knees, I look down. My chest is carved open, my heart dying on the ground at Brynn's feet. I fight for air, but it doesn't come, and she remains in Daryl's arms, oblivious to my presence.

A single thought splits my skull with truth.

I'll die without you, Brynn. A gypsy can't live without his heart.

Then I'm falling backwards, off the cliff and into the place where souls go to be forgotten.

I wake with a strangled cry, gasping for air around the knot of pain in my chest. It has to be my guilty conscience disrupting my sleep, eating into the only part of my life remaining where existing doesn't hurt. The things I've done are itching splinters in my veins that refuse to dislodge, the way I imagine a murder lives inside a man never designed for violence.

Where will it stop? What twisted lengths am I yet to reach in the pursuit of Brynn? If I stop right now, will I be absolved of my sins?

My fingers scrape through my hair as my exhale hisses. The things I've already done can't be undone. Or forgiven. It's all so futile, seeking to hold the one thing I need more than air while knowing I've already sabotaged our future. I growl into the dawn's chill, overwhelmed by the contradictions I've already become. For her.

The urge to beg her forgiveness before the chaos unfolds tightens my jaw until my head throbs. I could stop this now, and just maybe she will understand my reasons.

But the years of compounding rejection and prejudice make it impossible for me to reveal my heart to anyone, let alone the woman who owns my soul without realising it.

I'm used to being loathed and feared, but those feelings coming from Brynn would end me. I'll maintain my mask of impenetrability, belying the fact that even the casual shun from a stranger rips open those wounds that never heal.

***

Two weeks out from the wedding. Fourteen and a half days in which to change her stubborn mind. The distraction strips the satisfaction from the farm work, and I'm unable to set aside my irritability and focus on any task. When my phone rings, I'm grateful for the interruption.

"Hello?" I answer tersely without checking the number.

"Well, I don't need to ask you how you're doing, son." Mum's soft voice crackles.

"As well as can be expected when there's nobody cheering from my corner." I snap.

As soon as the words are out, the guilt replaces them, and I appeal to the cloudless sky for whatever crumb of patience it can offer.

"Sorry, Mum. You didn't deserve that." I murmur.

She doesn't. She's never said as much, but I know Mum and I share something special, something deeper than blood and more important than family, and Father has always been jealous of it. She's one of two people in this messed up world who really understands me. The other is Brynn, if she'd only open her eyes.

"If there's one thing I've learned, Kade, it's that arriving at the destiny you're allotted is never an easy road, but it's inevitable. I know I'm a broken record, but have faith that it's all unfolding as it should."

Its a mantra becoming harder and harder to believe in.

"Kade?" Her voice has a curious lilt to it that pricks my ears.

"Antony was finalising the documents this morning, and he's got the legal team going over it in preparation for the wedding and... what happened at that party years ago...*accidentally* slipped out of my mouth. I thought I'd give you a warning."

My lungs constrict. That damned party. The night where I watched the harmless flame between Daryl and Brynn catch fire; the heart wrenching glance that ended with Daryl's ring on her finger. The expression of fierce determination and honed desire as she followed my brother inside.

That night changed me on a molecular level. It stained my humanity and poisoned my morality. Even now, the bitter taste of my violated morals won't fade.

I couldn't set eyes on Daryl for months afterwards. Or Brynn. It hurt too damned much to face either of them, but I still tortured myself with news of them through Bella.

I know the contents of the document in question, because since I found out they were to be married I'd studied the pages thoroughly, scouring every word and every line for loopholes.

Now, for the first time in years, I feel the dormant seed of hope send out a tentative root, because Mum just stopped the wedding.

CHAPTER 12

BRYNN

*M*onday morning arrives abruptly, and I sit anxiously in the library, waiting for Antony to call me in.

"Brynn." There's no mistaking Kade's dark rumble.

I hear the leather groan as he sits behind me. My pulse spikes at his nearness, but I guard my expression, pick at an invisible speck on my top and ignore him.

"A true marriage should be the collision of two hearts beating to the same rhythm, a natural, intrinsic progression from passion and understanding. What it is not, is a clinical agreement between friends."

My mouth drops.

"What planet are you living on, Kade? You have no idea what Daryl and I feel for one another. Besides, love is built on admiration, mutual respect and-"

Kade yawns obnoxiously, then slits his eyes.

"Love is not a garden you need to nurture, Brynn. Love just is."

His steel gaze darkens to pewter. My blood warms.

Love just is.

"For your information, I love Daryl."

I'm drawn into those pewter pits for the longest time, then heat flashes in their depths. The inferno has me drawing a breath, the faintest gasp parting my lips.

"I don't think you do." He whispers conspiratorially as Antony's voice calls my name from the hall.

My throat is dry when I reach the office. It's all oak and class with an undeniable scent of money, just as one would expect of the owner of a billion dollar company.

Evie blends into the seat beside him, a silent support for her husband. Her brown eyes twinkle on me with kindness. My smile falters as Antony stands.

"We have a problem." He states without preamble.

"Oh?" I manage, my mouth parched all over again.

He clears his throat, a crimson stain climbing his neck.

"It seems you, ah, erm, I've been made aware that...you have uh, engaged in activities generally restricted to marriage."

What? I frown, and suddenly it dawns. I'm not a virgin.

"Are you asking me if I've been intimate with a man?" I gasp.

"Ah, yes. No. I have been informed that you have…engaged in such an activity, and I'm asking you to confirm or deny it."

My face burns. This is ridiculous. I glance around to make certain I haven't fallen back into the sixteenth century knowing that would be preferable to the current scenario where I discuss my sexual history with my future in-laws.

"Yes. Just once, but why is it important? Clearly Daryl hasn't been saving himself."

Like a nightmare unfolding, the door behind Antony opens and Daryl bursts into the room, expression twisting with pain.

"You were meant to be mine, nobody else's!" His accusing tone jars.

"It was only one time, Daryl, and it was with-"

"I don't want to hear it, Brynn. You've spoiled everything!"

I stare at him incredulously. I gave him my innocence, and now he's brandishing it like a weapon…or maybe a shield. He would have known this would come up, he was the one who mentioned the meeting, and he never told me to expect this, didn't even ask me to lie about it. I'm numb with shock at the panic radiating off him. The white knuckles, the muscles taut in his neck. But the look on his face; he's genuinely shattered.

"This is-" I begin, injustice boiling in my throat.

"No." Antony holds up a hand and the room falls silent.

"As trivial as you may feel this matter is, Brynn, this complicates everything. This…situation is in violation of the legal requirements of Daryl's future bride. We're grateful for your honesty, but that doesn't change the facts. You can't marry Daryl if you're not a virgin. Daryl will not be taking over the company and there will be no wedding."

I've taken my last breath as the future Mrs Daryl Walker.

***

I hear the tentative approach of footsteps on the lawn and I swivel my head, hoping for Daryl. My eyes collide with silver.

Kade.

The hollow ache in my chest takes him in. Tight, casual jeans and a shirt that clings to his body like a second skin.

"Are you okay?" He asks as he gracefully lowers to the grass, using the same gentle mannerism as his mother but without the stiffness of age. He'd have to be almost twenty seven now. There are six years between him and his brother, and I'm the same age as Daryl.

"What do you care, Kade? You have what you wanted. I won't be marrying Daryl. You must be on top of the world right now. I just don't understand what Daryl and I did to make you hate us."

I want to be angry, but I'm guttered. Empty.

"Christ, Brynn, I don't hate you or Daryl, I just…" He shakes his head.

"It doesn't matter, Kade. None of it does. Everything's broken and its all my fault. I just want to fix it."

I stare at the manicured grass, Evie's rose garden lawn.

"I can help, if you'll let me?"

Something inside his offer makes me look harder at him. "What can you do to help, Kade? Go on, tell me how you can solve all my problems. I can't see how throwing punches will fix anything."

The slightest flinch flits over his face.

"I can't solve them all, *pakvora*, but I can help with a few, and I assure you I will not be fighting. I have been made aware of the situation with your parents as well as the particulars of the legal documents that complicated your plans. What I suggest to you now is that I know of a loophole in the papers to allow Daryl to take over the company, and I might know of an investor for McAllister Farm that's ready to go should you wish it."

I don't completely believe the rot about the wedding not going ahead, but the thought of turning my back on my family home, their security and my youth strips me bare. It's all over town that McAllister Farm needs an investor. You can't hide anything in a small town. I'd spend the rest of my life married to damn Barnaby Coates in his floral dress rather than try and live with the guilt of letting my family down. This marriage business with Daryl and me…we have time to work it out.

Heartbreaking, but not set in concrete. Mum and Dad can't wait.

My heart thumps and I dare to allow the first ray of hope since Antony tore apart my future.

"What about Daryl and me? Got any magic wand to wave over that one?" I watch his jaw tic and the air dumps out of my lungs.

"No, Brynn. That document is too recent to have any loopholes. The new legal team they employ are exceptional-" He cuts off with a sigh.

"But nothing is free, *pakvora*. I can give you these things only if you agree on the terms."

"Which are?"

His eyes descend into deep pewter. "Marry *me*."

I choke out a cough and swallow the lump of insane laughter that threatens to spill out.

"You truly are insane, Kade. Why would I want to marry you?"

Kade flinches, his body tightening with tension. With a measured, weighted swallow, he steadies his gaze.

His focus is so deep I can feel him running his eyes over my soul and I rub down the goose bumps that crawl over my arms.

"Not many people know, but my farm isn't a branch of Walker Empire. It's mine. The problem I have is because I share the same brilliant legal team as them, I know that the only way to release the funds to invest in

McAllister Farm is to marry. Only my new wife will have access the term deposits prematurely, while the legalities are being sorted out and the finances are transferred into her name."

I taste the bitter reason in his explanation. It would dig my parents out of that hole they'd found themselves in. There would be next to no hope of finding a big investor, especially within the time frame required. And running the Walker Empire was Daryl's whole reason for existing. If that was torn from beneath him…

"And Daryl?" I press.

"That's just a freebie. I don't care about the company. It was always meant to be Daryl's. I just happen to have been made privy to a slight error in his favour that I can use if I so desire."

I swallow thickly. "And if I don't agree to marry you?"

He shrugs nonchalantly. "Then your parents have one week to find a new investor with a few million in their pockets, and Daryl has to wait until Antony dies to run the company, or…" His lips curl, "…he marries a virgin."

CHAPTER 13

BRYNN

*M*y breaths are too shallow. Bella's bony arms rope around me while I fight to stop the world spinning.

"Breathe, Bry. We'll find a way out of this. Just breathe."

But there is no way out. An hour ago I held the world in my hands, the key to every one of my hopes and dreams within reach, and now I have nothing, fingers closing on air.

I don't know what the answer is, but there's no way I'll find it within Kade's proposal.

My future was blonde and blue eyed, like our children would be, but where Daryl used to stand, the image in my head is nothing but shadows and holes.

Bella lowers me to her couch, my stomach rolling. I'd sent a quick text to Mum and Dad to let them know I'd be staying with Bella so at least I can delay the nightmare of seeing their faces and knowing I'd let them down. I won't have to witness their tired resignation when I explain to them that because I once defied them and snuck out to a party, I set into motion a series of events that would lead to them losing their home.

I know I'm in shock, but the only thing on replay in my head right now is the bewildering horror on Daryl's face etched in my mind. He gave me no warning, not even a hint, and it's so uncharacteristic of Daryl to be anything less than supportive, let alone react so violently to something he was well aware of.

My head pounds so hard that I swear it's going to burst open, and I don't even look when Bella shoves a glass in my hand.

I take a gulp to soothe my arid mouth, and my throat catches fire.

Choking, I gasp and huff.

Bella's laughter muffles and I glare at her.

"I'm sorry, Bry, but I figured you could use something a bit stronger than water. I expected you to look before you drank it. Never thought I'd see the day you'd swap water for Dad's top shelf whiskey."

Eventually, the scorch dies into a tingly warmth, and Bella wordlessly slops more whiskey in the empty glass.

"I just can't get my head around it, Bell. I was always supposed to be Mrs Daryl Walker. And with one moment, everything I was so sure of has disintegrated. How does that happen?"

In the silence that was supposed to reveal answers, Bella shakes her head, perplexed. "I'm more interested to understand why Daryl even entertained that clause in the first place, especially considering what happened at the party. He would have had to expect this, unless he thought he could get away with it…"

"That's the other oddity. Whenever I'd try to bring up what happened between us at the party, he'd give me an almost pained expression, like it hurt him watching me try and put it into words. I always gave up pretty quick, but looking back, maybe he thought that if I didn't say it aloud he could pretend it never happened."

Bella's forehead creases.

"But who else would know? If Daryl wanted to pretend it never happened for legal reasons, how could anyone know? Besides that look of bliss on your face when I bring it up, discussing something so personal with anyone makes you squeamish."

She's right. Only Bella knows the barest details of that night, and Daryl wouldn't have mentioned it to anyone. Even if someone were eavesdropping on every private conversation Daryl and I had, my awkward stuttering and trailing off into silence would be impossible to decipher.

I shake my head, the day's events still numbing my body from feeling that heartbreak that waits, and the whiskey anesthetizing my brain. I take another sip and recoil. I hate alcohol, but right now the heat in my core replaces the cold emptiness of reality.

"I don't care what happens, Bell. Daryl and I promised each other our happily ever after, and neither of us break our promises. We will find a way past this."

***

In the cold light of day, the shock and the numbness remain, and I use it to carry myself through the walk of shame from Bella's home and into the family kitchen. I glance around with cold finality, trying to imagine the shelves of trinkets and heirlooms empty and just can't. I wrap my arms around my waist, the smell of this mornings breakfast lingering like a bittersweet memory from my youth. When life wasn't so messy and complicated.

My exhale shudders out at the sound of gumboots, heavy with mud, advancing up the path. I square my shoulders as they shake with a thud to the verandah. I suck in a breath as my parents push through the door.

I never noticed before how the passing time has bent their spines and deepened the lines on their faces.

I love them, and it breaks me to see the doom in their expressions. If I accept Kade's offer, I will see them smile again. I can keep them safe. I can serve up their dream of living here with the echoes of our ancestors. But doing so will irreparably destroy the future I'd planned with Daryl. And if I honour my heart and fight for Daryl?

As Mum and Dad reach the front door, there's a moment before they see me. In that space I see the raw defeat anchored there, and I'm beaten.

Gutted.

My insides have been sliced open and cleaned out, and I'm empty and hollow.

I can't let them down.

When they see me, they light with smiles that can't meet their eyes, and I dash past them before I change my mind.

"I…uh. I have to go."

Daryl is white as a ghost. I wrap my arms around him and curl up on his lap. He strokes my hair absently, still consumed by the news I've just delivered to him.

"Please don't, Brynn. I just need some time to figure it out. That's all. Just…Kade is only doing this to hurt me, and you're seriously considering his offer?"

I swallow, still struggling to process my decision, trying to explain to Daryl that the lack of options has already decided me.

"Tell me honestly, Daryl. How good are our chances right now?" I ask gently, even though I know the answer will hurt.

His voice breaks, and it takes him two swallows to form the words.

"I…I've had three different solicitors check over it, Brynn. There's nothing they can find that changes where we are. I won't stop, though. I promised you we'd be married, and I keep my word."

I cringe as the bitter taste of betrayal fills my mouth.

"Daryl. I know you will. But right now, my parents need me. I can't let them down. They will lose everything if I don't do something immediately, and you won't be able to help until your father hands the company over to you. That transition could take years and you know it. Mum and Dad only have a week. The only way I can think of to help them is..."

I can't say it. The tortured growl that forms in Daryl's throat has me sobbing. I clutch him, and he holds me as if he'll never let me go. I wish for time to hold us here forever.

***

The exhaustion that turns my bones to liquid makes it impossible to do anything but sit in my car and try to summon the will to drive away. Once I do, though, there's no coming back. The second I drive out the gate I may as well be signing on the dotted line, officially waiving my right to own Daryl's heart.

I spot Kade's approach in the side mirror. So sure, so cocky. I grip the wheel.

He crouches so that his eyes are level with mine and doesn't say a word. We remain there for what seems like hours, balancing on the edge of indecision. I swallow so loud his focus immediately intensifies.

It's there, under the consuming pewter scrutiny of the devil that I sell my soul.

"I'll marry you, Kade."

***

That's the madness that led me to this moment. The frantic reassurances to my parents that I've secretly been in love with Kade all these years is one of the craziest things I've done. Kade stands beside me, arm draped over my shoulders, the heat radiates through his clothes distracting me. Their bewilderment is kinder to them than the thought their daughter destroying her reputation all those years ago. Bella's eyes glint with sympathy, and her reassuring hug is fierce.

Right now, instead of waiting for me at the alter, Daryl stands off to the side with the other groomsmen in his black pants, white shirt and blue cummerbund. The colour highlights the shine of his unshed tears.

I hold my head high as I make my way past the faces filling the chairs, trying to ignore the burning curiosity in their expressions. Evie apologised profusely to them all, citing an error in printing as the reason Kade stands in the groom's place, but their expressions tell me few of them actually believe it. Kade stands rigid and proud, like he was always supposed to be my husband. It's such a convincing act I give him a grateful half smile as Dad deposits me before him.

"You look stunning in that dress." Kade whispers.

I warm at his compliment. Without the pressure of finding a dress befitting of Mrs Daryl Walker, I chose the dress I loved. Nowhere near the price tag of the others, but so much more…me.

"You look like a man with a motive." I breathe back. He chuckles softly at my resistance.

"Be honest, *pakvora*, you like what you see."

I snort, but with a sweep of my gaze I know it's true. His suit hugs him, pulled tight against his arms and across his chest. His silver cummerbund snug around his narrow waist. His pants are equally mesmerising on him, tailored to cling to his backside and wrap lovingly around his thick, powerful thighs. Combined with the beautiful face nature bestowed on him, Kade is spectacular.

A man in perfect control.

"You need to know I won't be the submissive slave you want. I will fight you 'til the end."

His lips split in a genuine smile. "I love your fire too much to want to extinguish it. I expect nothing less from you."

He plays his part flawlessly.

Until the vows.

The celebrant feeds Kade his lines. "With this ring I thee wed."

Kade plucks a ring from the cushion, sliding it over the first knuckle. I gasp in awe. A vivid green stone, set in a simple white gold band, subtle yet utterly breathtaking in its perfect simplicity. I feel it expresses exactly who I am, like if I could design a ring by describing it as free, and wild, this would be it. Like it was made just for me.

"Oh!" I breathe in delight, catching his gaze. His eyes hold mine for so long the celebrant clears his throat.

"With this ring I thee wed" He prompts again.

"With this ring…" Kade chokes into silence and I search his eyes frantically.

He's disappeared inside himself, flickers of unknown thoughts race across his face like shooting stars, and I can't identify a single one.

Is he going to change his mind?

His lips part and he fills his lungs. His eyes anchor to something ancient within, then focus with crystal clarity on me. Understanding burns bright as his lips move.

"With this ring, I thee wed, and with it, I bestow upon thee all the treasures of my mind, my heart and my hands. My soul is joined with thee, the threads of our hearts forever entwined. I belong to thee, beyond the confines of time and spirit. Beyond our song on this earth."

I frown. They're not the vows we practised. But within those words, briefly, something makes perfect sense. Silver glowing and mystified, he seems to search inside me.

I recite the vow we practised stiffly, thrown by Kade's unexpected deviation.

"I now pronounce you, husband and wife. You may now kiss the bride."

His mouth is on mine before I can react. Warm, soft lips that moved with firm pressure that somehow lingers in every blood cell in my body. Incapable of thought, all I can do is feel. My spine relaxes and my body with it. I'm so close to him the heat radiating from his chest warms my breast.

Oh!

Flooded by sensation, saturated by the scent of spicy aftershave, I sigh softly into his mouth. So unexpectedly exquisite, his mouth. His arm burns around my waist. My hands seek his chest. Suddenly, he darts out his tongue, demanding entrance to my mouth. With a groan, I surrender, incapable of anything else.

Then he breaks the kiss.

No!

Boiling pewter regards me as I fight to steady my pulse. Those sinful lips lift at the corners like he knows exactly what he's done to me.

Flash!

The camera breaks the spell, the applause bringing reality into focus again. His hand engulfs mine as we stand before our friends and family, a grin on those swollen lips.

***

The reception is awkward. I feel like all my closest friends and family bore witness to the greatest lie I ever told.

"Oh, sweetheart" Mum whispers into my hair. "I wasn't sure about this sudden change of plan, but I understand, now. You two look so in love. I'm so happy for you!" Happiness shimmers and runs over her cheek. Dad stands straight and square with a grin plastered on his freshly shaved face.

Bella yanks me into a hug. She knows there's no need for words. She holds me for the longest time.

Kade is smiling with an older couple when Daryl steps up beside me.

"Brynn…"

There's so much pain in one broken word that I take a step back so I don't reach for him. I feel the distance like a knife blade.

"This was meant to be us, Daryl. It was supposed to be perfect."

He recoils at the low tone of my rage. His throat bobs, his tone plaintive.

"You think this is *my* fault?"

"I wasn't the one who stipulated in legal documents that my spouse was to come from the middle ages!"

"We were supposed to wait until we were married!"

"And you're regretting that *now*?" I seethe.

A shot of irritation fires in my lungs as Daryl's eyes widen in confusion. I'm so damned sick of this game; this ignorance he chooses to hold on to is what got us into this mess in the first place.

I feel Kade before I see him, fingers biting into the soft flesh of my waist. He smiles through fused teeth at Daryl.

"Do not come near my bride again, Little Brother, or I will remind you how my fists feel." He warns quietly.

Daryl's fists flex before he summons a stiff smile and shows us his back.

Kade buries his nose in my neck, the tickle of his breath warming my veins.

"People are already expecting a scandal, Brynn, but you are fueling the juiciest one of all by giving them a show at *my* wedding. You are *humiliating* me." He growls.

With a painted smile for the crowd that never reaches his eyes, he turns and I watch him retreat with a hollow sigh. For the remainder of the night I avoid Daryl and hang off Kade's arm like the doting wife I'm supposed to be.

Kade watches me with the expression of a man in love until the guests depart. Then like a shutter, his eyes once again become ice cold steel.

"Let's go home, Brynn." He commands.

My blood chills. So warm and sweet moments before; now arctic. I follow wordlessly, watching with unease as he snaps the strings that hold the cans to the bumper bar of the wedding car, dismisses the driver and jumps behind the wheel himself.

"Get in." He snaps, knuckles white on the wheel.

I climb into the back seat. The tires tear up the gravel as we peel away, my fingers biting into the seat.

"Thank Christ that damned circus is over!"

Shock keeps me silent as the trees flash past. It's the shards of ice in his timbre that rattle me. I can't apologise for the charade of a marriage, but I can for my behaviour.

"I'm sorry, K-"

"So am I." He deflates, his glare melting into gentle regret, exhausted and dejected in the rear view mirror.

CHAPTER 14

KADE

hat have I done?

I realised the moment I overheard the mindless natter about how my bride kept staring at Daryl that I'd made a mess of this. But it's done now. The small hours of the morning find me on the porch, keeping company with the stars. The thought that another human is now living in my house makes me uneasy; This is *my* place. My sacred retreat away from the bitter pain and ulterior motives of the world, but I went and destroyed that tranquility myself by inviting calamity in and giving her the spare room, unpacking her luggage of cruel taunts and stretched tension.

And I didn't have time to draw up a prenup.

She said nothing on the short drive home, not after her ashamed apology. I showed her to her room by dumping her suitcase inside the door without a word and slamming my own.

Welcome home, Mrs Walker.

The sun finally breaks open to fill the sky with light, my favourite time of the day. The farm lights up, bathing all the green rolling hills, teasing the dark valleys and filling the birds with musical tributes to the dawn. I let the tension subside while I fill my lungs.

I'll let Brynn sit today out. I feel my mouth twist in a bitter sneer.

Let her adjust to marrying the wrong brother.

I feed out hay, shut the tractor down and watch the herd eat. All fat and shiny. All in mint condition. Except one.

"Hows the leg, Cleo?" Her white head swings my way, hay moving either side of her mouth with every chew. She pinched a nerve years ago, and while it doesn't hurt her, she moves slowly. If she moves too fast, her nerves spasm and she takes a few uncomfortable stumbles on her knuckle.

Her spine is beginning to show. She's an old girl at 18 and hasn't had a calf in nearly six years, but I dread the day I need to play god for her.

"I got married yesterday, Cleo." She stops chewing and blinks those long sweeping eyelashes.

I scratch her neck as she leans into me. "Yeah, I know. Stupidest thing I've done."

The day unravels like every other day. I get the water working in the bottom trough, I rotate the herds, I repair the windmill. I normally don't work as hard as this, but I don't want to go back to the house. While I'm out here, I can forget yesterday ever happened.

But that kiss...I'll bet she wasn't thinking of Daryl then. I felt the second her body began to melt, how she near burst into flames when I gave her a quick taste, and it was merely a sample of what I had to offer. That expression of surprise telling me she had no control over how she reacted to me. She'd have let me if I deepened the kiss. In front of everyone I could have claimed her and she wouldn't have been able to stop it. I growl into the air.

Rocking back on my heels I drop the wire strainers into the grass. I was holding back, I realised. Not just by practising restraint and reining in the kiss, but making a conscious, real effort not to pull her closer and give her a real kiss, because it took almost everything I had to fight down that damn chemistry.

I delay lunch for as long as I can, so it's almost two when my guts threaten to eat themselves if I don't feed them. I take the quad bike to the house and feel the knot of tension twist harder the closer I get.

There's an empty coffee mug balanced on the handrail where I watch the sun rise each morning. She's dragged a kitchen chair onto the verandah and left it there. She's awake. Clenching my jaw, I climb the stairs and step into the kitchen.

An empty bowl and spoon sit on the table. The empty milk carton rests on its side, and the coffee and sugar containers are still on the counter.

Oh hell no!

"Brynn!" I call. "Brynn!"

Violet eyes appear around the kitchen door, wide and bloodshot. She's been crying. I ball my fist when I feel my resolve slipping.

"This is not a fancy hotel, Brynn. You make a mess, you're expected to clean it up."

The truth is I can afford a housekeeper, but there's something downright intrusive about a strange woman changing my sheets. Besides, it's an easy house to keep clean.

She nods those huge eyes. Eyes that lost their spark by being with Daryl. I shake my head as my heart bleeds. I need to find a way to breathe that fiery spirit back into her.

"You are free to do as you wish, but if you're feeling particularly generous, there is always an opening for someone to provide meals, wash clothes and maintain the house. I have lunch at midday most days, but if I'm later than quarter past you can leave it in the fridge."

I know I'm pushing a number of her buttons here, but after years of submissiveness and conformity, she needs to be shaken out of it. Her eyes narrow, the rest of her slipping stiffly into view. Tiny black shorts are barely visible beneath her white t shirt. Dark hair pulled back in a simple messy ponytail completes the picture. She crosses her arms over her chest, glaring defiantly at me.

A shiver scrambles up my spine.

"We may be married, Kade, but I will *not* be your slave. You will just have to learn to cook for yourself!"

I stalk towards her but she stands firm. *Brave girl.* I give her the full force of my stare.

"I don't expect much from a marriage, Brynn, especially from *you*, but this is a working farm and the jobs don't get done on their own. There are cows to be fed, fences to be mended outside and chores to do inside. You are more than welcome to help out if you don't want to cook, or clean. You can come out with me in the paddocks and get some dirt on your hands."

She radiates stubbornness. I sink into a kitchen chair and watch her storm through the kitchen. She slams two pieces of bread on a plate, applying the ham and salad the same way. Her rage is magnificent. I deny the smile that tugs at my mouth watching her hair flick with every flounce and stomp.

She lands in the chair opposite, seething and feral waiting for me to eat my sandwich.

"There's no mayonnaise…" I wing an eyebrow, wondering if I'm taking it too far. With a feisty snarl, she stomps to the fridge, and I bite my cheek to stop my delight showing as she squirts an unceremonious circle and slams the bread back down. I chew slowly, savouring her ire, delighting in the hypnotising rise and fall of her chest.

"I'm going dancing tonight." Her expression dares me to stop her.

"Give me your phone." I command, and she complies automatically, too surprised to defy me.

My fingers flick over the buttons before I hand it back.

"I'll need the car this afternoon, so take a taxi and I'll come and pick you up later. You have my number if you need anything. Thanks for lunch." I press a chaste kiss to her temple before she can pull away.

"Uh, you need mine?" She stands stunned with her phone in her hand.

In response, I grab my own phone and a second later hers comes to life. I leave before my grin breaks free.

Before she looks at her phone and sees what I listed my name as.

Sex god. *Let her think on that.*

I'm dripping with sweat by the time I reach the house that evening. She's cleaned the kitchen and the most glorious smell fills the room. I smirk openly, knowing I have the house to myself again in which to celebrate my victory.

Good girl.

There's a note on the kitchen counter.

> *Your dinner's in the oven. Don't get used to it.*
> *Don't come too early, I'm planning on having a few drinks.*
>
> *Your slave.*

My grin widens.

Oh, princess, no you won't. You don't drink.

I lean against the shower wall, feeling the water blast away the day's exhaustion. I groan as the warm needles massage my scalp, dig into my shoulders and flood soothingly down my back. It's the best end to the day. But it's not quite the end. Judging by our wedding day, I'm guessing she'll be spent by around nine, so I still have a couple of hours free before I go out to retrieve my wife.

I fall into the couch with a glass of iced water when the phone rings.

"Hi Mum. How did the clean up go today?"

"Come on, Kade, you know why I called. How are you?"

I sigh, unsure how to answer. I had a good productive day, perspiring out the negative thoughts of yesterday, but now they're back with a simple, loaded question from my mother.

"I guess I should have expected it, but there was no ignoring those pathetic looks at him all night. I can assume people will be talking about it for some time yet."

I sense her nod. Then I hear the depth of her silence.

"She loved the ring, Kade. And it was a perfect fit."

My throat locks and I rub the blur from my eyes.

"Kade" she hesitates, "Your vows...where..?"

I sigh, deflated.

"I don't know what came over me, Mum. The words just...filled my head and wouldn't go until I said them. I don't have the slightest idea where they came from. I must have heard them somewhere and they kind of stuck."

The silence stretches. "Mum?"

Her voice travels down the line like a hug.

"Just have faith it will work out the way its meant to, son."

I pinch the bridge of my nose as the burn in my throat softens.

"She's filthy, Mum. Can you believe she left all her dishes through the house? It's like she's got no idea how to be an adult. This is going to be harder than I thought."

Mum laughs. "If you think marriage was going to be easy, then it's you with the problem. It's the hardest thing you'll ever do. The trick is to work out how her needs meet with yours, and keep talking. That's your biggest hurdle. *Talking.* Not about who does the dishes, but about what it is that makes your heart beat. The important things. If you can do that, the trivial things can't grow teeth."

I drag my hand down my face. All that has done in the past is offered my chest to another's knife.

"I made her sleep in the spare room." It was a knee jerk reaction when I was drowning in rage and humiliation.

"You were angry, Kade, and rightfully so. When...when Dad and I confronted her, she said she only gave herself to a man once. She wouldn't lie. I know it."

"I have to go, Mum." I growl and disconnect, throwing the phone to the couch. I consider another shower, try and wash away the unwelcome waves of remorse and dread that keep intruding.

Instead, I finish my drink and slip on a shirt, grab the car keys and head out to fetch my wife.

The pub glows with dull coloured lights in the centre of town. I can see inside easily from where I park so I recline my chair and watch.

Brynn and Bella writhe on the dance floor, their skin shiny with effort. They're grinning, mouths enunciating as they attempt fractured conversation as they move. There's not many others on the floor, instead, cowboys and couples line the room with beers and watch. Brynn's slender arms lift , her eyes close and her hips rock gently like the tide. There's no denying my wife is a stunning creature. She loves to dance. Always has. I remember that storm, when we went to see her thinking we could beat the rain. But it pelted down, roaring with fat desperate drops. And there she was, spinning, arms out to catch it, smile soaking wet and long hair whipping around and sticking to her cheeks.

Not tonight, though. Tonight she's beneath electric twilight, her short dress simple and gorgeous. No make up. She's not here to impress. She's here to dance.

I lean back and watch for ages. Then I see it. Her movements slacken, her chin drops a little. She's tired. In a moment she'll meet with Bella at the bar where the cowboys wait with predatory eyes and hope. I take note of the time and walk into the bar.

I do it on purpose. Opening both doors wide, I stride inside, my attention already locked on Brynn. Her eyes widen when she sees me, scans me from head to toe and licks her lips. I smother a smile, knowing she's unaware of what her body tells me.

The cowboys scowl when I face her.

"Its time to come home, Brynn." I say it loud enough to ensure they all catch my meaning.

Yes, gentlemen, I'm pissing all over my territory here.

Brynn's chin lifts and sets. "I'm not ready yet."

"Yes you are. You're tired and stubborn. If you don't come now, I'll make you."

Her violet eyes deepen with challenge. And heat.

She sneers as she purposely sips her water too slow, widening her stance.

Bella looks between us and smirks.

"Good to see you again, Kade." I lift a brow at her and she grins.

Bella's acceptance of me spreads through me. She likes the idea of Brynn and me, and that's all the encouragement I need.

I step forward, slip the glass from my wife's hand and in a fluid movement, I spread my hands around her narrow waist, throw Brynn over my shoulder and carry her outside to the jeers and hoots of the patrons.

"Put me down!" The little hellcat grinds out.

CHAPTER 15

BRYNN

*P*ut me down!" I grate.

"Not until you admit you're tired and come home."

Smug bastard.

I grind my teeth. "I'm perfectly fine, thank you!"

Bella betrays me with a dramatic yawn. "Actually, I'm ready to call it a night, Bry, and you seem to be...distracted."

Kade laughs, his breath licking against the exposed skin of my waist. I palm the hard wall of his back feeling the way it flexes and tightens as he walks, but all I manage to do is get a better look at how his rear end fills out those tight jeans.

My tongue slides over lips gone dry from my rasping breath. Bella ducks into view and smirks at me. She's not out of breath, but I am, my pulse still hammers and my blood still simmers.

From dancing.

Not because this irritating mountain of a man went all caveman on me.

No. Definitely not because of that.

"You okay there, Bry?" She asks lightly.

I shoot her a glare, ruck up the tight material of Kade's shirt and slide my hand down over his hot flesh until I slip below his jeans. Kade stumbles and regains balance.

"What are you-?" The note of panic in his timbre tightens when I seek the elastic of his underwear. Nothing. I'm running my hands over the smooth, tight mounds of his backside.

Bella explodes in laughter, and Kade yanks me from his shoulder, sliding me down his hard chest. He drills me with those startling eyes as my feet find ground, so close I can taste his breath.

"I'm not wearing underwear, Bry, just in case you can't control yourself around me again." He smirks.

"Get a room, you guys." Bella giggles again and I growl at the Judas that was supposed to have my back.

Kade's lip twitches.

"Not interested." I bite, but there's a confident gleam swimming in pewter as I find the strength to push away from him and slam the car door.

"What time do you start in the mornings?" I ask when we get home.

"Seven."

I toss my chin at him and head for my bedroom, setting the alarm before I jump in the shower. I love the shower heads installed here. Like hard summer rain. I rinse the night from my bones and lather my hair.

Kade. Not a hint of anything more than irritating scowl on his face since the wedding, barking commands and laying down expectations. And not accepting no for an answer. I mean, the audacity of the man to drag me out of the pub against my wishes when I was having such a wonderful time.

I refuse to admit, even to myself that I was already thinking of heading home before Kade showed up like some herd stallion and rounded me up.

And I didn't really mind being tossed over his shoulder as if I were weightless. In fact, I liked it. And I think he knew it. Not that I'd ever admit it to him.

Would Daryl do that? No. He'd be civilised about it. Not even that - he would expect that I don't go out to dance at all.

***

I whimper into my pillow when my alarm sounds. It's still dark. The urge to roll over and bury my head is almost overwhelming, but I throw my covers off. I can't let Kade order me around like his damned housewife.

He needs to know he can't control me. I'm used to farm work from the years of helping Dad in the paddocks, and Kade Walker is about to discover just how capable his new bride is.

I drag on jeans and a long sleeved shirt, opt for runners in the absence of farm boots and head downstairs.

It's dark, and I mentally congratulate myself. Up before the cowboy. I make myself a coffee and head out to watch the sun rise.

The door swings open silently and I freeze.

Kade leans against the verandah rails, jeans low over his hips, coffee cup in hand.

And no shirt. And wow has he been hiding a treasure beneath his clothes. Sun kissed and smooth, the dawn touches every edge and corner on his torso, shows me the deep gully of his spine, the strong, purposeful lines of his shoulders, the powerful tilt of his neck. Unaware I'm behind him, he turns slightly to take in the mountain view, giving me a perfect view of his profile. His strong jaw, his perfectly shaped nose, the jutting swell of his lips. The ones I remember from our wedding day.

How could he have come from the same stock as Daryl? Kade's little brother is finer of features, slighter of build. Shorter in stature. But outside of that, there's no comparison. Daryl's energy is peaceful, controlled as an accountant, but Kade? Everything about Kade 's energy is huge. He's saturating, overwhelming and a single glance promises mind-blowing, untamed ecstasy. Unforgettable pleasure. I shake my head.

Kade flexes his biceps suddenly, drawing my focus to the hard boulders erupting from his arms.

"Or this?" He asks the rising sun, facing me with the tight bricks of his abdominals in full view.

"What are you doing?"

"You were standing there ogling me for so long I guess I thought you were waiting for me to put on a show for you."

I snort. "You're delusional."

"Oh?" He warns, stepping uncomfortably close to me. "Then how do you explain the sweaty hand print on the door from holding it open for so long, or how fast your little heart beats for someone just rousing from sleep? Your mouth says one thing, Bry, but your body tells me another."

I wipe my sweaty palm on my jeans, trying not to let my eyes fall back to his broad chest. My breath shallows and I gulp air.

"And what do you think my body is telling you, just so I can set you straight?"

He bends down so his eyes fill my vision, the coffee on his breath tickling my nose.

"Well, my bride, your heart's nearly jumping out of your chest. That tells me you like what you see." His finger lifts my chin higher, the sparks from his touch igniting my skin.

"Those tiny gasps I hear when we touch? They tell me you feel that chemistry between us, too. Your eyes darken on me, telling me you want more than your stubborn pride allows you to say. And your lips, Brynn…"

He drops his gaze, and watches my tongue moisten my arid lips. His throat bobs.

"Your lips tell me that they're dying for me to taste them."

My lungs squeeze and my pulse is a storm.

"You're wrong, Kade. I don't want that. I don't want you, and I certainly don't want you to kiss me. You kissed me yesterday and I'm sorry to break it to you, but it meant nothing to me."

I feel his breaths speed up.

"No Bry, your mouth doesn't want a wedding day kiss right now. That is too tame for a woman like you. Your mouth needs it like this-"

There's nothing sweet about the kiss. It's a living thing that takes and demands, that possesses and commands. His mouth crushes mine, fist in my hair holding me still as he claims me. His tongue doesn't seek permission, it intrudes. He dives in deep, tasting, licking, swirling over my tongue like a starving animal.

My resistance melts in the single moan that drowns and drives every other thought from my mind as my hands wind their way into his hair.

I feel *everything*. His mouth, his heart beating the same erratic rhythm of my own, the heat colliding where our flesh touches. The intimacy of breathing his oxygen, and giving him mine. Hard velvet feasts on my mouth, and those damned tingles flood my veins and conquer my senses.

The fist in my hair grips tighter, his other digging into the small of my back, jamming me hard against the concrete power of his torso. My own hand glides up his spine, my nails dragging a trail down his shoulder.

He shivers beneath my touch and I groan, moulding my body into his, knowing my surrender is imminent and rejoicing in it. Between us, the hot swell of his length twitches against my belly.

Then he breaks the kiss, abruptly turning away.

"Well its good to know I'm mistaken. I'll ensure I don't misread the signs again. We need to get the hay in today and some fencing done. You ready to go?"

I'm a burning, gasping mess, the ache between my thighs roaring in protest as he disappears into the house.

How dare he do this to me! I'm not some game he can play! Daryl wouldn't treat me this way.

Closing my eyes, I summon the image of Daryl, sweet and respectful and my breathing begins to settle. I let it play out in my mind, Daryl leaning forward, his soft lips giving. Not taking like Kade. The picture deepens, and Daryl starts scorching kisses on my neck and my pleasure spikes. Desire floods, and Daryl's lips become harder, hungrier. I feel it in my lower belly.

Daryl, I moan in my head and he looks at me. But it's Kade's face instead, wild with heat, and I reach for him...

No! My eyes snap open with a muffled growl.

Channeling the sting of frustration, I comb my hair out with my fingers and gather it into a ponytail while my heart finds rhythm again. Two can play this game.

When he comes outside I'm already on the quad bike.

"I'll warm the tractor up, then you can tell me where I should stack the hay and you can do the fences." I don't wait for a response.

My heart no longer threatens to explode from my chest by the time Kade joins me. He promises a tour of the farm another day, but until then, he shows me the empty hay sheds and the three paddocks full of hay bales.

The radio is broken. I huff my sorrow when I discover it doesn't even pick up AM stations, just an abrasive white noise on every frequency. I run the air conditioner and sing while I fetch three round bales from the long paddock into the shed near the house. One on the back, two on the tines in front. It would be much better with some real music to sing along to. Without the lively tunes the morning drags so I sing whatever song comes to mind, until Kade knocks on the tractor door.

I leap from the seat in shock, a strangled cry assaulting my ears. A smug grin lights up his face, then widens as I glare at him. He must have leapt up the stairs when my attention was on the precise placement of the bales. He drags a finger across his neck and I shut the engine off. He cracks the door and jams his head inside.

"I heard you singing." He smirks.

"So?"

"You sound terrible, Brynn."

"Screw you, Kade. That's why I sing for myself, not for your entertainment."

"I think that's self abuse, Brynn. Have you even asked your ears if they want to listen?"

"What do you want, jerk? You stopped me just so you can tell me I have an awful voice?"

He tips his head to the side like he's considering his answer. "I didn't say you had an awful voice, just a bad singing one."

I whack the arm he's shoved in the cab and he breaks into a laugh. A dimple balances on his cheek. Such a simple thing, but it sends a surge of fire into my lower belly and causes my lungs to crush. I swallow my reaction and narrow my eyes.

"What do you want, cowboy?"

Heat flashes in his eyes for a second, then he leans back.

"McAllister Farm never bucket-reared orphaned calves, did they?"

I shake my head curiously. There were so many things to do on the farm that whenever a cow would reject her calf, or had twins, the babies would be picked up by John Wright across town to raise.

His hand snakes into the cab and locks around my wrist. His touch burns.

"Then you're in for a treat. I want to show you something."

He keeps hold of my hand and leads me to the other side of the shed. From the outside, it's massive, and I question why the inside of the shed where I stacked the hay doesn't seem quite as deep. Rounding the other end, it becomes obvious. The rear of the shed is sectioned off into a smaller building. Kade opens a wide barn door and pulls me through. The entire space is a series of smaller pens along one side and a couple of large ones on the other.

Kade's grip disappears and I peer into the tiny stalls, unconsciously rubbing my wrist.

"Oh, Kade!"

A set of massive dark brown eyes bordered with long curled lashes blink up at me from a pile of fur half buried in the straw. Soft floppy ears twitch towards me, and the calf's leathery nose wiggles.

Kade's heat moves beside me.

"As you know, this year is K. This is Kelly, and in the other stalls we have Kyle, Kayla, Katherine, Khloe, Karen and Karl."

"Can I...can I touch one?" I ask.

A smile ghosts Kade's lips as he unlatches the small wooden gate. Kelly jumps to her feet as soon as I enter, stretching her spine and curling her tail like a pigs' before bravely approaching me.

She doesn't shy away like older cows do, stepping with absolute trust towards me. I touch her forehead, the fur like warm velvet under my fingers. I run my hand down the side of her neck, her baby body all scrawny and soft.

"She smells wonderful, Kade! How often do you feed them?"

Kelly steps closer, digging her nose into my leg.

"Twice a day. Six in the morning and six at night."

I laugh as her pink tongue pokes out, and I realise she's seeking something to suckle.

"She's hungry now."

"She'll have to wait. If I feed her too much or at the wrong time she'll get sick."

"You poor baby, Kelly. Are you hungry, sweetie?" I drop to my knees, so eager am I to be closer to her. I avoid her tongue, running my hand over fur covered bones on her back. "You're just adorable, aren't you!"

She latches onto my elbow somehow and starts sucking. It tickles, and I can't manage to break the vacuum she's created. I laugh so hard that tears form and my belly hurts.

"Oh my god, Kade, you have to help me! I can't get her off!" I manage to gasp before I'm helpless with laughter again.

Kade slips behind me in the narrow space, leaning into my back as he reaches around. His hand runs down my arm, sending sparks through my veins, slipping a finger into Kelly's mouth and breaking the suction easily.

My laughter dies when I feel his breath puff against my neck. I shudder and I'm sure I feel him stiffen against me.

"Quick, Bry, escape now before you're overpowered by your arch nemesis. She's ready for another round!"

His chest vibrates on my back and I huff out a snort, but he's right. Kelly is coming at me, tongue first, eyes crazy with instinct.

I spring to my feet and squeeze past Kade, sure that although he's shuffled aside, he doesn't move aside all the way. He watches me pass, focusing on my breasts sliding over his forearm. Liquid metal darkens in his face, descending further into the shadows when my sharp inhale reaches his ears.

He flicks his eyes to mine and the shimmer in them locks me in place. He holds my gaze as he snaps the stall gate. I can smell the saturating haze of oak and early dawn building as he closes the distance.

My back finds the wooden panels of the wall. My breath hitches.

Kade doesn't just notice. He sees me. Those silver drills bore inside me. They watch the rapid spasms of my heart, they see my lungs wage a war on the air. They look into my veins and watch my blood simmer.

I stare back, helplessly open and bare before him, everything I've ever thought and felt comes raging out of me. His palms land beside my head, caging me, causing my pulse to trip up. His own breaths burst out urgently, hissing through his parted lips. The lips I want on me more than I want my next breath.

This feels so wrong, loving Daryl but wanting Kade. But we're married, and surely it can't hurt to have one more little taste…

CHAPTER 16

BRYNN

*H*is warm breath curls against my lips, so close. I lean towards him, drowning in his blown pupils and the hard rasp of his lungs.

Then he blinks, twice.

"Break's over, Princess. Back to work."

"Sorry?"

"The hay…" He enunciates. "Won't shed itself. Back to work."

I'm grateful for the wall at my back as I shakily fill my lungs. My head spins with erratic thoughts and the almost-kiss. And his expression…my heart trips just remembering the dark promises I saw there.

What messed up game is Kade playing? He knows exactly what he was doing, and I'm the idiot letting him call the shots. That's not me. I'm not someone he can command without expecting a war in return.

"You were about to kiss me!" I accuse.

He doesn't even falter, just keeps walking away.

"Nope. Just wishful thinking on your part." Wide shoulders lift.

Smug jerk.

"You think because you married me that you own me? Is that it, Kade? Lay down the law, hand out ultimatums and mess with my head? Is it all a game to you?"

His spine stiffens but he doesn't turn. Rage crawls up my spine.

"I'm right, aren't I? I'm a social experiment for your own warped entertainment. What's the hypothesis? Can I ruin the lives of my brother and Brynn in one fell swoop?"

His shoulders drop and he balls his fist. I've hit a nerve. I should leave it there, but like the out of control train I am with a cargo laden with rejection and shame, I steam right ahead, and brace for derailment.

"I get the strangest feeling, Kade, that you only married me to get back at Daryl. You act all noble, pretending you're doing it to help me out with my parents, and it happened so fast I didn't stop to consider why. I've had time to think now, Kade, and I think you're game's to coax me into your bed so you can wave it in front of Daryl's face. I wouldn't bother, though. I don't think there's anything you could do to make Daryl hate you any more than he does."

Kade whirls, a raging cyclone on fury. His fury booms and bounces off the shed walls.

"There's only one thing worse than someone without a single damn clue, Princess, and that's when they open their ignorant mouth about it. I don't want to hear you mention Daryl ever again in this house!"

I watch his back as he retreats, sinking to the straw as he disappears from view.

I stare down at my trembling hands. Kade was so wild. I'm beginning to see a different side to him. Dark, broody and a fierce temper when pushed too far. It makes me wonder what happened between Kade and Daryl for them to be so bitter towards each other. Kade's reaction gave me an insight, though. While I may have been off the mark with my accusations, I managed to uncover some deep-seated emotions that only appeared at the mention of his little brother.

I stand up gingerly, dusting the straw fragments from my jeans and head back to the tractor.

Not long afterwards, a text comes through from Kade.

Sex god: *I'm going out for a bit. Don't make lunch for me.*

I roll my eyes. Sex god. I should change that.

***

My gurgling stomach tells me it's lunch time. I decide to head in for lunch, and I can grab my iPod at the same time. I'm grateful Kade is out. My nervous system can't handle another round with him just yet.

I shut off the tractor, and climb onto the verandah.

Kade is already back?

No, not Kade. The frame at the kitchen table lacks his width.

Daryl!

I gasp in surprise. It's been two days, and Kade just made it pretty clear he will not be pleased to know his little brother is in his home.

"What are you doing here, Daryl?"

"Brynn...I had to see you." His words break, and my stomach jitters. Because he looks shocking. Shadows hang beneath his swollen eyes. I've never seen him with a trace of stubble, but today tiny bristles of gold sprout untidily from his jaw.

"Oh, Daryl." I choke on the anguish in his expression.

"Jesus, Brynn, I can't begin to tell you how responsible I feel for this whole mess. I made you a promise to marry you and keep you safe, and I've failed you. I never should have added that stupid clause in. I'm so sorry, Brynn. I don't even know why I did. I guess I just expected that you'd wait for me, and I barely hesitated when Kade dared me to add it. Christ, I don't even know how it happened, I mean, I promised we'd be together, and now you're married to my *brother*..." He shakes his head as if he still doesn't quite believe it.

"I know, Daryl, but I had no choice. I couldn't sit back and watch my parents lose everything."

Sinking into the seat opposite I resist the urge to comfort him. I swallow thickly. Daryl is out of bounds to me now. Now and forever. I take him in, aware of how…distant he feels now, as if opposing magnets that were forced together have now been released.

"I've been wild with worry for you, Brynn. I mean, I'm a mess, but you're the one who's life has been uprooted."

Sweet Daryl, always so concerned about me. It's one of the reasons I love this man. He measures his own happiness on the security and joy I feel. But right now he's not sleeping, and he has a company to run. I love him too much to let him destroy his life for a choice I made.

"I'm managing, Daryl. Kade can be…challenging, but for the most part he leaves me to my own devices. I admit, too, that it's refreshing to be back out in the paddocks after all these years."

I should be reassuring him the way I always did, but It's no longer my place. My right. Daryl frowns when I lean away from him, then his eyes light up.

"You can divorce him, Brynn. I'll look into a divorce clause and see how soon you can get out of this."

I savour the idea a damned good while before I shake my head slowly. "It's not about me, Daryl. I don't want my parents to suffer any repercussions. I won't have them pay for my actions, do you understand?"

A strange heaviness forms in the bottom of my lungs. It grows in weight every time I point out another major hurdle in his logic.

"Besides, Daryl, even if I did divorce Kade, I still couldn't marry you."

The flash of panic I glimpse tells me he already knows that.

"I don't know how this will work, Brynn, but I keep my promises and I'll do whatever it takes to make you mine. I can't let you go."

You're mine now, Brynn. I can't let you go. That's what he said the night of the party. The night he short-circuited everything inside me, the night he chose to pretend never happened.

The chair tumbles to the floor with a crack when Daryl scrambles to his feet.

Kade's frame fills the entrance. He's dressed up in nice jeans and a good shirt. The comb lines still in his dark mop from the shower he took before he left, and the heavy cloud of aftershave finds my lungs. He's seen someone, and he put a lot of effort into his appearance for them. A weight settles in my stomach.

"Daryl. How…nice to see you. Its been, oh, never…since you came by to see me last. To what do I owe this…pleasure?" He curls his lips at Daryl.

"I, uh, just wanted to see how Brynn has settled in here." His throat bobs. Then again.

Kade prowls beside me, watching Daryl wince at the sound of the chair dragging. Slowly, Kade sits astride, leaning his elbows on the wooden back. The aftershave that hides Kade's real scent thickens.

"Oh? And what did my wife tell you?" I shiver with the chill in his tone and Daryl falls silent.

"Let me enlighten you, Little Brother. After a sleepless night, my bride spent the day acquainting herself with her new home. She made me a delicious lunch and the most tender roast dinner you've ever tasted before she caught up with Bella in the evening to share stories of her wedding night. When I picked her up to bring her home, she wasted no time at all trying to get into my pants. Who knew sweet little Brynn was such a firecracker. No. More of a hellcat, if you know what I mean? Then this morning we spent out on the farm together, and, well, that about brings us to this point right here, doesn't it?"

Daryl cringes with each blow until he's defeated.

"Oh," whispers Daryl, and my heart bleeds for him.

"Now, my bride and I need some lunch, so it's time for you to go."

The dry ice in Kade's glare chills me.

"Kade, he just dropped by to visit, it would be gracious if you invited for your brother to join us."

His glacial snarl whips to me.

"We're just married, Brynn. We should be left to be alone, not receiving visitors, especially ones who wish to interfere."

"Maybe, *Big Brother*, the proper thing to do would be to take your wife on a honeymoon. I had planned on taking her to Rome. And you take her to a dirty stinking dust bowl and put her to work?"

"Get. Out."

There's no mistaking the deadly undertones of Kade's tight monotone, and Daryl doesn't intend to push him any further. He jerks stiffly to his feet, lands a look of heavy betrayal on me and leaves.

The silence is tangible. I stare at the table, waiting for the inevitable fallout. I feel his eyes drilling into my head, but I refuse to meet them.

"What kind of woman are you to bring that man into my home within days of our wedding? I didn't realise just how underhanded you were, just after I specifically told you any mention of him was off limits."

"What kind of a man leaves his wife at home and runs off to meet up with another woman?" I snarl back.

His eyes burst wide. He searches for something in my face I refuse to give him.

"And that thought bothers you?" He queries softly.

I frown, realising my mistake.

"Yes. No. Damn you Kade. How can you do that? We've only been married two days."

His shoulders lift. "A man's got to eat, and if there's no meal on offer at home…"

"How dare you!" I rage.

"You know, Brynn, you treat me like I'm the bad guy, but if you hadn't spread your legs for some guy in the first place you wouldn't be in this position. Was it just one, *pakvora*, or could you not help yourself once you started? You would have let me take you on the verandah this morning, wouldn't you?"

Ouch. Yes. No. Yes.

He leans in close, slips a finger under my chin and demands my attention.

"And don't even think of spinning a story about that because I could smell your arousal, my bride. Only your stubbornness held you back from begging me to finish what I started."

CHAPTER 17

KADE

I find Daryl slumping towards his loud, obnoxious convertible, and I lengthen my stride. Even before I reach him, I can feel my rage weaken, and the old familiar sting of regret returns.

Little Brother, when did it all go wrong?

Somewhere between the laughter and freedom of youth, the poison found a way in and I could do nothing but watch the bond we shared slowly decompose. My little brother who would creep into my bed in the middle of the night when a nightmare woke him, tears and hiccoughing sobs only I could calm. The drawings he'd rush to show me first, before Mum and Dad could see.

Not now. Just hard loathing and aggression in his eyes.

"Daryl!" I snarl.

He spins, blue eyes bright with fear.

"Keep away from her, Little Brother. She's my wife, and she will not be divorcing me, so you need to just accept it and move on."

His glare prickles. "You were so damned jealous that I was happy so you had to destroy it like everything else. Dad was right about you. You can't be happy unless you're ripping someone's life apart and stealing their joy."

What?

I hesitate, chewing on his accusation.

"When did I steal your happiness, Daryl? What do you imagine I did?"

"You were always around, Kade. Following me everywhere I went and interfering, and you never listened when I asked you to leave me alone. Good friends would just one day stop speaking to me. Girlfriends who did the same, and I can't prove it, but I know you were behind it. You had to be, because you were always there! But this is too much. I love her, and you took her from me. I'm going to get her back, and I'm going to find a way to marry her!"

I glare back at him, swallowing hard to contain my guilt. Because he's right. I was behind it all, but he's not ready to find out the reasons why. Not like this. So I bury the remorse and growl.

"I refuse to allow you to do that, Little Brother. This is one time you will not have it your way. You don't understand how deeply I regret that you fell in love with Brynn. That part wasn't meant to happen."

"*Wasn't meant to happen, Kade?* How can you say that when I've been talking about marrying her since we were ten?" His fists tremble with emotion.

I dig my fingers into his shoulders, forcing him to look at me with a grip that he can't shake.

"Think, Daryl! Really think about how it was back then, because you have all the answers in that jumbled up head of yours. Now I offer a final warning, Little Brother. Do not get between Brynn and I, or so help me, I won't hold back!"

"That's your answer to everything, Kade. If it doesn't comply with your demands, just use your fists. That's all you'll ever be. A cruel and heartless bully nobody can stand to be around."

I rear back with a roar and barely manage to stop my fist from landing in his face, the rage born from hurt hissing with my rasping breaths. Daryl's eyes are impossibly wide, his own inhales dragging as he focuses on my fist hovering next to his jaw.

He's scared. Of me. I did that to him. Because in his eyes, I'm a joy-thieving thug who ruined his life.

***

"Why did you say that to him?" She spits.

"It was the truth." I attempt a shrug, but all I can feel is the weight of the evil that fills me.

"What is wrong with you? You made it sound like we barely left the bedroom."

"What does it matter? It's none of his business."

The spikes of adrenaline still remain in my system, and they're battling my remorse and feeding my irritation.

"I love him, Kade, and you hurt him."

There it is, the agony of salt in the wound. Because I deserve this, and she doesn't seem to understand.

"Let's get this straight, Brynn. You do not love Daryl, and he does not love you! Neither of you seem to be able to see that you were only ever meant to be friends!"

She snorts and locks her jaw in a stubborn resistance that infuriates and inspires me all at once.

"Screw you, Kade. You've got no idea what love is. Look at you. Where are your friends, your family? Not here, Kade, because you're not worthy of love. Your brother can't stand you, your father doesn't talk to you, and you resorted to blackmail to get yourself a wife. I can't wait to see what you're going to do next."

I teeter on the edge of imploding with the weight of it all. I want to shake her and make her understand why I did what I did, but she's consumed by her emotions, just like Daryl. But it's hearing the truths spoken out loud, the ones I have always felt that cut me deepest, and all I can do it walk away before I break.

***

For almost a week Brynn and I exist in a kind of distorted limbo where we work together without interacting. No matter what time I go for lunch, Brynn is gone and my lunch is in the fridge. A plate with a sandwich with wrap to keep it moist. I know she only does it to avoid having to communicate with me, but she's thought of me. Maybe not how I wished it to be, but I'm still on her mind. That's something, right? Even if her emotions are askew…

I loosen the plastic and place it on the table before me. Ham pokes out on one side. Mayonnaise smeared with a knife, lettuce and tomato with a slice of cheese against the bread so it won't get soggy.

I sit alone in my quiet kitchen with an ache in my chest and the meal my wife made for me and wonder how I can fix this.

***

It was the salesman assuring me she'd love it that convinced me to hand over the credit card. Brynn was out having lunch with Bella, her cold, brief text informed me, so I installed the radio in the tractor to surprise her, one of those ones that take a memory stick. I don't involve myself too much in technology, but apparently that's the newest thing, and therefore essential for a lover of music. Then I feed in the tiny plastic storage stick that the salesman loaded with music into the slot. It's amazing what people will do when you wave enough cash under their noses. I'm sure its the most expensive one of these on earth, but I don't care.

I test it out with a sense of achievement, grateful I swallowed my pride and took the instructions the salesman wrote down for me instead of trying to work it out myself.

I rub the humidity from the nape of my neck and search the sky. Thick clouds devour the sun, and the electrical bite in the air heralds a storm. I hear the car pull in the driveway and head for the calf shed, knowing she'll head straight down. She wants to spread the fertiliser before the rain, and she's running out of time. The tractor roars to life and moments later the music starts automatically.

After the calves are fed, I linger in the pens and listen to the soothing symphony of thunder and straw rustling under settling bodies. The sounds of contentment help me think.

Brynn, why can you not understand what is right beneath your nose? I'm here, exactly where I've been for years, waiting for you to realise it's me you're destined to love.

I don't know how this is supposed to work, and god knows I wish I could find the right things to say to make her understand, but I'm not great with people. I don't have the social skills like Daryl; instead, hiding from a world that looks on me with prejudiced eyes makes communicating virtually impossible. No matter what my heart says, my mouth refuses to utter words that could be weapons used to slay me. Whenever we speak it's to argue, and I'm beginning to fear that it's all she'll ever give me.

The rumble of the tractor grows closer just as the sky gives out. The drops pelt down on the shed roof, so hard I imagine the tractor is still idling and I move to investigate. At the door, I smile.

The tractor stands in the driveway, door wide open to the pounding rain. Music clashes with thunder.

And Brynn is *dancing*.

She's kicked off her boots. Splashes of mud cling to her ankles and cover her feet. Her long hair is plastered to her head, raindrops gather in her eyelashes. She grins as the volume drowns out her voice, but she sings anyway, sprays of water flying from her mouth when the deluge trickles in. It's a sight that ignites my blood. I feel the door frame at my back and allow the first real hint of hope to flower.

With arms wide to the storm and soaked to the skin, Brynn is being exactly who she's meant to be.

Maybe its not useless after all, because as long as Brynn is Brynn, there's hope that things will work out.

I watch because I can't not. The old sparkle flares to life beneath her skin. I can almost reach out and touch its return. She slips over in the mire and laughs at the mud in her hair.

Her smile falls when I come into view and she scrambles to her feet. She points slowly to the tractor where the music still cuts out between the raindrops.

"You?" She whispers, and I nod.

"You're soaked, *pakvora*." I murmur.

She blinks at me with eyelashes clumped from water. Such a simple reaction that I feel all the way down to my toes.

I keep my voice soft, following the instructions my heart gives. Her eyes darken slightly, but it's more than that. The windows to her soul are cracking open, giving me a glimpse of something deeper. Finally. And it's the rain and the music, and the freedom she's becoming slowly aware of. And it's me.

That I do feel, and its staggering. That first glimmer of curiosity, of her searching for something deeper within me.

An unguarded moment.

My heart expands painfully, and I hope she understands.

"What is *pakvora*?" She asks carefully. "You call me that, but I don't know what it means?"

I shift a thick strand of waterlogged hair from her cheek, and tuck it behind her ear, delighting in her tiny shiver my touch generates, feeling my soul's answering call.

"It means *'beautiful'*" I reply with a wary smile as I take in her filthy state.

Her laughter bubbles up uncontrollably, and she owns me. For her smile, her happiness, I would give everything. The rain, the music, they soften her. To the beat of some random song, Brynn allows me to touch the walls she's erected around her heart.

"Dance with me." I ask softly, tracking a new rivulet on her cheek as it cuts through a smear of dirt.

I hold my breath, so damned afraid she'll reject me at the first opportunity I've had to reach out to her in something other than defensiveness. Her soaked eyelashes shift as she searches my eyes, balancing on the precipice of breaking me. There's part of her that wants to do just that. I watch as it lingers in her expression.

Then it happens, Right there. The briefest nod, but she may as well have handed me the world by the exhilaration that surges through me.

I groan and pull her against me, mud and filth and soggy perfection in my arms. Finally in my arms. Willingly.

I chuckle when the water starts to penetrate my clothes. I push her away and spin her around to the music, and as the song ends I hold her against my chest for as long as she'll allow it.

"Thank you for the music." Her lips lift.

"Thank you for the dance." I murmur, needing to claim her mouth, but knowing I can't and brushing my lips against her forehead instead.

She pulls away, the sudden space between us catching the breeze and making her shiver and I step into her again, desperate to have her close.

"Here, shall we go up to the house together so you don't catch cold?"

She lands me with an odd look, but doesn't fight me. Like she wants to hold me as much as I want it.

I reach up and switch off the tractor as we pass by it, and we make our way in silence, saying nothing but making progress, and I wonder how long this truce will last.

Not long at all as it turns out. The very next day her indignation reappears.

"Why can't I help?" She stomps her tiny feet in the grass from across the laneway. I'm in one paddock repairing the fencing, and Brynn is in another after feeding out silage, the laneway stretched out between us.

Brynn is a wonderful help on the farm and is rather perplexed when I let her know Bobby would be coming to help me move the bull. She's stubbornly resistant to anything I do to try to keep her safe, and it's infuriating. She knows how dangerous bulls are, doesn't need me to explain how hazardous it is to move a randy bull past two paddocks of cows, but I can see she's set her mind. Her father never used a bull, most likely choosing to artificially inseminate the cows just so he didn't have to have this exact conversation I'm having with his daughter.

"I told you, Brynn. You're not helping with the bull. It's not negotiable."

"In one breath you tell me I can do anything on the farm, but in the next you forbid me to try something new because it doesn't suit you? I'm not a child!" She hisses.

I love the way her entire body pulls taut when we spar. The way her violet eyes flash like lightning at sunset because she believes so passionately in her argument. It's not only that; Brynn is passionate about everything. She's genuine; every expression and smile comes directly from her heart. Her fists ball at her sides, injustice coursing through her, and the paddock of cows crowding around curiously to watch could be her army. She's not afraid of them, like some folk are. Cleo licks at her shirt with her long tongue and stretched neck, and Brynn lets her. I want to kiss her for that alone.

I rake my fingers through my hair, distracting myself from the flare of arousal in both of us that always accompanies our disputes. I could tell her she can watch, so she can see the way he bellows and snorts, charges and bucks, but I have an overwhelming need to see her as furiously aroused as I am.

"You're inexperienced, and you'll just get in the way." I growl.

I'm almost ashamed of the excitement I feel when she clamps her teeth and drills me with those incredible eyes.

"And how do you expect me to get experience, arsehole? Should I spend the next fortnight googling 'how to open a gate so a bull can walk out'?"

I'm so enthralled by the tremor hurtling up my spine at her curse that I fail to see the danger lurking in her expression.

I lean on the horizontal post on the stay set, trying to take in as much of her as I can. That faint flush surges from her chest, up her smooth neck colouring her luscious skin the shade of rage and passion I have grown familiar with. I can almost feel the heat rolling off her, only some of it from anger. The rest...the rest is mine. They're the parts of her that embrace our chemistry, feeding off it while knowing it fuels her hunger for so much more. I see it in the way her pupils blow out, her breaths labour and her body kind of bends in like her core is drawing down.

My own pulse thunders as I struggle to refrain from walking right through this barbed wire and pinning her to the ground beneath me. I adjust my tightening jeans.

"You might need one with pictures, Princess." I bite.

The flames rise in her eyes, and I'm too consumed by all of her to twig until its too late.

An eyebrow lifts with silent vengeance. She traps my focus while her fingers manipulate the latch on the gate.

The sound of rattling chain not only grabs the attention of the herd behind her, it also shocks me into clarity.

"Shit. No!" I plead.

Her lips spread, showing all her teeth. And the chain drops with a hollow thud against the wooden post.

"Brynn!" I growl, but even I hear the panic in my tone.

She swings the gate open, and forty-nine cows, with Cleo bringing up the rear, push to escape their bare paddock and into the long, lush rye. The paddock I've locked up for hay.

It takes an hour and a half to convince reluctant bovines to return to their paddock. The long grass they regretfully left behind was now flattened by their hooves, clumps of green torn and missing from hungry mouths. Slipping the latch on the gate, the mournful bellows curse their captivity as they gather around the bale of silage and feed their loss. All the desire and lust I delighted in earlier is replaced by exhaustion.

The quad bike pulls up at the bottom of the stairs, the glow of the kitchen lights making me aware of how much time has passed. She's showered, the fresh vanilla scent of her shampoo lingering in the air, her long legs curled beneath her. She lowers the tablet and eyes me suspiciously when I enter. She looks relaxed, but she's not. Her stiff shoulders hard and ready for anything more I might send her way. But I'm spent, and it's my own damned fault for pushing so hard for my own sick enjoyment.

I watch her with a flood of pride. My little hellcat, refusing to accept the limitations anyone allocates her, mowing down every obstacle that fails to slow her. Including me. Especially me.

At the doorway to the hallway, I pause, a swarm of satisfaction in my belly. Brynn lifts her chin and hardens her face. She never backs down from a challenge. From the time I watched her as a child dancing in the rain like it was hers to command, I knew there was lightning in her soul, but it is for me and only me she unleashes her storm.

A wolfish smirk tugs at my face, and that hot flush I see more frequently now crawls up her neck.

CHAPTER 18

BRYNN

ll we do is fight, Bella. It's all so useless." I sigh.

"Less a fight and more a battle of wills, I think." Bella smugly informs me, spooning the cream off her iced chocolate.

"What's the difference?"

Bella smirks, absently poking the scoop of ice cream into the base of the glass.

"The difference being, one is in anger, the other is a challenge."

"I wish it were none of the above, Bell. It's wearing me out."

She watches me with narrowed eyes as I sip my own drink.

"No you don't, Brynn. You love it. You're radiant with it. You love a challenge, and that's what Kade is providing for you. You think being miserable is the right thing to feel about it, but inside you know that's not what you think of it. You barely gave the divorce Daryl mentioned air time, and if I'm honest, you rarely even bring Daryl up any more. We've been friends far too long for you to start bullshitting me now, Bry. You're happy. Or you could be if you allowed yourself to be."

I draw the cool chocolate drink through the straw slowly. She's wrong. I miss Daryl so damned much, but it's not that gut-wrenching, soul-decaying grief I expected. I've loved him for more than ten years, and if I'm honest the guilt of not being torn up eats at me in the dark more than heartbreak does.

"I think I've blocked it out. Like what happens when people go through some pretty traumatic events. I haven't been able to process it yet."

Bella snorts. "So you're dealing with the trauma by smiling and glowing."

"I'm not smiling and glowing, Bella. Right now, actually, I'm furious. Every two weeks, Kade gets dressed up in nice clothes, puts on the same aftershave every time, and leaves for a few hours at a time. He insists I remain faithful, but he obviously has a different set of rules for himself."

"I don't believe that!" Bella gasps.

"Why not? He's cold and aloof towards me, and he's pretty consistent with his scowling. The only time that changes is on that one day a fortnight when he's all wound up and agitated, like he's anxious to impress someone. He paces and watches the clock, so distracted he doesn't notice me watching him. What else could it be?"

Bella shakes her head adamantly.

"No." She rejects, and that's when I see it.

"You like him!" I accuse.

Bella has the grace to look guilty.

"Please understand, Bry. If you let him, I know he'll be perfect for you, and he celebrates who you are instead of trying to rein you in. He supports you dancing because he knows you need it, he puts music in the tractor for you, and with him you're becoming the Brynn you used to be; you have your sass back."

Her voice lowers.

"And I can see how much he loves you."

I choke on my chocolate.

"Are you broken, Bella? He's only married to me to get back at Daryl. They hate each other. And he's cheating on me, and he definitely doesn't love me. He's made it clear with his snarky comments how much he hates me in his house. And did I mention the cheating?"

Bella leans back in her chair. "Why don't you just ask him what he does when he goes out each fortnight?"

"Because he can do what he likes. See who he likes. We are *not* a couple. Anyway, I don't care." I shrug.

Bella shoves her glass aside.

"Clearly you do if you're calling it cheating. If you ask me, I'd be more worried about the fact that he's getting under your skin. He's a good guy, Brynn."

"He is not! He's just the hot topic, actually the *only* topic when I'm suddenly living in his house because I'm *married* to him!"

Bella suddenly looks tired and I'm aware that all I do when we're together is complain about Kade.

"Sorry." I mumble.

She blows out a breath and fingers her straw.

"Just…maybe give him a chance, Brynn. All you've done since you got there is fight him, and it must be exhausting for both of you. I get that you're determined to see him as a villain, and maybe he is at that, but I think you owe it to Kade to work that part out yourself instead of relying on hearsay and Daryl's jaded opinion."

Thoughts erupt of the gentle expression and soulful eyes. The ones that keep drawing me in and conveying so much more. The ones that darkened on me and made me want to dance with him.

Consumed by flashbacks of Kade dancing with me in the rain, I pull the car to a stop before the looming gates of Walker Manor. I swallow hard, knowing Kade won't be pleased with me being here, but I need to do this. I shut off the engine and sit quietly for a moment. Shame floods through me when I remember the last time I saw Daryl here, expression twisted in betrayal when I admitted to not being a virgin. I grip the wheel.

What kind of idiot puts a stipulation like that on legal papers?

In front of Evie and Antony, too. I squeeze my eyes shut and try to shake it off.

I walk the same path I used to skip along in my childhood, asking if Daryl could play, but I hesitate uncertainly before the huge wooden door, and shift my weight. As a child I'd push it open and walk right in. But now? What is the right course of action now? Technically I'm family, but with the chaos that surrounds my presence, am I welcome?

When the door opens, I cry out in fright. Evie stands in the doorway, her trademark smile releasing all my tension in a harsh exhale.

"Hello, dear. I hoped you'd come by. Daryl isn't here, though."

I watch her smile weaken as she mentions Daryl.

"That's okay, Evie, I came to see you."

Her happiness reaches her eyes again and she wraps her arms around me. I sigh in the realisation that all this craziness between Kade, Daryl and me hasn't stained the love she has for me. Evie's hugs heal.

"Come in dear, Antony is in the city for a few days on business, so I have the house to myself. We can relax in the lounge room with some tea."

Her brown eyes have already registered the tangled thoughts inside me, reassuring me in one flippant remark that we can speak freely.

She leads me into the kitchen, loading biscuits onto a plate and retrieving mugs as she chatters happily.

"Tell me how married life is treating you, dear? Kade tells me you love the farm."

I train my attention on her, and she notes my surprise with a chuckle.

"We speak most days. Always have."

Her chocolate eyes sparkle with mischief as I try and picture Kade openly having a conversation with anybody. He rarely says more than a handful of words at a time. Evie watches me. No, she burrows into me and pokes at my thoughts.

"It's difficult for Kade to open up, dear, but once he feels safe, you'll find my boy has a great deal of depth to him."

It occurs to me we've had a conversation and I haven't managed to utter a word. Her gaze is intense. Unwavering. Like Kade's.

"How do you do that, Evie? How can you look inside me and know what I'm thinking?"

"It's a little something I picked up along the way, really." Her satisfied grin twists as she speaks in her gentle tone.

I shake my head. "Just like Kade, it's easy to see where he gets it from. He looks at me almost the same way, like he knows who I am better than I do."

Her eyes twinkle.

"Yes, I guess he did get that from me. Close to the only thing he did get from me. That son of mine is his father all over."

She watches me closely when I frown. I summon an image of Antony. Blonde and blue eyed like Daryl, I mentally match physical traits and fail. Even the personality doesn't line up.

Evie clears her throat delicately.

"Not Antony, dear, Kade's *biological* father."

My mouth hangs while I wait for my mind to catch up.

"Ohhh."

A secret smile dances in the corner of her mouth.

"Brynn, dear, everyone has skeletons in their closets and the ghosts that come from these invade each of us in different ways. It's how we manage to fight those ghosts that define who we are. Some wrestle bigger demons, and others find a way to banish them for good. That's my ghost, Brynn. I'm haunted by the man who filled my world with light and gave me Kade."

"I never knew…"

"There's not many who do. Antony wanted it that way. He wanted the world to think he had the perfect life. Married, two sons. That's why we moved out here, somewhere where people wouldn't look deeper into our family than what we chose to show them."

My head spins with questions. Kade looks like his father? Where is he?

"Tell me about him. Please?"

Brown eyes shimmer with memories.

"He was a magnificent man, Brynn. Almost the spitting image of Kade. Right down to his incredible eyes. I met him by chance one day, not far from where I lived at the time. My parents were strict, but this one night I decided to defy them and crept out with some girlfriends. We were trying to see a movie, not that I can remember which it was now, but as we turned the corner, there was a crowd gathered in the street. My friends and I pushed through to see what was happening, when I was knocked to the ground. We'd stumbled into the middle of a street fight and got too close. Anyway, I scraped my face when I hit the ground and my lip was bleeding when these brilliant gray eyes appeared before me. He asked if I was okay and pulled me to my feet. It was instant, dear, that bolt of electricity you read about but never believe in. One of the fighters moved too close and bumped him, and before I knew what happened, he flattened the man with a single punch and led me away to get ice for the swelling. We talked into the smallest hours of the morning. By the time I climbed into my bedroom window, I was madly in love and my fate was sealed. I saw him every moment I could sneak away after that. Now I like to think I am a woman of strong morals, but there was something…exceptional…about him, and six months later I discovered I was pregnant with Kade."

"Oh wow, and your parents didn't even know you were seeing him?"

Evie throws back her head and laughs in mischievous delight. She gives me a glimpse of the spirited and carefree girl she used to be.

"Oh, no, dear. No idea at all. But there was no way to hide it after that, of course. I told Kade's father first. Oh, Brynn, I'll never forget the look on his face. The news blew him away, and I've never seen a man happier than he was that moment. But we made a mess of things. My parents were out for blood, and it didn't help that I was from a society family, and Kade's father came from lowly gypsies. We decided that to stop a potential bloodbath, the two of us would get married before anyone could stop us, and started a new life."

My heart melted. The love story most dream of was Evie's reality. Only for a time, I realised. Now she's with Antony and there's no mention of Kade's father.

"Does Kade know? About his dad, I mean?"

"I'm not sure. He used to talk about him all the time, but he knew Antony hated it, so he only spoke of it when we were alone. Then after Daryl was born, he stopped mentioning him altogether. I don't think he's forgotten, but I don't know how sharp those memories are any more."

So many questions beg answers, but Evie's phone rings. She snatches it and smiles as she accepts the call.

"Kade, I was so worried. Thank you. No, I'm having a lovely chat with Brynn. No. She came to see me. I love you too."

My lungs squeeze as she ends the call. He told his mother he loves her? I wonder how those words would sound tumbling from his lips. When I glance up, I see a secret smile tug at the corner of her mouth.

"You're doing it again, Evie, you're looking inside me?"

She nods. "Like Kade, I see more than you'd think."

What does she see? How hopeless this whole situation is? How somehow

I've managed to hurt Daryl with a single mistake and steal the future of her other son?

"What can you possibly see that still has you smiling when I've torn apart your entire family? Daryl's upset, Kade's trapped in a marriage he doesn't want, and Daryl and Kade are looking to tear each other's heads off."

The woman laughs, bright and honest.

"Dear, only when you step out of the storm can you see it's merely a light shower. It's not at all what you think, but if you were to explain the Sistine Chapel to someone rather than let them see it for themselves, or show them Mozart's sheet music instead of having them listen to it, you strip away the magic of experiencing it. Finding that exquisite epiphany you only get from taking the journey and living the pain. I'm not going to spoil the journey for you, Brynn, but I will say this; at least my sons are talking again."

My head spins as I turn the car towards home.

Home. I huff out a laugh. When did my autopilot decide Kade's house was my destination?

Down the road a little I pull over and shut off the music and let the overload in my brain settle. Antony isn't Kade's father. Daryl is his half-brother. Is that the reason they can't see eye to eye? Is that the reason Antony treats him differently?

I suck in a breath, because Daryl could never do any wrong in the eyes of Antony, but sifting through my memories, there was never the same consideration for Kade. He would have watched Antony dote on his brother, knowing he was barely tolerated, and I know this because even as a young girl I was aware of the hostility Kade received. Guilt seeps in. I never stood up for Kade when Daryl yelled at him to go away, and I ignored him as much as any of them. I swallow the lump forming in my throat.

I was never close to my parents, but I loved them and they loved me. I can't imagine how much it would hurt if they took it away. I summon an image of my father's face, dark with anger the day I felt sorry for the cows waiting in the yard, and set them free before the truck arrived to take them to market.

He was furious, but I still saw the love there.

All Kade would have known is that his father didn't love him, and his brother hated him.

All you've done since you got there is fight him.

Bella was right. Maybe I should put away the gloves for a while. There's every possibility that this woman Kade sees is the only one besides his mother who shows him kindness.

It makes me feel sick.

CHAPTER 19

KADE

*T*he sun paints the sky red as the new morning is born. Always my favourite part of the day, I feel my heart step up and glance around, knowing Brynn will be in the shadows. It's uncanny the way I can perceive her long before she's in my sight, how the air shifts sideways when she's near. My heartbeat tells me, too. Like an echo of my own I feel her.

Thump. Thump (thump-thump). Her heartbeat walking beside mine.

"Red sky in the morning, shepherd's sure warning." I murmur.

I feel the heat of her desire like fingers brushing my skin as she looks upon me.

One day she'll want more than just to look, and the anticipation of that keeps me on edge. I clench my jaw and watch the sun, because every day is a day filled with the possibility of her touch. I gave her something to think about, those tastes I gave her, but my patience is taut and frayed.

"What's on today, Cowboy?"

She leans her elbows on the rail beside me, coffee mug cradled in both hands. Her hair falls in messy waves down her back, waiting for the stroke of the brush to untangle last night's sleep. I lean slightly and drag that sexy smell into my nostrils so she doesn't notice.

"I have an appointment before lunch, so I'll be out for a couple of hours. Think you can handle the farm while I'm gone?"

"Hmmm. I'm concerned if I'm left to my own devices I might break a nail."

I hide my smile in my coffee. She's so very capable of this life and she loves it, even though she doesn't say. The longer she's here, the more I see her relax. She never would have made a good wife for Daryl. She'd die inside the cage he would build for her wild spirit so she could conform to his pretentious needs. She's got too much zest, too much appreciation for life to become his husk.

"I knew you couldn't hack it here." I bait, and she rises, glorious ire and indignant fire.

"I could run this place on my own, Kade. You like to think you're so damn integral to this place, but I don't need you here."

I catch a whiff of her arousal and it sends me crazy. She loves the banter as much as I do, only she thinks I don't know it.

I let the musky ambrosia of vanilla and spring mornings curl into my nostrils a moment longer before I step away. The fragrance fades and I manage to restrain myself again. Barely.

"I will be out for lunch, *pakvora*. Don't make me any." I smirk and wait. She doesn't disappoint.

"I'm not your damned slave!"

I'm up at the house early. I can't be late. It's quiet in my house again with Brynn in the paddocks, almost like it used to be, but much better. As I do before my appointment every fortnight, I shower, shave and find the special bottle of aftershave I keep just for this purpose. Then I perch on the edge of the bed and lift the photos from the top drawer beside my bed and flick through them. Although it hurts, I bury the pain and allow only the good memories through. My heart is in these pictures; snapshots of an alternate reality that was so damned perfect. The last two are new photos. I replace the bulk and study the crisp vivid colours fresh from the photo lab. I paid the photographer double for this image alone. We'd just exchanged our vows and my mouth was still so close to her. The expression on her beautiful face, frozen in time and perfectly captured.

She looks at me like she just realised who I was. Perfect mouth cracked, violet recognition so hot I can feel it as she stares *into* me. A look that breaks my heart into a million pieces, then puts it all back together again.

***

The house is an unassuming brick home in the centre of town with child proof gates and an orderly garden. I feel the smile bend my lips as I crack the door without knocking. It betrays me with a creak, and a young boy tears down the long hallway, leaping into my arms with a faith that blows me away.

"Kade!" Marc squeals in delight and I squeeze him close.

Such a different child from when I first met him, before he found a way to let hope in again. When his legs hit the floor his tiny hand grips mine and drags me outside.

"Come on, Kade. You gotta draw with me. I've been practising drawing dragons but I can't get the fire right. You have to help!" I feel laughter bubble up at his exuberance and flash Charlotte a friendly greeting before I manoeuvre into the plastic seat beside the little boy.

"How is school going? Did you and Tommy end up friends?" I ask.

"Uh-huh! I found out he didn't know how to be friends, so I told him he had to be nice to be a friend, and then he started learning so he's my best friend and he likes dragons, too!"

I select a brown pencil because I know Marc will want the green, and pull a blank piece of paper in front of me.

"That's great, Marc. Some people forget how to make friends because they're scared of people hurting them, and it takes someone pretty special to show them it's okay to be afraid."

My own words haunt me. I'm handing out advice to a kid like I'm not a hypocrite. I push the thought aside as I listen to Marc chatter excitedly about school, and nod as more men and children start filtering through the doors.

The familiar lump in my throat burns as the quiet little girl, Erin, bursts into life for the first time when the man she's been anxiously waiting for arrives.

"Paul, you really came, I hoped you'd come but I thought you wanted another kid instead!"

"Erin!" I hear his reply muffled in her embrace, "I've been so impatient to see you again! No way I'm going to let someone else steal away my Erin!"

With a hug and the right words, Erin starts to heal.

"Look!" Marc commands as he shoves his drawing over mine.

"Well done, Marc! I can see you've been practising your fire. It looks fantastic!"

Marc beams with pride.

My pencil freezes mid-stroke when I feel the blood echo in my chest. Leaning back, I seek the source in the window. The open plan lounge room has a window on the other side, offering a view of the street. I find a familiar figure in the distance, standing uncertainly on the opposite sidewalk, glance swinging between my car and this building. I swing my smile to the boy in front of me.

"Hey Marc, do you want to meet a friend of mine?"

Huge brown eyes look up curiously.

"She loves dragons, and I know she'll love to see your drawings."

Marc whips the paper to his chest, grabbing an orange pencil. "I want to show her what colour goes into dragon fire!"

"Piggyback!" Marc demands halfway down the hall, and I relent with a laugh.

I open the door and spot Brynn immediately, poised indecisively across the road. She starts when she sees me with Marc on my back, reluctant to move.

"Kade says to come here!" Marc bellows beside my ear. I smile at his lack of filter. She hesitates for a moment, then I watch her lift her chin and walk into battle. She wears a flowing white shirt with a wicked glimpse of cleavage and a black thigh length skirt. I run my gaze over her hungrily.

She looks brave and proud, but her eyes narrow with suspicion as they dart between Marc and me.

"Is she a Princess?" Marc asks.

"She likes to think she's one." I smirk as I watch her stop at the front gate.

"Brynn, this is my friend, Marc, and Marc, this is the friend I told you about."

His little hand releases my neck as he extends it to Brynn.

"Hello, Princess." He giggles mischievously as she greets him and quirks an eyebrow at me.

She studies us, no doubt trying to spot similarities between Marc and me, and it fills me with satisfaction.

Marc wriggles down and hands her his drawing. "Kade says you like dragons. I brought this to show you."

Brynn crouches down, smoothing the crinkled paper over her knee.

"Oh, Marc, this is wonderful. You are truly talented. Oh, and look at the fire from his mouth, he looks so fierce he might eat me up." The more time she stares at it, the more his chest puffs out.

I lay a hand on Marc's head. "Now Marc, maybe Brynn would be happy to wait at the coffee shop a few doors down until I have to say goodbye to you. Our time's up in half an hour and I want you all to myself until then."

I pray my expression conveys my hope for her understanding and patience.

Marc's face slides into a scowl, then brightens.

"Okay. See you Princess! Come on, Kade, you have to show me how to draw wings!"

***

I expect her to be furious. I could see what she thought, finding me in some random house with a young boy and dismissing her without explanation. I couldn't, though. Not without taking away from Marc's day, but as soon as I spot her it's obvious how wrong I am. She wears a strange look, but it's not one that causes me tension.

"Want to get out of here?" I ask.

She grabs her purse as she stands, but says nothing until we're in the car.

"Who are you?" She whispers.

I shrug.

"You have to know what was going through my mind when I found you..."

"After you followed me instead of simply opening your mouth and asking where I was going?" I clarify lightly.

She ignores me, frowning.

"And this lady approached and asked if I was one of the mothers. When I asked her to explain, I find it's a service provided free to young children whose fathers have left suddenly, are in a bad place or have passed away. Apparently it helps the child reconnect with another male and remind them that they are special. Kade, why do you do it?"

I'm on the verge of a witty retort when I think about what Marc said about his friend learning to be nice.

"I do it because I fund the charity."

Her eyes widen.

"Why volunteer your time, though? I mean, all you need to do is fund it. You don't have to-"

"I do it because I want to, and Marc needs me. His father died of a drug overdose a year ago. He doesn't know details of course, but unfortunately his mother is heading the same way, and his little world is full of fear. When he lost his father, his mother was too busy feeding the needles into her arm to help him process his pain, and he was forced to deal with it alone. I know what it's like, to have something so precious ripped away and struggle with a pain that shouldn't belong to a child. It leaves a gaping wound you're expected to just cover up, and once a new fellow comes along, there's always awkwardness, and often distrust. It's always the child who is expected to compromise, more adult expectations forced into the lap of a child unable to understand. Marc's stepfather can be quite cruel at times, and having this few hours each fortnight gives them a sense of worth that is otherwise lacking."

"You know what its like? How do you know, Kade?" Brynn tethers me with her scrutiny.

"Antony isn't my father. My father died a long time ago. Antony likes everyone to believe I'm his son, but he's never been kind to me. Merely tolerates me."

"Daryl never told me." She mutters.

"Daryl doesn't know."

She bites down on her bottom lip, staring out the window, but there's no surprise on her face. My mother told her already. I mentally roll my eyes. Of course she did, trying to force me to open up.

"Oh, Kade, I'm so sorry. Do you remember him?"

The familiar bittersweet memories float behind my eyes, snapshots that have grown heartbreakingly fuzzy the more time passes. It breaks me a little more each time, to see him step into the shadows a little more. His smile vanished years ago, but I still hear it, in the weakening sound of his voice.

"Yeah. I was only little, but he was always around. I was always in his arms, or hanging off his hand. He'd take me everywhere with him, like he just had to show me off to everyone. I don't know what I ever did, but he was so damned proud of me. No matter where he went, I was his little shadow, and I don't recall a single time when there wasn't a smile on his face. But more than that I remember how I felt when I was with him. Like the world was mine because I was lucky enough to be loved by him."

My breath shudders and I fall silent, suddenly aware of Brynn's warm hand on my thigh. Her thumb rubbing circles that burn in my lungs.

"Turn here!" Brynn points, and I take the car down an overgrown gravel path, because there's nothing I wouldn't do for her. When I reach the end, I cut the engine and Brynn climbs out, gesturing me to join her. The track winds through the gums, opening into a clearing at the end. A massive rock fills the opening, and she clambers up, patting the boulder beside her. I stretch out so I'm lying beside her, head propped up to see the view. And her. Wearing a simple shirt and skirt, she's as beautiful as ever. Her hair is pulled back in a loose ponytail and stray wisps tickle her cheeks with the breeze. Trees fill the scene, the thin clouds waiting for a zephyr to take them. I suck in the fresh air.

"Do you have pictures of your dad?" She blinks down at me when I shake my head. Her eyes flick to my fists flexing.

"Nothing. Antony wanted to erase my Dad completely, and he succeeded." My jaw clenches..

CHAPTER 20

BRYNN

Who is this man? So far from the snarky Kade I've grown familiar with, this version overwhelms me with his openness and honesty. There's so much I don't know about him, and I'm more curious than I'll admit.

"How did he succeed?"

His voice thickens with bitterness.

"My father loved to take me in his car, an old 1967 Mustang Fastback, midnight blue. The thing he loved most after Mum and me. He told me that one day it would be mine. When Mum married Antony, he made a big fuss over not wanting to have anything from her past in his marriage. I remember that day because Mum and Antony argued in front of me, and they rarely did that. Anyway, it seems he had a buyer all lined up and Mum arrived home when he was giving the buyer his sales pitch. When they shook on it, I got so angry I grabbed a hammer from the bench, determined to break the sale, but all I managed to do was put a nice big ass dent on the edge of the bonnet. I thought the damage would put him off, but the new owner took it anyway."

The breeze picks up, moving the clouds along and disrupting the treetops. The day is warm, but I shiver, empathy for a young boy who lost everything but his memories of a man he loved deeply. I lie down beside him, not close enough to touch, but enough to feel his heat.

"I envy you, Kade."

He snorts.

"I do. I mean, I know my parents love me, but neither of them showed me the kind of love you had with your dad. I sometimes wonder if I hadn't loved the farmwork and followed Dad around begging to drive the tractor, would he have actually made time to spend time with me? When there wasn't work to do, he never once sought me out or took me places just to have me there like your Dad did. He obviously adored you so much that he spent every moment he could with you, and I never had that. Most people never get that, and I'd give anything for Dad to tell me he was proud of me."

Kade rolls to his side so he's facing me.

"How could he not be proud? You have a beautiful heart. Very few would go to the lengths you have to care for their parents. You're more capable than a lot of farmers on the land. You're resilient, fierce and independent. But way deep down, Brynn, you find the courage to be all of that when you're so scared of losing control of your life."

"How do you do that? How do you look so far inside me and just know who I am?" I ask when I feel his eyes.

"Because you're so deep under my skin that I can't help tuning you in."

I gasp, my heart tripping and spine straightening. The music, the farmwork, being unnaturally aware of the moment I'm too tired to dance and appearing at that precise moment to take me home. He's not assuming he knows what I want, he's somehow able to know my desires before I'm aware of them.

"That's it. *Tuning*. That's what it feels like, you picking up on my frequency all the time. It's almost spooky. I mean, how did you even know I was at the home? Did they have cameras?"

His jaw twitches. He wears that expression well. Almost a scowl with wild and vulnerable edges, the tension emphasizing his strong cheekbones. He's so guarded right now that I don't expect an answer until his heavy sigh dilutes it.

"I don't know, *pakvora*. Its hard to explain, this...awareness...I feel when you're close. Today, I was in the backyard with Marc, and I knew with such clarity you were there, and I was drawn to you. It's so strong that I know I could find you in a crowd with my eyes closed."

I watch him, notice the smell of his aftershave. "I prefer it when you smell like Kade." I whisper absently.

His lips lift. I like that, too.

"That's for Marc. Early on when we'd just met I took him to get an ice cream, and he kind of...zoned out for a bit. He gave me this look and told me the man behind the counter smelled like his dad. Fragrances are a powerful trigger, and I saw how happy it made Marc, so I wear it when

I see him."

"You'll make a wonderful father one day, K-"

"Stop!" He snaps at me.

I roll to face him, shocked by his tone.

"Don't say it, Brynn. You and I both know how that will end. I'd let them down. They'd look at me with the same contempt everybody else does, and they'd leave."

His face hardens, but I hear him swallow.

"Do I look at you with contempt?"

"Yes."

I open my mouth to respond, but falter. I *have* been treating him with disdain, and I won't do him injustice by denying it. Instead I consider this enigma of a man. So cold and hard on the outside, I see now it's merely armor for his crying soul. His shoulders, stiff and coiled to carry on despite his wounds, his wild eyes constantly scanning for invisible dangers that lurk in the dark hearts of man. I'm slammed with what was behind Kade's aggression towards his brother's visits. He expected me to run off with Daryl at the first opportunity. The way he approached me after he'd finished with Marc, hesitant. Wary. Ready for a fight. Kade isn't scared, I realise, he's anticipating doom. I spread my fingers and rest my palm over his heart. I close my eyes and concentrate.

Thump. Thump.

So strong, yet so fragile.

Thump. Thump.

The heat from his chest swarms up my arm, and when it reaches my chest I become aware of how fast my own heart beats. I feel the beats merge, a clattering tangle. I smile at the broken notes falling over themselves and wonder if we were a concert would our audience have walked out long ago. I picture ladies in evening dresses clutching their ears in horror.

And then our beats sync.

Thump-*thump.* Thump-*thump.*

"Kade?" My eyes slam open and collide with his. They've darkened to rich pewter, swirling with unnamed thoughts. He hasn't moved a muscle, just holds me captive with his stare and breathes with me. His lips part slightly, and I watch them exhale to the rhythm of our hearts.

"You feel that, *pakvora*? It is us." His velvet timbre softens in wonder.

Us. Such a simple word with so much weight. So intimate, like acknowledging it invites him into my very soul. My breath catches, and my heart free falls into space.

Thump-*thump.* Images flash through my head, none of them mine, but feeling that they should be. Overwhelmed, I fall into his eyes once more. *Us,* they echo.

"Dance with me, Kade." I whisper.

He moves with feline grace, ever so carefully folding my hand in his huge one and pulling me to my feet without breaking contact. I feel his chest brush my cheek and press my ear against him.

Thump-*thump*. Thump-*thump*.

I sigh when his arms wrap around me. It feels so good to be held in them, to feel the muscles tighten around me until I'm pinned against the hard heat of his chest. I rest my ear over his chest, the beat of his heart a soothing tattoo.

We slow dance on that rock in the middle of the woods to a tune only we can hear, our bodies fused, the breeze unable to penetrate.

The rhythm speeds up, and us with it until-

"Brynn." He rasps.

I lean up, giving him my mouth. He takes it, hungrily, possessively. Urgently. His fist secures in my hair and holds me steady as his tongue dives in. This isn't Kade being sweet, or making a statement. This is Kade, raw and ferocious with a need to claim me. And I want him to. I cling to that awareness with nails digging and moans of desire tumbling free. His chest thunders. I feel his body vibrate with a throaty growl and feel my mind slipping away.

"Kade. Stop."

He staggers backwards, pain and regret splashing through the palpable desire. He thinks I don't want him.

"Sorry, Brynn. I couldn't…I just needed…"

I can't catch my breath. My lungs heave as his eyes dip and he steps away. It's not what he thinks. I've never wanted something so badly before, but his eyes veil and drop to the ground. He's turning away when I catch his hand. His eyebrows float in confusion until I lead him off the hard surface of the rock, and down to the grass.

"Brynn?" His whisper is raw with urgent hope.

I answer with my fingers winding through the dark hair on the nape of his neck.

His breath explodes as he crushes my lips under his and I moan against his tongue as he invades and conquers.

This is what I need. Unbridled, all consuming desire. My blood vibrates with pleasure as his fingers dig with bruising lust into the small of my back, my breasts pressing hard into his chest, my own fingernails biting into the flesh on his neck. He growls, so wired and wild as he dips and dives with insatiable hunger, and my body shudders in his grip. The sheer intensity of his craving holds me on the brink of sanity, and I've never felt so alive.

He feels it too, breaking the kiss and drilling into me with liquid silver. And this time, instead of holding back, I allow myself to fall into them.

I see it in that moment. The endless sea of warmth and integrity that ebbs and flows over a shore of suffering and despair that he buries so well beneath a scowl of self-preservation. I want to dance in the waves, even for a moment, and let it carry me away.

His breath breaks as he feels me traipse through his most vulnerable places, watching me carefully.

"You are beautiful, Kade" I breathe, and his exhale shudders.

He draws me to him, burying his face in my neck, dragging his nose up to my ear. Leaning back, I see his nostrils flare and something primitive stirs to life.

He's scenting me, storing it to memory.

One last glance, heavy pewter lost beneath the weight of desire before he lifts me off the ground.

Oh, my god! The grass is at my back, and his wide body covers me. My moan stretches, and he growls in response.

"Kade!" I gasp when his lips run a scorching trail down my neck.

It's been so damn long since I felt this. The party, so far away now, was the last time I gave myself to someone, and every cell in my body is hard wired into Kade, overloading my circuitry with his burning touch and the song of his breaths.

I cry out when he drags up my shirt, and I ruck his. The torturous contrast of cool air licking gently against the roaring fire of my flesh merged with Kade's has my eyes rolling back in my head.

"You're a vision, *pakvora*. So perfect."

I gasp when his mouth finds the mound of my breast, his tongue swirling over the soft skin and bringing my aching nipple to life. I press into him, loving the perfect pressure of his fingers as he works my other breast.

"Oh, god, Kade! Oh, yes!"

Kade's hand scorches its print into my thigh. My blood slams in my chest I'm so worked up, and Kade's flaring nostrils tell me he knows it. He's breathtaking like this, wild and open, his desire refusing to be confined to earthly limitations.

I tug on his shirt in desperation, grunting my pleasure when he yanks it over his head with one hand, the way only a man can. It drives me wild, and the heat that grows in the base of my belly intensifies. He pauses, sniffs the air.

"You smell so damned good, Brynn."

I roll my hips in response, feeling the thick swell of his arousal on my thigh. He presses it against me, watching my reaction when I feel it. I curl my fingers into his backside, needing him closer.

"I'm trying to go slow, but you're making me crazy. I want you to feel good." He rasps, and I see the tension in every fibre as he struggles to maintain control. It's so damned sexy I release a groan of agonised yearning into the air. I want him. I need him. *Now.*

"Kade." I whimper.

He holds my gaze as his fingers glide the loose fabric of my skirt to my waist, and I'm wanton animal. The simple, mundane task is suddenly so erotic that I roll my hips against him, needing to feel him against my core. When his palm curls around my exposed thigh, I buck into him.

The silver trap of his eyes holds me captive as the cool air finds my legs. The soft grass cradles my backside and tickles my shoulders as he lowers his head.

A cry tears up my throat when his tongue swipes through my folds.

Oh my god!

My spine bends with the pleasure that ignites through me, coiling as he works his mouth. Arrows of rapture find their mark, the nonsensical sounds they elicit making perfect sense.

When I look down at him, twin pewter sunrises still pinned to me, I almost come apart at the sight of him. He's so intense, like he's completely absorbed by me and that every response I give is a treasure, and it's the most sensual feeling I ever experienced. His fingers pressing into my hips, holding me in place, his stare burning into me and that mouth of his summoning wave after wave of mounting pleasure. My eyes blow out as it crashes over me, again and again, my mind empty of all but...

"Kade!" I scream into the air.

CHAPTER 21

KADE

*W*atching Brynn come apart is the sexiest thing I've ever seen. She's still panting, hair clinging to the fingers of grass, pupils blown out from the pleasure that consumed her.

I see it in her eyes though, she's far from sated. She's reaching for me with urgent hands, her sweet gasps begging for more, and her soft skin burning to be touched.

I keep her gaze as I slide my jeans over my hips, watching her tongue dart over her lips when I spring free. She's never seen me before, and I note with satisfaction when her eyes dip and her breaths explode.

She wants me, and for the first time since I can remember, I feel like I'm enough. My wife finds me acceptable.

And that's the greatest feeling in the world.

I cover her body with mine, knowing instinctively it's what she needs. Her mouth finds mine, and our groans clash when she tastes herself on me.

"Kade" she pants, "Oh, god, please!"

My name on her lips. It's me inside her thoughts. Nobody else. My head swims with the wonderment of it. Her tiny hands exploring me, kneading my back, tearing tattoos of desire in exquisite lines down my spine.

I swallow thickly, burying that flare of guilt that rises. I can regret later, not now. I grit my teeth and line myself up.

"Ready, *pakvora*? Are you ready for me?"

She gasps my name and wraps her legs around my waist.

I nudge her entrance and her buck almost undoes me. I revel in the hot, slick channel as I slide my tip in. Her head falls back, her mouth stretched in a strained O, like opening her mouth will make more room for me inside her.

Sweet Christ, does she feel good! So tight and wet for me, the noises of ecstasy the most beautiful sounds on earth.

"Kade! I need…"

I know what she needs. But this is for me, first. I struggle to rein in my control as I penetrate deeper, feeling the silken passage stretch and give, allowing me full access. Until I'm seated so deep inside her it's impossible to tell where I end and she begins. My breath explodes in awe. She writhes beneath me, hunger sending her out of her mind. It's beautiful.

"Eyes on me, *pakvora*." I command, and her head swings to me.

She implores me with her sounds and nails, and I steal one last kiss...

And then I give her what she needs.

I draw back and plunge deep, growling when I reach the very end of her. Her hips meet mine at every dive, pulling away in the beautiful dance that brings us ever closer to rapture.

But it's more than that, because with every stroke I give her my soul, with every breath I hand her my life, and with my eyes locked on hers, I show her my heart.

"Oh!" Her eyes open impossibly wide; a redeeming epiphany.

The friction of her bunches in my sac, and I let myself go. With my body pinning her to the ground, one fist in her hair and the other on her shoulder, I drive harder, deeper, faster, until, on the edge of deliverance, her muscles grip my length in convulsing surges, and I roar my own release as my body shudders and my seed fills her.

Her spent legs slide off me, but while her arms still hold me, I remain deep inside her. The ultimate connection. Brynn and I with the sun on my back and hope in my lungs. I drop my head and nuzzle the fluttering pulse in her neck, tasting the beads of perspiration as our breaths even out.

"What was that?" she whispers.

"It was us, *pakvora*." I murmur into her hair.

"It was...everything." She breathes, eyes dancing between mine for answers.

I smile carefully. Now that the moment has passed, I feel vulnerable and raw. I drop my eyes, but when I start to pull out, her legs wind back around me, and I sink back inside her.

"You don't get to hide from me any longer, Kade." She purrs, running a finger down the side of my face.

But I can't meet her eyes for the ache in my chest, and the cloud of impending doom laced with guilt that never lets up.

***

We ride home in silence, but I steal glances every chance I get. Every now and then, she sucks in a quick breath and her body quakes with aftershocks. I still can't believe she let me inside of her.

When we pull up, I head straight to the barn to feed the calves, and Brynn goes inside. I smirk as I watch the door close. She's probably exhausted.

And then I feel the air change as my wounds open up again. She's too good for me. Her light, her spark and her innocence is too pure for the likes of me.

I'm a bully, Daryl says, and he's right. I've used my fists so many times I lost count, the layers of scars themselves covered in scars. The most recent ones from my own brother. I flex them, the purple indents where the scabs fell away yet another regret to add to my list.

I've tried to do the right thing and be a son that my father would have been proud of, but now I fear I've let him down. Every good intention has been buried in my manipulations and betrayal. Things I never thought I was capable of. Yet here I am, realisation dawning that I'd do it all over again in a heartbeat if it brought me back to this point.

I think of Brynn, curled up in her bed with a flood of remorse.

The house is silent when I return.

I shower, resting my palms against the wall as the needles of water sting the nail scrapes on my back, and I shudder with flashbacks. I wrap the towel around my hips and smear the fog from the mirror, noting with awe the marks of Brynn's pleasure carved in my shoulder blades.

It's barely seven when I emerge, but I'm so worn out that I consider sleeping. My breath catches when I see Brynn, curled up and deep asleep in my bed. Her lips hang open, a tendril of hair across the space moving slowly with the rhythm of her breaths.

What's she doing here? Did she come to find me, to tell me she regretted it and fell asleep as she waited?

I swallow thickly and sit on the bed, smoothing the hair from her face. Her eyelashes flutter, then burst open as clarity hits. She sits up, my covers held to her chest, her face flushing.

"Uh, Kade…I came to find you…I guess I fell asleep."

I smile warily, waiting for her to climb out, but she doesn't.

"I fed the calves. Are you okay?" I reach out and cup her cheek.

I feel the moment her guard drops, where every front she's trying to hide behind melts away.

"It's silly, really, but earlier, you had on that aftershave and..." She sucks a breath and braces.

"I wanted to smell *you*, Kade. The real you, before I could sleep." Her frown is adorable.

"Well, now that I have..." she throws the covers back. She's leaving.

"Or you could stay here the night?" I offer, a little too fast.

She pauses, questions dancing in her eyes.

"Please? Please stay with me, Brynn?"

I don't realise I'm holding my breath until she runs her warm hand over my chest. I crawl in beside her, and gather her into my chest, her breath pluming against my heart.

"I was so afraid you'd say no, Kade. You seem so detached most of the time that I thought you might not want me."

"No, *pakvora*. I've wanted you for longer than you know. I...I find it difficult to explain how I feel."

"Mmnn I had no trouble understanding you earlier." Her smile tickles my chest, and I chuckle.

"I think it would be uncomfortable if I communicated with everyone that way."

She giggles, tilting her face up to mine. I land my mouth on her just because I can.

"How do you taste so sweet?" I murmur as I let her bottom lip slip from between my teeth.

"Who would have thought bad boy Kade Walker was such a romantic?" She smirks.

"Don't spread it around. You'll ruin my reputation. Besides, I'm putting on an act. Just wait 'til the morning when I kick you off my side of the bed."

She quirks an eyebrow in challenge.

"And which side is your side?"

I dig my teeth into her neck and she squeals in laughter.

"Both sides are mine!" I grin.

Her giggle evaporates and her focus drops to my dimple.

"That's dimple's enough to melt the panties right off a woman, Kade. You're packing some pretty heavy arsenal right there."

"Is that so? So are you telling me that whatever I ask you will agree to if I flash this at you?"

She pulls her lip between her teeth and nods coyly.

"In that case, Brynn Walker, can you stay in my bed every night?"

I watch her smile shrink and I cringe inwardly.

Too fast, Kade. Way too fast. I watch her eyes shift and know she's thinking of Daryl. I open my mouth but close it again when I see the distance in her expression.

I can't do this.

I slip out of bed and drag my tracksuit pants on, scraping my fingers through my hair.

"I'm making scrambled eggs, do you want some?" I deadpan, but I don't wait for her answer.

I pace the kitchen as the eggs cook, cursing myself for being too needy, for destroying a good thing. She looked at me like...

No, Kade. Don't do this to yourself, I sneer. *There's no way she can grow to love you. You don't deserve it, especially after what you did.*

"Kade?" I spin when her voice reaches me. She's wearing an old t-shirt of mine and it reaches mid thigh. Her nipples jut out above her crossed arms. She looks at me with...

Pity.

Christ, no! The last thing I want to see on her face is pity.

"Eggs?" I ask, the chill back in my tone.

She flinches, another layer of guilt to add.

I empty the eggs into a bowl and carry it to the table while she watches silently. I add salt and pepper, because anything to delay the inevitable is good.

"Kade, can we talk?"

Here we go, I think, pushing the bowl from me. I couldn't eat anyway. I glare at her.

"Don't do that, Kade. Please. It hurts." Moisture wells in her eyes and the thought of me causing her pain breaks me. Really destroys me. Her honesty shakes my walls down with a single drop of moisture on her cheek. I track its path, breathless from the calamity inside. My normal reaction to raise my armour and ready my sword conflicts with the instinct to wrap my arms around her and keep her safe at all costs. I've never experienced this utter confusion before, and I fist my hair in distress.

"I told you, Kade, you don't get to hide from me. You need to *talk* to me."

"Why? What can I say to you, Brynn? What do you want to hear from me, because I'll say whatever you want. But it won't make any difference in the end, because of this delusion you hold onto that you are meant to be with Daryl. You grip it so tightly, Brynn, that you don't see what's right in front of you, and I don't know how to change that."

"I've loved him for years, Kade. That doesn't just go away."

I seethe. "Its a seed that was planted when you were a child that died years ago but you're still watering it and hoping it will flower."

She swipes away her tears angrily.

"Then what *should* happen, Kade? Am I supposed to decide I want to stay in this sham of a marriage forever? With you? Can you say you'll be happy to look back on this in twenty years time and know that it wasn't you that I loved?"

My lungs shred with pain. She's stripped me bare with her soft skin and sweet surrender then tore out my heart.

Nothing hurts like the rusty blade of reality, and I respond the only way I know how. I tower over her until she feels the full force of my rage.

"No, Brynn." I spit. "Because we won't even make a year. There's no way the likes of you could ever love someone as loathsome and contemptible as me. You were right all along; it's a game of mine, see? Find out what buttons I can press to make people hate me as much as they can. It's why I married you, Brynn. I wanted to find out just how much my brother can hate me. Because driving people away is what keeps me going. Is that what you wanted to hear?"

My pain hisses through my clenched jaw, but Brynn straightens and stares me down.

"Is that truly how you see yourself, Kade? Do you really believe everyone will leave you in the end? What about Marc?"

There is no anger left. Now there's just pain, and through the pain, I find her eyes and show her every last drop of my regret.

Barely audible, I acknowledge my curse, searching her expression for anything I can salvage from the wreckage I've set in motion.

"You will hate me too, *pakvora*, when you find out what I've done."

CHAPTER 22

BRYNN

*B*ehind his eyes, ghosts and demons loom. "You will hate me too, *pakvora*, when you find out what I've done."

The door slams behind him, and I watch his bare torso stalk into the twilight until the marks I left on his back can no longer be seen.

What has he done? What is it that would make me hate him?

I release a shuddering breath, shaking my head. He was glorious in his rage, and even though I love Daryl, its Kade my body catches fire for.

I love Daryl.

I mouth the words, wishing they didn't cut so deeply. I've always loved Daryl, and I can't just switch that off because Kade says to. I think about Kade's accusation as I absently bring the bowl of eggs in front of me and poke at them with the fork.

A seed from my childhood that I water long after it's dead. It was an idea born as children, but the years kept us close. It wasn't from the expectation of our future that we stayed close, we remained friends organically, and the future never wavered in our minds. Even Bella said I rarely spoke of Daryl, but we'd made a promise to each other. We fit, Daryl and I. We spent time together, and it was always pleasant. He was safe, reliable, and we shared similar interests. Mostly.

I have to admit I do prefer the farm life with space and sky for miles over the electric stars of the city. But that's the compromise all couples experience, right? Like how Daryl always wanted me to wear my hair a certain way, and suggested I wear those tight skirts even though they didn't suit my shape.

And he was a gentleman, unlike Kade, who could be an animal at times. My core burns at the thought of Kade's wild eyes on me as he claimed me. My pulse quickens.

That's one thing we have, Kade and me. Mind blowing chemistry, in bucket loads.

The fork clatters to the table.

"I slept with Kade." I groan to the empty kitchen. I cheated on Daryl, unable to control myself, and I hadn't felt remotely guilty. Until now.

I race to my room, pulling on a clean pair of jeans and head for the car.

I need to see Daryl.

***

The queasy feeling of betrayal launches dangerously close to my throat as I climb out of the car. Again I pause in deliberation at the door until Daryl cracks it, peaking through the crack with my text message open on the phone in his hand.

"Brynn?" He blinks as if he's been asleep.

"I needed to talk to you." I stare at the ground, unable to meet his eyes.

"Come in, I think Mum's still awake, but Dad's asleep."

I realise suddenly how dark it is.

"I'm sorry, Daryl...I didn't realise how late it was. Maybe I'll come back."

"No, Brynn, don't be silly. I'm here for you. Always."

I meet his eyes and see the truth in deep blue.

He leads me past the kitchen, and the strangest feeling encompasses me.

I shouldn't be here.

"Brynn, Dear? Is that you?" Evie pokes her head out with a frown.

"Hi, Evie. I just came to see Daryl for a few minutes." Her eyes widen, then narrow.

"Oh." She says, and in that one word I decide.

"Please, Evie, won't you join us?"

Her shoulders soften and she gives me a smile, announcing she'll bring tea and biscuits in a moment.

Daryl rests a curious frown on me and leads me into the parlour. I select an armchair, less comfortable than the couch, but the only chair that seats one.

"What's going on, Brynn. You're scaring me."

"Daryl, when did we decide we'd get married? I mean for real. Not when we were kids messing around, I mean as adults. When did we decide?"

Daryl frowns, searching the air for his memories. "I can't say, Brynn. I think it was just always a given."

I shake my head. "No, Daryl. It's a decision to be made between two adults at the fulcrum of their future."

"Where is this coming from? It's what two people do naturally when they're in love."

I shift in my chair, leaning forward. "But Daryl, what *is* love?"

Love just is.

Daryl frowns, exhaustion tugging his face. He shrugs in confusion.

"Love is the natural progression of friends who have grown into something much more."

And with that, my blood chills. A strange ache takes flight in my stomach. I don't know what I expected, never even understood why I needed to be here, only that Daryl has always been my safe place to land. Reliable, dependable and every other safe and predictable virtue. But for the first time, I understand that Daryl is Daryl. He doesn't exist on deeper plains. There's no guessing, no frustration with Daryl. He's the calming light, steady and sweet. An angel.

And Kade is the devil.

He's a passionate, overwhelming presence that rattles my world and keeps me guessing; a fierce, unpredictable and exciting man who envelopes me in fire and steps into the flames beside me.

I stare at the face etched in my future since I was a child, and find I'm no closer to resolving the puzzle Kade planted in my mind...

Daryl draws a breath, but his words are silenced by the clatter of the tea tray.

Evie places the tray on the table and sits where she has a clear view of both of us.

"How's Kade?" She smiles, sliding a glance at Daryl.

"He's good. The farm is looking great and it looks like it will be an excellent hay season..." I trail off when Daryl shrinks against the couch, and deflect.

"Daryl and I were just discussing our childhoods." I say.

She chuckles behind her hand. "Ah, yes. You two were so good to Kade, letting him hang around. He was always so overprotective of his little brother that he would have been beside himself if he couldn't watch out for him."

"*What?*" Daryl's spine locks, his head whipping to Evie.

"Oh, yes, dear. He worshipped the ground you walked on. I'm surprised you don't remember it, since the two of you were inseparable. I lost count of the times I found you snuggled up to Kade in his bed after a nightmare. And, oh, boy, when you started kinder he almost lost his head. He couldn't fathom you being without him for more than a minute, and when he found out he couldn't be with you, he raged for weeks. Even after, when he realised he had no choice but to let you go, he'd walk you to your room before running to his own class down the road. It was the same every lunch time and after school. He was so worried someone would hurt his little brother. He was so consumed with you he never had time to make his own friends. Not that that ever bothered him. You were far more important to him."

Evie seemed oblivious to the silence that cloaked the room, taking her time adding sugar and stirring her tea.

"You should have seen him the first time someone took a dislike to you. I thought he'd kill the kid. Huh. Funny how time changes everything."

Evie smiles that light, wholesome smile, but her eyes add weight to her words.

Kade was protecting Daryl.

A memory bursts to life in my mind. I remember coming home from school, the police cars in the driveway blinding me with their flickering lights. Kade full of bitter rage and defiance struggling against the handcuffs.

Evie had confronted Daryl to ask about Damien Wright, and Daryl's voice, so thin and scared saying all he knew was that Damien wanted his lunch money, but didn't come for it that day. And I remember the expression of triumph on Kade's face.

Daryl sits, pale as a ghost.

"Oh, my god. I remember that now. I'd forgotten." He lifts bewildered blue eyes to hers. "How could I forget? Mum, what happened between us?"

She shrugs. "I have no idea, Daryl. Maybe one of you will remember. So, Brynn, tell me how many calves are you rearing this year."

I force the conversation until I take the final sip, and say a hurried goodbye to them both. Daryl barely registers my departure, just sits rigid, wearing a severe frown, and Evie slides her eyes to him, but keeps her smile for me.

"You have no idea how much I appreciate you dropping in tonight, dear. Give Kade my love."

***

I set out tonight with the intention of finding answers. I needed to understand this vague and cloudy history Daryl and I have. I do love him. I know I do. I felt it in the warmth that spread in my chest when he answered the door, and in the way the tone of his voice just…fitted me. Like my favourite pair of pyjamas that I slip into at the end of the day. I look forward to Daryl, but Kade? He sets me on fire.

Instead of enlightenment, all I have to show is more puzzles to piece together.

My feet take me to Kade's room. I know he's not there, but I climb in, inhale his scent and wait for him. I need to unravel this mess, because while I love Daryl, I want to be in Kade's bed, and I'm not sure I know what that means. I always thought love was black and white; you either loved someone completely or you didn't, but here I am, loving Daryl with no desire to sleep with him, and craving Kade's touch again.

I groan with frustration. When Kade asked me to sleep in his bed every night, it rattled me. I had to bite my lip before I blurted out an immediate yes, and in that hesitation, guilt poured in. Only then had my thoughts turned to Daryl, and that damned remorse kicked in when the pain-stricken twist of his face flashed in my mind.

I couldn't hurt Daryl any more than I had. If he knew what I'd done with Kade, it would upset him. But when I saw him tonight, I couldn't deny that something had changed. Compared to Kade's intensity, Daryl seemed like the heartbreak that was supposed to be debilitating was diluted. He seemed more put out than devastated. And when I laid eyes on him, there was no quickening in my belly, no bolts of charge darting through my bloodstream. No desire to feel his lips on mine. Outside of the night of passion at the party, there never had been anything electrifying about our love.

Daryl seemed different, too, like a foreigner was wearing his face, or perhaps it was me. But he appeared less devastated and more…guilty. It fed my own guilt. Daryl and I shared our lives, but lately I've been avoiding him, not once asking how he's handling this upheaval.

I blame Kade, who consumes me so entirely that he leaves me breathless and fully charged every time we are in the same room, and when he leaves, I'm tingling for more. He leaves me no space to consider Daryl's plight.

The enigma of Kade bleeds into every cell. The bad boy image he lets people see? It isn't him. He's been scarred by Antony's attitude towards him, and whatever turned sour with Daryl.

Kade spent his childhood protecting his little brother, and something happened to break that. Something Daryl couldn't remember.

I try to recollect, but all that comes to mind is every time Daryl told him to leave us alone, and the sad pewter eyes that followed us everywhere in spite of it.

On the edge of slumber, a memory surfaces.

Daryl and I are ten. We are watching the storm from the shelter of the big oak tree. I squeal in delight at every drop that manages to wind its way through the canopy of leaves to strike me. Daryl hugs the trunk to avoid them, inviting me to do the same.

But I step into the deluge, arms wide, face angled towards the heavens.

Daryl looks up suddenly.

"Kade! You're getting wet! Come under here with me! There's plenty of room for all of us."

Kade, a sturdy sixteen, grins, dimple deep as those startling eyes soften on Daryl, but when he turns to me, there's the strangest expression on his face. I feel it in my bones and wonder what it means, but Kade shakes his head as if to clear it, then smiles at his brother.

"Come to me, Little Brother. Feel how warm the rain is."

Daryl and I both race from the cover of the tree and into Kade's open arms, his laughter like music.

"Come, Kade. Dance with us." I command, and with an indulging smile, we move to the rhythm of the pelting rain, twirling and laughing and feeling the storm while Daryl hangs back, not understanding what the fuss is about.

So beautiful was that moment, that I feel the emotion slide from my closed eyes and into Kade's pillow.

What went wrong?

CHAPTER 23

KADE

*S*omething's wrong.

My eyes snap open and take a moment to focus. I fell asleep in the barn in a bed of straw. It had been months since that happened. The calves hadn't yet stirred for breakfast, but my own stomach gurgles in protest, reminding me I hadn't eaten dinner last night.

I'd slept with Brynn. My morning erection twitches hungrily at the prospect of repeating that.

It was more than I imagined. The way her head fell back, lost in the sensations I was giving her. The glorious feel of her, so tight and slick, how she opened to me finally and let me see how I made her feel. And I saw it all, everything she stubbornly refuses to acknowledge herself.

Then I pushed her too far.

I fist the straw and drag my other hand over my face. I told her I married her to get back at Daryl.

I curse, and the calves begin to rouse.

My lungs tighten, reminding me I need to be alert for whatever it is that woke me up.

I thank the stars for a warm night because I'm dressed only in the tracksuit I dragged on last night after Brynn and I argued, the cool morning air clearing my head as I stride to the house.

Daryl's car. I growl in the back of my throat. He just has this knack of showing up when I'm not around, or at a time when Brynn is most vulnerable.

The door slams open, and there they are, Daryl and Brynn, sitting at the kitchen table. Both looking like they haven't slept, Daryl's perfectly combed hair uncannily mussed up. I glare and scan them both. No evidence of swollen lips or passion on either of them, I note with fleeting relief, but that's not to say it didn't happen. I swallow the urge to send Daryl to hell simply for being here.

"What do you want, Little Brother?" I block the doorway with my frame and cross my arms over my chest.

Brynn rises from her chair, shame colouring her face.

"Kade, he's here because…I went to see him last night, and he-"

I didn't let her finish. With a snarl I grab Daryl's arm and he leaps out of the chair. He covers his face with his arms, and I should feel guilty, but I don't. I drag the shirt out of his slacks and expose his back.

"What are you doing, you psycho?" Daryl chokes.

I run my hands over his unmarred skin and shoot a glare at Brynn. She's sunk in her chair, head buried in her hands, humiliation glowing red.

I yank his shirt back down and smirk, showing him the marks Brynn gouged in my back.

"Making sure you didn't have marks to match these, Little Brother."

His mouth falls as he takes them in, torturing himself by examining each one.

"Daryl." Brynn whispers, her voice filled with pain.

My brother looks at her. Swallows. Then without another word, he pushes past me and out the door.

I round on Brynn, but she's out of the chair and in my space. The fury that darkens her eyes makes my heart stutter with her vengeful beauty. Her lips twist, and my pulse hammers.

"You're such an arsehole, Kade!" she snarls like a vengeful warrior.

I want to apologise. I know I should. What I did was jealous and cruel, and unforgivable, like so many other things I've done, but my nostrils flare as her scent reaches me. Summer rain mixed with…me. She slept in my bed last night, and the smell of me on her as if she truly belonged to me is too damned intoxicating.

I'm overcome by the ravenous hunger to taste her, and I crush her mouth with mine, groaning at the sweetness of her. Her hands slap against my chest as she struggles to escape.

"How dare you do that to Daryl, Kade! You didn't even give me a chance to tell him!" Her fury is perfect. So full of emotion, but it's misplaced.

I pull back, still holding her tight, snaring her eyes with mine.

"His car hasn't left yet, you can still catch him if you want to." I offer breathlessly, but the moment I plunge my tongue against the seam of her lips, demanding entry, she submits with a sigh. Her palms rest against my chest and my head swims as she melts into me.

Her mouth moves against mine and I fist her hair. This isn't about worshipping her body. It's not about giving and connecting. This is about claiming what's mine, raw and feral. Her arms snake around my neck, giving me access to her sleep shorts. I yank them down her thighs, lifting her off the ground and pinning her against the kitchen wall in my haste to flick them off her feet. Her legs wrap around my hips, her breaths harsh and needy in my mouth. I slip a finger between her thighs and she moans and rolls her hips as I feel the slick centre of her. I press my shoulder against her so hard I feel her heartbeat while I free myself and line up with her.

Remember this, Kade...

I slam in and roar at the sensation, her own cries cutting through the air. She tears at my back, opening the old wounds and forging more in searing ecstasy. I pound relentlessly into her, watching her mouth gape in wonder, listening to the sounds of her pleasure.

My sanity slips, drowning in the feel of Brynn, the ambrosia of her arousal, the awe of being inside her body. The heat, the sound of our skin slapping together, our breaths fusing, its too much.

Thrust. Remember. Thrust. Remember.

I catch her eyes. I need them on me now.

"You're mine, *pakvora*." I snarl, driving into her with punishing force. She cries out in pleasure, fingers gripping, eyes wild with the frantic rhythm of us.

When it's all over, Kade, remember this moment.

I feel her muscles clench and bunch a heartbeat before I find my own release, our cries a perfect duet of euphoria as stars burst behind my eyes.

She's kissing my shoulder when my head clears, gentle and sated and pliable in my arms.

I smirk down at her through heaving breaths, and feel a shiver run down my spine as her eyes narrow. She squirms, but I pin her there, not ready yet to pull out of her.

"You're such an arsehole, Kade." She growls softly.

"Mmm. And you love it." I dare her to deny it.

"I waited for you last night." She murmurs, glancing down.

I can't have her look away. I twitch inside her and she gasps, snapping her eyes back to mine.

"I know."

"I…I wanted you to know that I was here last night. Alone. Daryl and I just talked."

"I know."

She frowns. "No you don't, Kade. You can't know that, you uh… checked his back…"

"Mmm, yes I know, but I know you slept in my bed last night because you smell like me. No, like us, and damn if that scent doesn't send me crazy."

The corner of her lip curls up, and she runs those warm hands sensuously over my shoulders.

"That wasn't a nice thing to do to your brother." She frowns, but she lacks conviction.

"Probably not, but you didn't chase him out to fix it, *pakvora*. What do you want me to do? Apologise for a moment with you I'll never regret?" I nip at her ear, loving the gasp that tumbles from those delicious lips and is all mine.

If it weren't for my seed slowly dripping out of her and down my shaft, the moment would have been perfect. Instead, like a faithful hound the guilt comes back, breaking the spell.

I'm terrified that when you find out what I've done you'll walk away from me.

She groans when I pull out of her and put her gently on her feet.

"What does this mean?" She asks quietly, watching me tuck myself back into my pants.

I shiver.

I'm terrified I'll never be enough, and it's my brother who owns your heart.

"It means exactly what it means." I press my lips on her head.

"Damn it, Kade. Stop talking in riddles." She snaps, and I bristle.

"Well stop asking questions you already know the answer to." I retort.

***

She spends the morning in her head, and I spend it searching her expressions for the epiphany she needs to reach. While I'm relieved she makes no move to chase Daryl down, by midday its agitating me.

"Let's get out of here, *pakvora*. Today belongs beyond the farm."

With a grateful sigh, we jump in the car and head away from the town. We wind through the hills, the wheel turning where it wants to until we find a small town I've never been to before. The streets are filled with people milling around the stalls lining the footpaths.

I find a park and reach tentatively to take Brynn's hand in mine. I know she's raw, trying to make sense of what her heart is fighting the mysterious familiarity of me for. She frowns at it and stabs a quizzical look at me, but to my delight, she doesn't pull away.

We wander past the stalls of fruit and vegetables, the stall holder's booming invitations and promises of freshness making me smile. Brynn inspects the handmade jewellery of a young woman, fingering the choker with a silver sun charm. I hand over the cash with a smile while she's still absorbed in the detail.

"It is yours, *pakvora*." I smile at her. She grins back, but I'm distracted by the woman in my periphery who's head jerks towards me at my words. She's an older woman, probably the same era as my mother. There's a gentle beauty to her that lingers despite her age, and her gray eyes go impossibly wide.

"*Pakvora?*" She breathes, "That is the word of Lash if I'm not mistaken."

There's something familiar about her that I can't put my finger on, but I know I've never set eyes on her before. Shaking my head I correct her.

"I'm sorry, but I don't know what you mean. I'm Kade Walker. Kade Lasher Walker." I don't know what prompted me to give her my full name.

She scrutinises me, boldly scanning for something only she can see. Her lips thin.

"You are Lash's boy. I'd recognise you anywhere, and If I didn't, you recognise your heart with the same term Lash used." She nods decisively, then indicates to Brynn with her eyebrows. "And this is…?"

"This is my wife, Brynn." She glances between us, completely unaware of the silent conversation that's going on between words.

The woman's eyebrows disappear into her hair.

"She does not know, yet." A statement, but one that instantly validates everything I believed.

I shake my head, the smile playing on my mouth. "And who might you be?"

"I am Masilda." She says simply, holding out her hand. When I clasp it, she snatches it to her, opening my palm.

"You are a farmer." She grins, some of her teeth missing, but she turns my hand and runs her finger over my knuckles with sadness. "But you are also a fighter."

"Only when I have to." I lower my voice, and Masilda looks at me with a piercing stare that I feel right inside me.

"You will use them one more time, and then never again, son of Lash. That time is gone. Come back and see me again later, and bring Evie." And with that, she lifts the back curtain of the stall and disappears behind it.

"Well, that was the strangest thing I've ever seen." Brynn gapes at the empty stall, then back at me.

I laugh, weightless for the first time in far too long. With Brynn's hand in mine, I feel invincible, and whatever went on between Masilda and me touched a place within that needed to know I belong somewhere.

I clasp the choker chain on Brynn and kiss her forehead before continuing our exploration.

"This is lovely, Kade. I can feel the happiness in this place."

As if to reiterate, a group of boys race through the crowd, laughing as they pass the ball between them as they weave. A young boy catches the ball and collides with the rear end of a woman carrying bags. She laughs at his quick apology, but the ball is gone.

"I've got it," Brynn calls, and the boys run towards her.

"Catch me if you can!" She taunts them and runs towards the grassy park.

The swarm of boys pass by. Brynn laughs, dark hair flying out behind her as they lunge at her. She laughs, holding it out of reach.

My heart floats.

"I'll get it for you!" I announce, and, as if I could do anything but, I chase after Brynn.

One lad has scaled Brynn's side, levering himself up using her shoulder. I snatch the ball out of Brynn's hands and the children fall away from her and turn their focus on me. I'm waiting for them to reach me when I'm knocked to the ground from behind.

Brynn's laughter rings in my ears as she falls on top of me. The ball bounces away and the boys chase it in youthful exuberance.

"I caught you." She laughs victoriously.

I wind my arms around her and nuzzle her ear.

"Only because I let you, *pakvora*." I snigger.

"You're such a sore loser, Kade! I beat you fair and square. Now let me go!"

"Not until you kiss me."

"That's not fair! You can't keep changing the rules like that!"

I grin and watch her struggle uselessly to break my grip. Feeling her wriggle around on me is a distraction I didn't consider when I entered this battle. The warmth of her, the scent of her consuming me again...

"Hah!" She cries triumphantly when she slips from my grasp, dancing around me like a sylph of light and joy.

I shake my head, conceding defeat. Is it really defeat when losing makes me feel this good?

I climb to my feet, brushing the grass from my jeans when Brynn launches at me. I catch her as her arms wrap around my shoulders, and her legs encircle my waist.

And then the world stops, because my wife spontaneously, willingly, and genuinely kisses me.

CHAPTER 24

BRYNN

*B*ella places the napkin on her lap and sips her water. "So what happens now?"

I sigh. "That's the million dollar question."

She leans forward, her blonde tresses spilling over her shoulders, reminding me we need to dance again soon.

"So let me get this straight. You love Daryl, but you slept with Kade, then when you felt guilty, you went to see what Daryl's definition of love was, and that you thought it was stupid-"

"I didn't say it was stupid-" I protest, but Bella dismisses it with a wave of her hand.

"But it *was* stupid. Then you slept with Kade again, and then spent the day with him and had actual fun with him, and now you're *finally* realising that Kade is a pretty awesome guy."

"Argh! When you say it like that it sounds so simple!" I bury my head in my hands.

"It can be that simple. You think you love Daryl, but how is it different to the way you love Kade?"

I frown while the waiter places the mushroom risotto in front of me. Bella stabs her chicken salad and looks at me expectantly.

"It's very different. Daryl is…Daryl. He knows more about me than anyone. But Kade is exciting. It's hard to explain, but it's like he understands me better than I understand myself. And he seems to know without asking me what I need, to the point it verges on irritating. And the way he looks at me, Bella, like he's devouring me and I don't even know it yet. He fills my life, just by being in the same room…" I shrug, but Bella grins at me.

"What?"

"You admitted it. I asked how Daryl compares to the way you love Kade and you didn't bat an eyelid. You love him." She replies smugly.

The air vacates my lungs in a loud whoosh.

"It's okay, Bry. I think you were the only one who hadn't figured it out. Now we're all caught up and can get on with moving forward."

I gape at her, speechless. She's right. I didn't hesitate. Didn't deny, didn't falter.

I love Kade.

I love Daryl.

"Can you imagine a life without Kade, Brynn?" She asks, and the thought stabs at my heart.

"No!"

"And Daryl? Can you imagine a future without him in it?"

"No." I'm slower to respond, but its the honest truth. My heart hurts with the thought of losing either of them.

With an evasive promise to go dancing again, I drive home, grateful Kade is at the neighbouring farm for the evening so I can be alone in my thoughts.

***

I'm still drowning in confusion when Evie shows up.

"Hello dear, I wanted to check in on you after the other night. You seemed a little out of sorts."

I kiss her cheek and make tea as she settles into the chair. With quiet speculation I watch her. I never gave her credit before, but she's shrewd. She seems, like Kade, to see more than she lets on.

"I'm much more settled, thank you, but I'm pleased you came. I don't know if Kade has spoken with you, but we bumped into a woman who thought she knew Kade. Called him Lash."

Evie's hand springs to her mouth.

"Did she say who she was, Brynn?" Her voice trembles.

"Masilda."

Tears well up in her eyes. "Ahhh, Masilda. Such a beautiful woman. How is she?"

"I have no idea, Evie. Masilda and Kade started this strange conversation, if you could call it that. It was like they were having a deep and meaningful, but someone had taken away most of their words. I can't even imagine what they spoke about, even though I heard every word."

Evie roars, a hand-on-her-chest laughter that shakes the room.

"Yes, that was undoubtedly the woman I knew. Gosh, I miss her." I watch the warmth fall from her, replaced by a heavy sadness.

"But that is my lot no longer." She sighs.

"Was Lash Kade's father?" I ask.

She nods with a smile, settles into her seat and sips her tea.

"Kade's father begged to get married immediately. He said a gypsy knows when he finds the one who owns his heart. He described it once as being a blinding flash of insight or awareness, or an irrefutable knowing that he feels in his blood, and that there was no point in waiting. I agreed, of course and we made plans. Modest ones, my dear, because we had very little with a baby on the way. When I mentioned sending an invitation to my parents, he was beside himself. He would honour my decision, but he made it clear that he would prefer them to be absent at our wedding."

"What? I thought he was sweet and thoughtful. How could he be so cruel? Did he become nasty to you?" I lean forward in angst.

She chuckles. "Oh no, dear. He was the most perfect, most gentle creature I've ever met."

"But he wanted you to exclude your parents?" I query, far from understanding.

"Yes dear, you see, Gypsies are unique people, and they love with their whole hearts. Unless you have experienced the love of a gypsy, you do not truly know love. Everything else is a poor substitute. They are consumed by it and they fiercely protect the object in their hearts beyond every limit. They are destined to love only one other in their lifetime, and their need to fight for their relationship exists even if there is not a battle to begin with, because if they lose the one they love, their heart dies, and so do they. The term 'to die of a broken heart' is more than an expression, it's a gypsy truth.

"To him, allowing my parents access to me to potentially brainwash me into leaving him would literally kill him. Sometimes to guard your own life, you find yourself making irrational decisions and taking actions so far removed from normal behaviour that you question yourself. It's a natural instinct for those with gypsy blood. That's why Kade's father needed the threat of my parents removed, and since my relationship with them was never...close, there was never a choice for me to make.

"No man in the world is perfect, Brynn, and neither was Lash, but when what you have is so wonderful, it's important to look past the errors and see them for what they mean instead. Kade isn't great at communicating, just like Lash wasn't.

"One day I will tell you our biggest hurdle, but I will reveal this much. What Lash did went against every value I hold. But it also went against his, and I can't tell you the countless times he woke screaming from the nightmares it caused him, knowing he crossed that line. He found it harder to live with than I did in the end.

"Anyway, I digress. I cut ties with my parents, and we were married before a celebrant with a stranger bearing witness, but I didn't care. He was all I needed. Him and our baby."

She fell silent, a smile ghosting her face. She'd sacrificed so much, and instead of growing old with Kade's father, she's with Antony.

"Do you love Antony?"

Her eyes widen remarkably.

"Oh, I suppose so, in a way. He's so different to Kade's father on every level. I'll never have again what I did with my first husband, but I'm ashamed to admit that our relationship only bloomed because I was afraid of being alone. The absence of Lash made the world a cruel, cold place, and Antony found me when I was weak with it.

"Kade took the loss of his father harder than I thought possible, but at the time I didn't factor the gypsy blood flowing through his veins. In hindsight, I should have called Masilda, but my broken heart made me believe I was alone, and I managed the best I could. As Kade and I began to heal, Antony caught sight of me in a restaurant with Kade, and started pursuing me. He was, and still is a fine man, and he was prepared to take Kade on, so I relented…

"You must never utter this to anyone, Brynn, because I will deny it till my dying day. Daryl was born when Kade was six, and I never thought I could have room in my heart for two boys. I love them both so much. They're such completely different personalities that I can't help but adore them. But between you and me, Kade always received the lion's share of my heart. You see, I had to make up for the loss of his father's love. Daryl had Antony and me, and Kade…he just had me, and he's seen more pain than Daryl."

Her smile clouds.

My heart bleeds for Kade. The way he loved his father, and the cold, underhanded presence of a man who did his best to erase the love that filled Kade's heart… my mouth dries with the injustice Kade has suffered.

"Anyway, I probably should leave you to your day, dear."

She deposits her cup in the sink and pauses.

"Oh, and you're good with that Internet rubbish. You might be able to find something on Kade's father. His name was Lash Greyson."

Perhaps an obituary. But I snag my phone and type his name into the search bar so I don't forget it and automatically activate it. On the edge of setting it down on the table, an image flicks up and I gasp.

I may as well be staring at a current photo of Kade, silver eyes shining into the camera, so full of life and trust that it takes my breath away. There are a few differences, though. Lash's face is a collage of scars that, combined with that unaffected grin, simply makes him seem more exotic and untouchable. His nose is off kilter from more than a few breaks, but he has more laugh creases in the corner of his eyes than his son. The same shock of untameable hair.

"Oh my god." I mutter. Evie appears at my side and I can hear the sound of memories in her sigh.

"Isn't he the most beautiful creature? That was just before he died. I never knew the Internet had all this."

"Don't you have photos, Evie? Anything?"

She shakes her head without moving her attention from the image on my screen. "I think Antony knew my heart would never completely belong to him and he jealously insisted I get rid of them. I posted them all home to Lash's family years ago, but I might have to learn how to use this technology after all. I've missed his face so much."

She runs her finger reverently over his face. With her touch, the image scrolls. In the next photo he's topless, tears of joy streaming down cheeks hard with his smile, arms raised above his head. In his hands he holds a golden belt, the caption below reading;

Bobby Kade undefeated in world titles.

"*Bobby Kade* was your husband? Everyone knows him!"

Masilda's sorrowful words sprang to mind.

But you are also a fighter.

Evie glows with pride. "Bobby was what his friends called him, and

Kade, well, he carried his son's name to every fight. He said Kade was his good luck charm, and he must have been right, because the only fight he ever lost was the only one Kade didn't make it to, and it was the same one that took him from us."

She disappears in nostalgia, hand hovering reverently over her first husband's image before her determination finds me with a bold smile.

" I think it's time my son knew who his father really was, don't you?"

CHAPTER 25

KADE

We find the perfect balance of existence over the following week. We speak easily and freely, but the guilt is always waiting in the shadows. I look for any sign she might be unwell, or unsettled.

"I was hoping to go out dancing tonight." Her voice is unconsciously sensual as the fencing chain slides through her fingers. Seeing a chain in her hand sends electricity scampering through my blood.

"I need the car this afternoon. Can you take a taxi again, and I'll come and pick you up?"

"I can get a taxi home, too. That way it won't put you out."

There is no damned way I'll give cowboys with a gullet full of dutch courage a chance at her.

"You are not taking a taxi home at that time of night. It's too dangerous. I'll pick you up."

"I hate relying on you for everything, but I understand that taxis can be expensive-"

"Damn it, Brynn, its not the money. It's the cowboys in the pub. I watch them try and swoop in for a piece of you when you leave the dance floor. I refuse to give them an opportunity to approach you while you're alone waiting for a damned taxi."

Her eyes flash with fire.

"Bella is with me. I'm not alone."

"Brynn, unless your companion is a male, you may as well be alone. I'll not hear any more. It's not safe. I'll pick you up."

"For heaven's sake, Kade, I'm not a teenager. I can look after myself." She snarls like an angry kitten, claws out with rage in her veins.

"Really, Princess? Really?" I growl, adrenaline already coursing through my body. She sets her chin, but I don't intend to start that fight. Instead I take two short steps towards her, wrap my arms around hers, effectively pinning them uselessly to her sides.

"Kade! What are you doing? I-"

I need to show her how easy it would be for one cowboy to overpower her, let alone a whole bar full of them. Claiming her wasn't my intention, but became the inevitable result. I crash my mouth on hers, that warm softness I crave constantly. I swallow her grunt of surprise, forcing her surrender with my tongue. It happens faster each time, I note, like every touch we share brings us ever closer to where we both want to be. She softens in my arms and presses her breasts into my chest.

Oh, lord, so soft and warm is this temptation. I want and I want…

I hear that tiny groan that makes me crazy. I feel my core coil and vibrate with the sensation of her, her sounds, her scent. She smells like a storm, that electrical zing mixed with summer rain, and I don't want to stop. I never want to stop. I want this woman in my bed, her skin beneath me. I want all her noises, her gasps, the screams of ecstasy I could wrench from her again if she'll let me. So feisty; making love to her is a beautiful war. And this is our battle cry.

I lose myself in the taste of her, only realising I've lost my head again when I come up for air. Her slim arms, still pinned by mine, slip beneath my shirt, leaving a lava trail where her fingers stroke. The light scrape of her nails makes me shudder and my zipper threatens to burst out. I press my arousal against her, dragging a low moan from her throat.

Damn it, Kade. Her eyes are closed, feeling my touch but thinking of another. *Daryl.* Summoning the last of my restraint, I push her away roughly with a hot snarl.

"See, Princess? I didn't even try and you had no chance of fighting me off."

She stares at me, mouth slack in disbelief, her pupils blown and pulse still racing in her sweet chest.

"Damn you to hell, Kade." She whispers, slamming her tools down and stalking towards the house, her incredible curves moving like a sinful taunt, and I wish that just once I could find it in me to say the right thing and stop driving her away.

***

At nine-thirty I find a park, recline my seat and settle in to watch her before it's time to bring her home. Her movements are sloppy tonight. A little more free, but less Brynn. I sit up, suddenly hyper aware of the difference in her tonight. Bella giggles and stumbles to the bar where she scoops up two shot glasses and slips one into Brynn's hand. Brynn tips it down her throat.

"What are you doing, Bella?" I breathe anxiously.

They've been drinking. I grip the wheel and watch. A cowboy, younger than me but older than Brynn approaches the girls. I see the moment Brynn becomes aware of him dancing closer to her.

What will my wife do when I'm not supposed to be here for another hour? She lifts her head, startled by his presence, then turns away from him, dancing closer to Bella. The cowboy closes in, daring to grip her waist.

I'm out of the car before I'm aware, slamming through the doors like a raging bull. The cowboy sees me and snatches his hand away, but my fist is full of shirt and his face is in mine, strangling out useless apologies.

"That's my fucking *wife* you laid your hands on." I rage. The fury engulfs me, testosterone needing release, wound tight, needing blood.

"Sorry, mate, I thought she wanted-"

"Bullshit. She's drunk, and you were trying to take advantage. Don't ever touch a woman when she's been drinking, and *never* touch my wife when she's dancing." The air reverberates with my anger.

I pull back my elbow and land my fist in the man's eye socket, sending him to the floor with a single blow.

The music stops. Adrenaline pumps through me. Brynn is slower to notice me, but when she does…

"Kade? What are you doing here?" She gasps.

I watch her pupils dilate the moment they land on me. They don't falter, or fall to the cowboy groaning on the floor with his head in his hands. They hold on to me with their violet flames like they know how I feel.

I snarl as my thoughts dissolve, scooping up my wife in my arms.

She leans up, kisses me with a mischievous smile and says "Not like this, Kade."

I smile then, my temper muted by her playfulness, and heave her over my shoulder. The thick scent of her arousal as we walk out the door has my blood screaming through my veins.

A taxi waits in the bay; the driver a plump woman I know from town. Brynn still over my shoulder, I hand her my card.

"Take Bella wherever she wants to go."

Bella giggles and climbs in. Brynn waves with her whole arm as I unfold Brynn into the passenger seat.

"I danced so much tonight, Kade. And I found a drink I like." She giggles into her hand. "Wanna know what it is?"

I shoot her a glance. She's leaning towards me, zeroed in on me, like a hot promise.

"What drink do you like, Brynn?" I play. She leans closer, palm open on my thigh for support. I feel her scalding heat and groan inwardly, wishing instead they were on my flesh.

"It's a cock-sucking cowboy." She throws her head back, roaring with laughter. My jeans tighten and a lump forms in my throat.

When the laughter dies, she goes quiet for a bit.

"You're a cowboy, Kade. All smooth and broody with a kick of fire at the end. I wonder if you taste like that." She murmurs, and my knuckles whiten.

"I'm not a shot, Brynn." I warn her, images biting on the edge of my sanity.

"Brynn. *Brrrrynn.* Why does it always sound so sexy when you say my name, Kade? A hundred people use it to communicate with me, but when you say it, Kade, I feel it here."

She runs a palm over her flowing top, the fabric showing off the gleam of perspiration on her chest. The material ends above her belly button and her hand slowly strokes along the smooth bare flesh of her belly and down, down.

She holds her hand over the seam of her jeans, runs a finger along it, then collapses into the seat.

"This is where I feel it, Kade." Her eyes implore me, beg me to touch.

Oh sweet Jesus.

"Do you feel it, Kade? Between us? Sometimes it's so strong I just want to do dirty, dirty things to you."

My erection agrees with her, pressing so painfully against my zipper I choke on my urge to free it.

"Like what?" I ask. I don't know why I feel the need to torture myself.

Her eyes widen and she licks her lips. I choke on a groan.

"I don't know, Kade. I've had a pretty limited experience with that stuff, but I do know I've been thinking a lot about what you're hiding in your jeans and how I want to run my tongue over it, just to see how it feels."

I skid to a stop in our driveway, my jeans suddenly way too tight to be anything but excruciating.

"Are we home now, Kade?" She grins at my nod.

"Tonight, I want to sleep with my husband. I'm so tired of relieving myself every night when I have a virile husband barely a room away."

God damn! My thoughts enter a dangerous place, imagining her taking care of herself only a room away.

But I can't. Not when she's been drinking.

It's a bitter disappointment to find that in amongst all my deceit I found a line I couldn't cross with Brynn. I wish I was the guy who could, with clear conscience, indulge this reachable fantasy. I wish I could just throw caution to the wind and accept her tempting offer. But I also want to know what it's like to wake up with her in my arms, even if it only happens once.

"You can sleep with me, but no sex. I am not going to take advantage of a drunk woman, even if you are my wife."

She pouts, disappointment printed on her face.

I open her door, but she shoots me a cheeky grin, shaking her head.

"Oh, no, cowboy, you know how to take your wife home."

I smother a smirk and laugh silently as she squeals over my shoulder.

In my room, I dump her on my bed. Heat flashes in her eyes. She's killing me, watching with her bottom lip crushed between her teeth as I peel her top and jeans off, revealing black lacy lingerie. Of course.

I will not get any sleep tonight.

"Oh, Kade! I love how you smell. I could bottle it and be forever happy. Forever happy." She giggles at herself. I take my shirt off and turn at her gasp. I feel her glance like an erotic stroke, travelling from my head and pausing below the hem of my jeans.

I slow it down, popping the buttons on my jeans before gripping the zipper. Her eyes are glued to my hands. I moan with instant relief as my erection bursts free.

"Holy shit, Kade. Do you have any idea how utterly *perfect* you are? Every time I see you I feel like I've slipped into a dream with all my darkest fantasies all squooshed into one." She purrs, her eyes on my arousal.

It takes every last inch of control I have not to push her into my mattress and take her. I climb into bed, pulse hammering and erection raging, and pull her back against my chest.

She huffs sweetly.

"But Kade, I want to kiss you. I want to feel your mouth on me." She moans and I grit my teeth.

"You don't know what you're saying, Brynn." I growl.

"Oh, yes I do, Kade. I want your mouth all over me, and I want mine all over you." She's drowning in desire. The smell of her arousal is so strong I can almost taste her, and her pupils are so dilated there's barely a hint of violet to be seen.

"Princess, you're killing me. But I can't. Do you understand? But if you still feel that way in the morning, I'm all yours."

"You want me again?" She blinks up at me with innocent uncertainty and I pull her hard against me so there's no space for air between us. She settles back on my pillow, and I pull a shaky breath.

"Always." I whisper.

But she's silent and her breaths find a slow rhythm. I roll my eyes in the darkness and my erection aches. At least one of us will be getting sleep tonight.

CHAPTER 26

Brynn

J'm aware of the most delicious smell I've ever scented. If dawn had a smell, it would be this. Exciting and crisp as a new day. My nostrils seek more. Dawn with woody undertones, like the oasis I always wanted to be lost in. I pull it into my lungs, and I feel the weight of an arm on my waist.

Kade. *I spent the night in Kade's arms!*

The memories return slowly. I was dancing. Bella heard all about my animalistic interludes with Kade and began feeding me drinks. Then that guy wouldn't leave me alone, but when I turned around, Kade was there and then suddenly that guy wasn't bothering me. He was curled up on the ground. Kade was so sexy. He tossed me over his shoulder, but I can't remember what happened to Bella. No, the memory returns. Kade found her a taxi and sent her safely home.

My mouth is dry, but I feel his chest wedged against my back, warm and hard like an invitation. It feels so good I wriggle closer. He lets out a sexy sigh, his grip on my waist tightening briefly, before his breath evens out again.

Then I freeze. I came on to Kade last night, and now we are in bed together. His bed. I feel his hard body against me, recall my bold conversation and groan my embarrassment.

I initiated it, but he knocked me back.

No.

Princess, if you still feel that way in the morning, I'm all yours.

His exact words. He's all mine if I want him. And oh, lord do I want him. I wriggle against him, slowly grinding my backside into his groin. I feel the monster in his boxers twitch. With a sly grin, I turn my head to look at him. His eyes are closed, lashes resting thickly on his cheeks. His mouth is parted slightly, hair scrambling about in sleepy chaos.

Oh wow. My husband is beautiful.

The mere contact of him sends that exquisite dull ache inside me that I want him to soothe. I turn in the loose grip of his arms, sliding myself beneath the sheets.

Do I even dare? How do I dare not? He already gave his permission. I suck in a lungful of courage, slip my fingers below his boxer waistband and free his morning arousal. It's thick, and long, and hard.

Before I lose my nerve, I part my lips and slide the tip of his manhood between them.

He jerks, the movement driving him that little bit deeper into my mouth.

"Oh, Jesus." He growls.

He's hot in my mouth. The broad head fascinates me so I allow my tongue to explore it. The smooth tip, the thick ridge where it meets his shaft. I feel him shiver as I run the tip of my tongue over it. I intrude into the slit at the top, drawing a moan from him. Keeping my mouth poised around the tip, I wrap my hand around the base. So hard but so soft, like satin stretched over steel. I find the vein protruding along the underside of his shaft and I rub the flat of my tongue along it. I feel his groan through my palm on his stomach, and I dart a shy glance towards him.

Silver eyes, blackened with desire, drill into me. There's something about his eyes that makes my pulse race so fast I can barely distinguish one beat from the next. I pant around his erection.

I hold his gaze as I slide my lips down along his shaft, drawing back before sliding him deeper inside my mouth.

"Brynn…" He groans. I clamp my lips tight, sliding up and down his length. The sight of his arousal, the way he wears it on his handsome face, it tugs at my core. I groan long and deep.

He rips me off his erection with an animalistic snarl and slams his mouth on mine. I love the way his lips take and give; taking my surrender, giving me pleasure. I arc towards him, revelling in his bare skin burning mine. I press my pelvis into his erection.

"Christ, Brynn, I can smell how ready you are for me."

The rumble of his words accelerates my pulse.

"Oh, please, Kade." My whisper begs.

He slams me into the mattress, nipping, biting with such hunger I'm barely able to think. I don't need to think. I have Kade and he's all I need right now.

"I love your hunger." I moan, offering my neck. He takes it in his teeth, sating and then building my desire in sure, confidant strokes.

"I love how responsive you are, Brynn. You're a fantasy come to life." He's panting with the same need I have. He slides a hand expertly behind me and releases the clasps of my bra. With a growl he slides a rough palm over one mound, possessing the other with his mouth. His tongue flicks and teases my nipple, sliding over the hard peaks of my breasts. He bites down gently, and my body arcs towards him with a low groan.

His head moves down, those lips of lava burning trails down my belly, the heat scorching towards the place I crave him. My brain ceases to function, saturated with Kade and his lips, and his fingers.

"Kade" I moan, and his fingers hook into the elastic of my underwear. They drag downwards.

"Tell me to stop, Brynn." He holds my hips hard.

"Oh, don't stop, please." I gasp.

He takes a few breaths before he continues. He dips his head, sliding his hot tongue between my folds.

"Oh, Kade!" I mewl.

His tongue swipes again, causing me to buck against his lips.

"Kade! I need you, Kade."

But he ignores my plea as his mouth begins to move. I buck and cry out with every lick, every swirl of his incredible tongue.

His mouth expertly brings waves of tingles over me, and I clench beneath his attention.

"Oh, Jesus, Kade!" I beg.

He slides a finger inside me and I scream my approval. Oh, that thick, heavy pressure inside me. I need it, I want it.

My hips flick forward, sending his finger not quite deep enough inside me.

His mouth moves, his finger curls, strokes and teases, until the waves crash over me.

A scream rips free, my nails clawing at his shoulders. Pewter fire catches mine.

"I need you, Brynn." I can only answer with my nails and moans, but he understands, covers his body with mine.

I feel his erection press against my entrance. My heated moan demands he satisfy this ache inside me. Silver bursts into flame. My head bends backwards and my scream fills the air as that stretching burn fills me as Kade impales me with one hard thrust.

"Look at me, Brynn." He commands.

I lock on his eyes, my mouth working uselessly as it tries to assist the intrusion of Kade deep inside me. I feel his pelvis against my entrance, evidence that he's deep inside me. With a deep growl, he pushes even further inside me, the electric pinch of him at the very end of me, the weight of him reminding me who owns who. My lungs fail, so consumed by the arousal his possessiveness and power invokes.

"Oh, Jesus, Kade." I whimper, my eyes rolling back in my head. He's inside my body. Kade. He's everywhere.

Muscle caging me in. Hot, hard chest pressing down on me.

"Oh, Jeez, Kade, Move. I need. Something." I gasp, and my husband provides. He pulls back slowly before plunging so deep he touches my soul.

"More!" I scream, and he wastes no time, pounding deep and hard and fast. Every stroke brings an explosion of friction, another pressure against every nerve ending, another dive into that sweet spot that sends me over the edge.

"Kade!" I scream into the atmosphere with a gouge of my nails and a bend in my spine.

The spasming muscles of my channel grip him with convulsions so strong he roars with me.

"Christ, Brynn!" He digs so deeps he nicks a nerve in pleasure pain and I buck as he jerks his release inside me.

***

His eyes anchor me. Breaths, so ragged they burn, tear from my lungs as he holds me with pewter intensity. This is where I'm supposed to experience regret, that guilty cloud that rebukes whatever insanity that shoots through my head that drove me into the arms of this man. But instead I feel sated, complete. Happy. He nuzzles the crook of my neck, reluctantly withdrawing from me. I protest when I feel him leave me, but he chuckles and manoeuvres himself beside me, resting a corded forearm protectively over my stomach. He reaches down, silver locked on me, and I gasp as he swipes a thumb through the thick moisture spilling from me. I watch him as he brings his hand up, smearing his thumb over my collarbone.

I feel the cool air find it and he shivers as if he's the one who feels it.

"You're in my blood, Brynn. You make me so damn crazy." There's an open wonder in his tone, like he's giving his inner thoughts a voice. He glances his mouth over my hair.

"This is your bed now. I never should have allowed you to sleep in the spare room."

"Kade, don't you go all caveman on me. What if I like my own space? What if I don't want to sleep with you every night?"

He runs a finger down my neck, following its path between the valley of my breasts, dipping into my belly button, skimming his finger further down. He stops when I gasp, withdraws his hand.

"You don't want space from me." He says simply.

I snort.

"Oh, I forgot you can read my mind. Tell me again what I feel. What do I want for breakfast, Kade?"

He huffs out a laugh, then his brows pinch.

"I have no idea what you feel most of the time. I know you can't decide if you hate me or…feel something else for me, but sometimes, straight out of the blue I look at you and I…understand. Like now. I don't know much about what you're feeling beyond…sated, but I just know you like the idea of me holding you through the nights."

He looks momentarily vulnerable and somewhat perplexed by what he told me. I reach for his jaw, just because I can.

"You're so intense, Kade. The way you give me your full attention, it should freak me out, but it doesn't. It turns me on to think you're always watching me. Like you're somehow keeping me safe."

Something dark flashes across his face.

"What?" I ask, but he buries his face in my neck, inhaling deeply.

"God you smell so good. You smell of arousal, temptation, and me."

He captures my mouth again, reigniting the fire he lit inside me. My weariness evaporates with Kade's lips and hands on me. This time he owns me, giving me no doubt as to where I belong.

***

"Why don't we spend the day in bed?" I mutter as Kade rolls languidly beside me. His chuckle rolls down my spine.

"We need to eat." He reasons.

"You might, I've got everything I want to eat right here."

I can't get close enough to him. I need him so much closer. So close that our bones weld and we share a single skin. Still not enough. The only time I feel satisfied is when Kade is so deep inside me that the stars themselves shatter around me, but my stomach grumbles and I reluctantly admit defeat.

There's a soreness between my legs that brings me a smile as we take our coffee outside. The sun beat us up this morning, its dazzling rays climbing onto the verandah.

It must have been last night when I was out dancing that Kade had assembled the wooden swing seat.

"Oh, Kade." I grin.

He shrugs, huge shoulders lifting and dropping.

"We both like to watch the sun rise. I figured I'd make it more comfortable for us."

He sprawls over the seat, one long leg stretched out along its length and invites me with a wide arm. I accept with a deep sigh, leaning my back against the steady rise and fall of his chest and his thick forearm rests on my stomach. I sip my coffee, the farm highlighted by the morning sun, the scent and heat of Kade against me.

Perfect.

"What made you decide to run a farm?" I ask.

"I love it. " Kade snorts. "That, and it pissed Antony off to know I was making my own future, independent of his name. He hated it, but he spent a great deal of time making it appear it was his idea and we were still a perfect, wholesome family."

"So Antony didn't set this place up for you?" I frown.

"No. Antony made it abundantly clear I was his son in the eyes of the public only. He would look after me, certainly, but everything that fell under the Walker banner was always going to be Daryl's alone. But when Dad died, he had some money locked up for me. Antony tried to get his hands on that, too, but Dad must have had some good legal advice and there was nothing Antony could do. It was getting unbearable living with him, so as soon as I turned eighteen and the money was released to me, I brought this place and moved out. Best thing I ever did."

"Is that why you hate Daryl?"

He jolts. "Where on earth did you get the impression that I hate him?"

"You don't talk, Evie says, and Daryl is…unfriendly when he speaks of you. And of course, when he invited himself over the other day."

Kade stiffens.

"I don't want to talk about him today." He dismisses.

In the stillness that follows we watch the morning rays warm the earth, coaxing it awake.

"Oh, here. I keep forgetting to give this to you." He wriggles as he retrieves a credit card and rests it on my knee.

"What's this for?"

His chuckle vibrates in his chest. "Never seen a credit card before? You're my wife, and that's my wife's card for when she chooses to purchase something."

I slap his leg playfully, then tap my lip with my finger as I make a show of taking inventory. "Oh, good. I need a new wardrobe, a holiday home in Hawaii and maybe a car. What's the limit on this bad boy because it's about to be hit?!"

His mirth explodes, the sound nestling snugly into a dark place inside me and flicking on a light.

"Seriously, should I be hunting for a condo or a caravan?" I giggle.

He leans forward and drags the tip of his nose along the curve of my neck.

"There is no limit."

I crane my neck to look at him, weighing his sincerity. He blinks his liquid metal eyes.

"My Dad, he, uh, looked after me, and I don't really have any expensive needs or hobbies so…" He shrugs.

We spend the morning mending fences, the sun on our backs and the fresh air in our lungs. Kade fastens the wire and I hammer in the insulators and fasten the wire to them, singing 'Me and Bobby McGee'. I let the chorus take me over, swaying my hips as I fix another length of wire in place. When the final word leaves my mouth I spin, straight into Kade's steel chest.

"I love it when you sing, Bry." He growls as he slams his lips on mine.

I'm ready, so ready to feel the things he does to me and my own hunger breaks free. I claw him, running my hands underneath his shirt, below his tight jeans.

"Christ, Brynn, you make me crazy. Let me make you feel good."

I groan as he fumbles with my jeans.

"On your knees sweetheart." He growls, and I obey, the sun warming my bare backside.

"Oh my god!" I gasp shakily as he mounts me from behind. It feels like he slides in forever, that stretching burn wreaking havoc with all my nerve endings before we even begin our exquisite dance.

"Jesus you feel so good, Brynn. So tight and slick for me."

"Oh Kade, I love being full of you!"

Then he starts to thrust, sending me to the stars.

CHAPTER 27

KADE

I can't get enough of her. The moment I'm done and we separate, the craving begins all over again. It's the freedom she radiates, the way she rejoices in her happiness, it's the indigo that lights up her beautiful soul. It's her flame. She saturates me and short-circuits my brain.

To wake up with her in my arms is heaven itself, to find her sweet lips wrapped around my shaft blew my damn mind to pieces. The mere thought of her brings a lump to my throat that never goes, because I feel our time slipping through my fingers already, because the damning truth lingers like awaiting destruction at the end of every breath I take. It's been beyond perfect between us recently, but all good things must end. Just like Daryl's love, Brynn's will also inevitably turn sour. The calm before the storm.

The sand sprints through the hourglass.

I have no right to be holding her this close, touching her and losing myself in her like the world won't unleash its vengeance upon me.

I lay a fingertip on her cheek where her lashes rest in slumber against them. As light as smoke I trail a path over her jaw, down the warm, perfect lines of her neck. She shivers in her sleep, and my heart snags.

When my world implodes, Brynn, will I be able to breathe without you?

Consumed by those dark thoughts in the smallest hours of the morning, I wonder if coming clean would change the inevitable outcome, or would it send us hurtling towards the end at breakneck speed? It's that latter possibility that stops me, because I'm too weak to do anything but clutch at every second with her, and free fall into this sweet lie with arms wide.

I push the thought away, bury it so deep I can pretend for a while that it won't surface again.

Every time, I brand her to memory. I try and capture forever the way her mouth drops wide open when I breach her like she's trapped in a silent scream of pleasure. I need to remember the way her body arcs for mine, needing to feel all of me against all of her. And will I be able to recall the pitch of her tiny noises and whimpers? The ones I interpret instinctively that instruct me where she needs to feel my hands and my mouth when I'm inside her. Let's not forget that throaty moan, long and drawn out that tells me I'm delivering exactly what she craves.

My blood hums when I look at her.

Her eyes flutter open, sleepy and raw on me. That expression right there, I can pretend its love.

"Good morning." I mutter.

"Mmmmm" she smiles sleepily, and my lips twitch in the corner.

I scent her, running my nose up the smooth skin in her neck and she shivers.

"This feels so good." She murmurs groggily.

"What does?"

"This. You, me. *Us*. It feels…easy, comfortable, you know what I mean?"

Do I ever. Listening to her melodic voice admit how she sees us makes my heart spasm in my chest as her fingertips score a line down my chest.

"Yeah" I say with careful tones, "Like I'm in the sweetest dream I've had, and I'm terrified to wake up."

Her finger stops and she blinks up at me, clear crystals I feel in my soul.

"Terrified? That's a pretty strong word, Kade. If it's a dream I'm in, I certainly wouldn't want to wake up, but I'm not terrified to…"

She frowns lightly, concern flicking over my face. It's unsettling, and I take her lobe between my teeth to distract her. She shuffles back a little.

"Kade? What are you so scared of?"

I take her in, wanting to say it all but frozen in fear.

"You." I whisper eventually against her neck. "The way I feel… everything…when I'm with you."

I pretend that flash in her eyes means something.

"Talk to me, Kade. I see the things you try to tell me without words, but I don't recognise them. There's so much about you that I feel like I understand, but then like a light switch you snap out, and I'm a thousand miles away from you, and I don't know where I'm supposed to be. What are you hiding from?"

My lungs fill with lead as she sees me, dissects me with her insight.

"I destroy everything that holds meaning for me. I'm trying to protect you." There's a hint of panic in my tone as I beg her to understand, but there's another lie. I'm not doing anything to protect her. She doesn't need a guard, she's fierce and resilient enough without one. I'm protecting myself.

"You don't want me to get too attached, Kade? Is that it? You're worried I might fall in love with you?"

Oh, those words that give me hope and cut like a knife all at once. I rear back and study her face, searching for something I can anchor myself to.

She frowns gently. "Or are you afraid because you might love me?"

Therein lies the answer to it all. The beginning and the end and everything in between this crazy situation. The familiar sting of painful truth. I'm not afraid I might fall in love with her. She's owned my heart since she was ten; when she caught the raindrops in her outstretched hands my soul fell with them and she never let it go. But I'm the evil that lingers on the edge of every one of her smiles, and she's way too virtuous for the deeds I've carried out. Our ending is inevitable.

"Everything I touch with my heart decays, and the pain of it resides in my bones. Whatever this is between us is already broken, damaged long ago by actions I can't understand and regrets that I should have but don't. There's no *if* this ends between us, Brynn, it's *when*, and I already bleed."

***

Brynn tenses up the closer we get to her family farm. The one she left to live with me. When Stan and Janette made Brynn, they signed up for a sweet, malleable daughter who they could shape into their ordered and predictable life, but instead they got a free spirit who broke their mold and forged a new one with mud and filth and fresh air. They know what to do with her as much as the world knows what to do with me.

Brynn and I, we are fated to find each other because we are the only people on this earth who can understand each other. Brynn still needs to reach that conclusion, but I've sat with it for years. Hopefully, I won't have to wait too much longer. She's warming to me, slowly surrendering the fight against destiny, but it makes me crazy that she's still fighting.

This is the first time since we were children that she has led me with pride into her family home. It feels like a victory, like she's finally admitting to the most intimate parts of her childhood that I have importance in her life.

Now, Brynn mentally pulls herself in, an unconscious attempt to meet the expectation of conformity she feels she owes her parents. She wears it about as well as her parents' attempt to understand Brynn.

It's nobody's fault. It just is.

She looks stunning in simple shorts and tank as we push through the gates of McAllister Farm. I fall behind so I can watch the way her backside moves when she walks.

"Did you bring the rolls from the car?" She asks over her shoulder.

I lift the plastic bag in answer and return to her rear. Brynn opens the door without knocking. I'm hit by how comfortable and domesticated this all feels. Off to have dinner with the in-laws, my wife on my case about the damned bread. My heart aches, because I'd give my life for this to be my 'normal'.

"Oh, here's the happy couple! Brynn! Kade! Congratulations again! How's married life treating you?"

My thoughts dive into the bedroom this morning, and I smirk when Brynn instinctively elbows me.

"It's great, Mum. How are you and Dad?"

Stan walks up and hands me a coke, handing his wife a glass of wine. Obviously Brynn worded them up about my drinking preferences.

"We're good, sweetheart. I can tell you now that it's all past, but it was a little concerning when the investor pulled out of the farm. The chances of someone stepping in last minute like they did was virtually zero. But now we can relax again. It's freed us up and we were thinking we would go on a cruise if you didn't need us here?" Stan's concern flits between Brynn and me.

Brynn laughs. "Oh Dad you look so serious. We're fine, really. You and Mum have done so much for me that I'm delighted to hear you're going to spoil yourselves."

On the back porch he gestures for us to sit, and we raise our glasses.

"To Mr and Mrs Kade Walker."

I spent my childhood hanging around McAllister's farm, but this is the first time I've been chosen by Brynn to be the one at her side. The first time she's chosen me over Daryl. And it feels so damned good. I rest a hand on her leg and she lands that smile on me that steals my breath.

***

Cruel reality invites itself in the form of Daryl. It's almost uncanny the way he knows just when Brynn and I are most contented, appearing like a death knell.

I wore her out last night. Indulged in her so completely that her voice was still hoarse this morning, so I left her asleep and feed the calves. In the crisp morning, I catch myself humming and smile. For the first time in way too long, I'm happy.

Or I *could* be happy, if only my deceit didn't dig its tiny hooks into my conscience, reminding me that I've sabotaged Brynn and me long before I made my vows. Years before. With regret, I think of her sweet face, frozen in sleep, and set the empty milk buckets to dry. Before my world falls apart, I'm heading back up to the house, and my wife's arms.

The morning sun warms me as I follow my shadow up the gravel lane, already imagining her dancing around in one of my old shirts.

But instead of her sweet voice belting out some feel good song from inside our home, I find Daryl's distinct and agitated tone. Stomach churning, I silently climb the veranda stairs to listen.

"...Said we might have a chance if we get a good lawyer." Daryl says.

"Daryl, can we not do this today? I know we need to talk about it, but we need to meet, somewhere we can't be interrupted and-."

"Brynn, Kade's like a lingering bad smell. He's just doing this to piss me off."

"Daryl-"

"You don't know him, Brynn. He might pretend he's doing you a favour marrying you and sealing this merger with your parents, but Kade doesn't just do spontaneity. There's some hidden agenda here, I can smell it. The best move to make is to find a good lawyer and get them to look into a divorce. Then we can work on our future after that."

My mouth is a desert. Damn Daryl for being so switched on. But he hasn't worked all of it out though. He hasn't put all the pieces together yet.

The thought of Brynn discussing divorcing me when things have been so perfect between us cuts deep. I did everything in my power to show her happiness, and I truly believed she was happy, even though I knew it wouldn't last. Nothing does. Not my father, not the relationship between Daryl and I.

My little brother used to look up to me, shadow me on tiny pudgy legs. His innocent dribble-shined lips grinning out a tsunami of adoration every time I played with him. I was his first destination when he managed to work out what his legs were for, his first smile, his first word. I grind my teeth, because that blue-eyed angel in my heart is now encouraging my wife to leave me, and she's not opposing it.

The sand spews through the hourglass in an arid torrent as Daryl's words bring us closer to the end. My chest burns.

The sunlight captures the ring on Brynn's finger and I sink heavily into the swing chair. My mother's ring. I wonder, will she give it back, or pawn it when the time comes?

"It will all work out, Brynn. It has to because I love you and that's the way it works."

My ears hone in. Will I hear my wife say those sacred three words for the first time to another man?

I'll never know if the words are on her tongue, because at that moment, Daryl steps onto the verandah and freezes when he spots me.

"Kade!"

Brynn bursts from behind him, violet orbs wide with guilt when she spots me on the seat.

"Kade, I-" My palm flies up, cutting off her lies. I can't take them from her. *I just. Can't.*

I get to my feet, glaring at them both before stalking away.

***

My knuckles burst open on the wooden beam, the explosion of pain is a fleeting distraction. I suck an inhale through my teeth and swallow the need to roar out my pain, because I deserve this.

The deception and manipulation that brought Brynn to me is now unravelling, because good always triumphs over evil. I crept into the garden and stole one perfect rose, and now I watch helplessly as the petals shrivel and fall, one by one. The rose is dying, and I'm left holding the wilting bloom, its thorns biting into the hand that holds on too tight and can't let go.

Brynn. Too good for the likes of me.

I stare at my fist, so damned tired of being Kade Walker, son of a dead man, brother to the enemy and lover to a woman whose dreams do not know me.

She was supposed to feel this connection between us. When I opened up to her and lay my heart and soul at her feet, she was meant to do the same. She was destined to love me. I felt that ancient instinct in the centre of my bones gravitate towards her, ready to claim her, but she doesn't feel it. She doesn't love me, and she doesn't want me.

How did I get this so wrong?

My despair is a heavy, hollow ache that burns my heart and scratches at my throat and it takes everything I have not to fall to pieces when I hear her approaching footsteps. I choke on the urge to tell her how much it hurts, because it won't make a difference in the end. I've learned that. Telling Dad I loved him didn't keep him alive. Telling Antony I loved him didn't heal the hatred in his heart. Loving Daryl wasn't enough to stop him turning against me, and admitting to Brynn that I love her won't keep her with me either.

I'm so bone weary of exposing my heart to people who use it as a doormat, that maybe it's time to protect myself instead.

As her tentative footsteps approach, I clench my teeth and wait.

CHAPTER 28

BRYNN

My feet take me to the calf shed. I know he's there. The morning sun filters in through the cracks in the doors, and through the dusty windows, the rays catching the particles that hang in the air from the milling calves.

On any other day I'd be celebrating how glorious and refreshing the morning was, but today I'm filled with guilt. I don't know how long he'd been there or how much he heard.

Somewhere, in the middle of the village outing and our visit to my parent's farm, I've felt a shift between Kade and me. The fortress he's built around himself is starting to weaken and split, and the light streaming from the spaces almost blinds me. Even when he's not here I seem to be able to feel him like an ember warming me from the inside. The way he makes me feel with a touch of his eyes or a glance of his finger strikes the deepest wells of my soul.

And it scares the hell out of me, because I love Daryl, but when the chaos erupted, I gravitated organically towards Kade. I slow my steps, remorseful that poor Daryl has been deserted by me yet again in favour of his big brother. The first time had been nothing more than doing what my parents had drummed into me: stand by your spouse. But that's changed, too. I chase down Kade because I want to. Because I can't fight that pull even if I wanted to.

That's what I'd tried to explain to Daryl, but I watched his eyes cloud in confusion when I'd told him I needed space. My heart bled as I struggled to find the words to tell him that I wasn't sure I wanted out of this marriage, but he wasn't able to comprehend that I love the farm life, that I feel free here. And happy. When he still couldn't seem to understand, I'd admitted my feelings for Kade are changing.

Daryl's face hardened with dawning realisation, wildly hurling accusations about Kade's ulterior motives I no longer believe.

I think Daryl had already suspected my feelings for Kade had grown, but that odd expression on his face when I asked him if he truly loved me continues to unsettle me.

It could have been guilt, or panic, or something more convoluted entirely, but whatever it was, his response wasn't that of a man with a breaking heart, and that's what consumes my thoughts.

Up until I see Kade.

As if he'd planned it, he stands with his back to me, head bent as the ray of sun glows on his back like an angel without wings. There's an otherworldly quality to him, as if he's fallen to earth, vulnerable and lost. His broad shoulders rise and fall as if he's waging some internal battle he's losing, and every beautiful sinew in his body is strained and taut.

I stop and wait, knowing he'll turn, and when he does my heart jumps to my throat.

His gorgeous face shines on me, the light picking up the light stubble on his strong jaw, and I realise in that moment that while I might love Daryl, there is no comparison any more, and probably hasn't been for a long time. The ghosts in his heart, the way he carries his pain, everything he is calls to me. Bella was right.

I'm in love with my husband.

"Kade?" I whisper, needing to see his eyes.

They are cold, hard steel. Just like the set of his beautiful mouth.

"What do you want, Brynn?" His icy tone chills my blood.

I swallow. "I want to talk to you."

He lifts a contemptuous eyebrow.

"I don't want you to talk, Brynn. Right now I need you to listen."

He moves through the beams of light towards me. That feeling of uncertainty fades with the slam of sudden understanding. My man is coming towards me, and whatever way he arrives, it's because I need him to.

"I don't want to hear anything you have to say, because I don't care. Daryl's right. You don't know anything about me. You're trying to convince yourself I'm a good man, but you're wrong. Look around you and see what's under your nose. There's a reason why nobody stays for long, it's just that you haven't worked it out yet. I don't care how you feel or what you want. I don't care if you stay and I don't care if you go." His tone dulls.

I'm frozen in place. I can't breathe. This is a side to him I've never seen, never even suspected was hidden inside him. My blood pounds in my head and I blanch when his words bite, but realisation dawns. They're only words, and they're not the meaningful components of the conversation we're having. Words that are at odds with the agony peeling from him with every beat of his heart, and that's what tears me apart inside.

"Kade?" I whimper, but he sneers in my face, those sensual lips twisted and cruel. Defensive.

"Not a word, Princess. I. Don't. Care." He spins away and I clutch at the wooden support beam for balance from the pain in his voice.

He aims a painfully empty glance over his shoulder, his face in the shadows and eyes glinting like moonlight, then prowls close again, so close in fact that I can feel every hard line and edge of him radiating his resentment.

"Kade, I thought...I thought we shared something." Damned hollow, useless sounds.

Words are flat and empty. What I really need is to touch him. Rub away the shards on the edge of his wound and stroke until he's healed, but he's closed up like a fort and my hands lay limp and useless at my sides.

He barks out a caustic laugh, his neck bobbing.

"Do you honestly believe someone like me is capable of anything more than a few fun nights?"

My heart bottoms out and I gasp at the blow, but he's relentless, burying his pain in the arms of bitterness.

He breathes on my neck, and even as my heart cries, my body springs to life beneath his attention, and he smirks, running a finger over my lips.

"Don't delude yourself. You have no idea just how cruel and heartless I can be. I've already destroyed every last piece of light in your soul and every time I touch you I find another broken shard to shatter beneath my feet, and when you find out, you'll be finished with me for good. If I was a different person, I'd have never stolen you in the first place but..." He holds a loose tendril of my hair in his fingers, frowning as he gently tests the softness and weight of it. He tucks it behind my ear with a hard swallow.

The fragility of him can't be hidden from me any longer. I feel it all, the futility that burns inside him as he looks on me. It interrupts my heartbeat. His pain is my pain, and it's only within the excruciating battle he's losing against himself that I finally realise it. As if he knows, his anger slips, and his voice softens unintentionally.

"No matter what I do *pakvora*, you invade me. Every thought centres around you. Every lungful of air carries more of you into me. You are the only sound I crave, the only thing I need to touch. And your taste? I'm addicted to it. I need it every second of every day. I need it now."

His eyes illuminate, ignite and then fade out, the flickering steel of his eyes becoming lifeless and flat.

"But it's nothing more than lust and it's time I accept this. I am not a good man, Brynn. I am a man who has done things I never thought I was capable of to get where I thought I needed to be, and maybe it's me that's been wrong all this time. I thought you were someone else, someone who would stand with me and fight the dark at my side, but your heart belongs to Daryl. I should have known, *pakvora*, that my dreams belonged to someone else. I'm tired of being a soldier fighting on the losing side. I'm done, Brynn. Do your worst, because I deserve it."

"I don't-" I choke, but he cuts me off with a wave.

His agony scrapes my bones like a blade and he turns away. He shuts down, walls rebuilding in the space around his heart like the time we spent together never penetrated. It hurts, and I want to enclose him in my own heart and take all his suffering from him.

But when he turns back to face me, something has shifted. His expression is locked, his armour impenetrable, even to me. Everything beneath he used to show to me is buried, the icy steel of his gaze turning him into the cold stranger who used his fists to get what he wants. The man nobody could love.

Except I do love him. I love the way he fires me up, constantly challenging me . The way he encourages me to be exactly who I am and celebrates it with me. The way he seems to know what I want even before I do, and he does it. The music in the tractor, the swing seat to watch the sun rise. The way he turns up at the pub the same moment I decide it's time to go home.

In fact, there's not much that Kade does that isn't done with me in mind. And the way he always spoke so convincingly about Daryl and me, like he could see us better than we could see ourselves.

The conversation Kade and I had in the restaurant, just after Daryl had proposed springs to mind.

"It's not real, pakvora. It was never written in the stars. It's just the promise between two children that should have remained in your childhood. Deep down you know it. I know you do. You ask yourself where the passion is, the hunger you crave, the flames you want to be consumed by. What makes you hold on to that dream instead of chasing the reality?"

I slide bonelessly to the concrete floor. He's right. It's Kade's hunger that makes me burn. It's the intensity of his passion that brings life to my soul and shows me there's nothing in this world he wouldn't do to feel it again with me.

And I would do anything to taste it again, too, I realise. Even now, with the cruel things he said to me, I crave the inferno of his touch. But it's more than that. As Kade walks away, I can feel the chill creeping into my blood, because he's not meant to be leaving me. He belongs with me.

And now he's giving up, because he's convinced himself that he's done something so bad that when I find out I can't possibly forgive him, but I know him. I know he's not capable of anything that could turn me against him.

He won't listen to me, but perhaps I can show him what he means to me. With his birthday coming up, I'll give him the gift of his father, and remind him that once upon a time, he was one man's entire world. And maybe he will believe that he could be mine, too.

"No man in the world is perfect, Brynn, but when what you have is so wonderful, it's important to try to look past the errors and see them for what they mean instead. What Lash did went against every value I hold. He found it harder to live with it than I did, in the end."

Was Evie warning me, when she told her story? Does she know what lies behind Kade's fears?

CHAPTER 29

KADE

Sometime during the night, Brynn climbs into bed with me. She slides in so gently so as not to wake me, but I couldn't sleep without her anyway. In the darkness she slips beneath the covers, wrapping herself in my arms with a whispery breathy shudder as if she's been crying.

I pretend to stir, dragging her intoxicating scent into my lungs, drawing her harder against me. She fits against my body so perfectly I feel every beat of her heart through our touch. I'm consumed by her, suffocating in the incredible connection that is us as I listen to her breaths even out. Only when she's asleep do my own tears slide free.

When I wake, she's gone.

The following night is the same. In the small hours she sneaks into my room and falls asleep in my arms, only to be gone when I wake. She can't sleep without me; I know it as well as I know that I can't sleep without her. Her body softens in my embrace, and she plummets into sleep. Why she fights this is beyond me. All it would take is for her to look past that damned stubborn streak for just one moment, and she will find me woven deep into the walls of her soul. She's mine. She's always been mine, but she refuses to see it.

As the nights pass, she comes to me later and later, until one night she doesn't come to me at all. I lay there all through the night waiting for her, the light from dawn casting shadows over the ache in my chest. I haven't slept a wink, because she's found a way to sleep without me.

I blink in the cold and empty room.

The tension between Brynn and me takes its toll. Although I crave to reach out and touch her, I can't open myself to the pain of futility, and I focus my energy into protecting the shredded remains of my heart. And Brynn? Instead of embracing work on the farm like she used to, she's out most days. But she used to love farm work as a girl, and I'm sure I watched that tiny spark in her soul become a flame every day she spent in the sun. Now she spends the evenings sitting on the opposite end of the couch, flicking through whatever's on the Internet, sometimes completely missing the sunsets she loves so much with whatever it is on that electronic screen that captures her attention.

She's there beside me, but she may as well be in another postcode. I can almost see that bubble around her that keeps her away from me.

The beginning of the end. It crawls up my spine and burrows into my temple, pounding away. I deserve this. I know I do, but knowing it doesn't ease the pain in my chest.

Why can't you let me have her? Why do you give me a taste just to rip her away from me again?

There's a general sense of trepidation in the house, and I don't know how to fix the damage I've done. Ironic, since it was broken before it even started, but those times in between when she smiled and everything else just fell away were a heaven I'd sell my soul to have back.

She's absorbed by her tablet when I steal another look at her.

Beautiful and wild with eyes that glow and long dark hair like an exotic sylph. My hand flexes with the urge to touch her curves, craving one last sad, mad night where I can let my body say what my mouth can't.

Because from that moment years ago when I saw her dancing in the rain I knew I loved her, and the layers of manipulation and deceit that hide the things I've done to have her by my side have come to nothing. She wants to leave me. Because I'm not enough. I'm not Daryl and my wife is in love with my little brother.

***

Two days later my bank manager contacts me to question the cash withdrawal of over $250,000 made by my wife from a bank close to the city where the cut-throat lawyers sit in their sky rise offices built with dirty money. The cold fist of impending doom tightens.

She's divorcing me.

CHAPTER 30

BRYNN

Opening the cabinet in my bathroom I reach for the paracetamol. My head pounds relentlessly with queasy dread. I haven't been able to get to sleep after our argument, my stomach rolls and my mind whirls with Kade's cold words.

I don't know how to repair this rift between us. I don't know how much he heard of our conversation, but judging by his icy attitude, he heard just enough to fuel his anger.

But what would I say? I could explain I was placating Daryl, waiting for him to get it all off his chest before I set him straight? I could picture Kade's expression, disbelief twisting his mouth into a sneer. He'd shut me down.

I sigh. This messed up battle between Daryl and Kade is escalating, and I'm stuck in the middle. Daryl wants me to divorce Kade, and Kade condemns me for conspiring. I can't win. Not once has either of them asked what I want.

It's easier to stay away and give him a chance to warm up a bit, but it seems to have made things worse. I miss Kade. I miss his eyes, so intense and focused on me, his smile that lifts his lips when he thinks I'm not looking, and I miss him teasing me. He has a way of riling me up and finding a way to make me take the bait each and every time that works me up. It's obvious he loves it, watching me furious and indignant with a smirk on his handsome face. Judging by the way he'd ravish me afterwards: the best kind of foreplay.

My stomach rolls again, and I pop out two tablets, reaching for the glass when I freeze. My hand hovers over the space I keep my tampons, and I'm instantly aware that its been a long time since I used them. My lungs seize as I send my mind back.

When did I use them last? I was due last week, but it wasn't unusual to be a few days late. Then I realise I completely missed last month, too.

I barely make it to the toilet before I empty my stomach, the heaves that grip me like aftershocks driving the truth home. I don't need a test to know that I'm carrying Kade's child. My palm spreads open over my flat stomach while I catch my breath. A tiny miracle sprouts from a seed Kade and I planted. I lift a thumb to wipe away the tears that spill out.

I'm wound so tight, adrenaline coursing through my veins. I want Kade. I want him to hold me and tell me everything will be okay. Filled with fear, I tiptoe into his room. I hesitate at the door, listen to my heart thumping in the darkness, wondering if he'll tell me to leave.

When I'm met with silence, I can only assume he's sleeping, finding that elusive respite from the harsh reality of day that I can't find. Part of me wants to wake him, to tell him and feel his arms around me again.

But if he sent me away? Then I wouldn't be able to pretend that we'll be okay, and I can't face that right now. So I creep into his bed. In the arms of sleep he pulls me into him, an unconscious response that binds me to him one more time.

I inhale his scent and ignore the futility of this because Kade is unhappy. He's never once said he loves me, and he's not tried to convince me to stay or show he'd fight for me. It's as if he's sitting back waiting for a divorce to happen because he doesn't care what happens either way.

***

Kade's birthday is in two months. I tremor with excitement. His main gift is already tucked away in a place he'll never find it, but this gift will blow him away. I find every photo I can and store it in a folder on my tablet, knowing Kade won't pry. He has no patience for technology. Maybe this will be enough to show him how much he means to me.

I read with fascination the articles of his successes, finding an early one that brings a tear to my eye.

Champion welcomes baby boy.

The world knows him as Bobby Kade but the baby in this champions arms will know him as Lash Greyson, or simply 'Dad'. Asked what he thought of his little bundle of joy, the fighter simply replied "He's perfect." With his father's signature steel eyes, will Kade Greyson follow in the footsteps of his father?

"I hope not." He laughs, referring to the ribs broken weeks ago by opponent James 'Jimmy' McLean. Clearly besotted by his new son,

Kade was asked if he intended to continue his career or retire as an undefeated champion.

"My priorities have shifted without a doubt. I'm taking a break while my family settles in, then perhaps a few more fights before Bobby Kade will leave the ring forever."

The next one breaks my heart.

World mourns Champion's tragic death.

The fighting world is reeling today with the news of Bobby Kade's tragic death. Kade was set to win yet another championship against Ronnie Doyle when Doyle landed a surprise right hook on the seasoned champion. Ronnie was awarded the TKO, but when Kade remained unresponsive he was rushed to Lancebrook Hospital for treatment. Kade never regained consciousness. An investigation into the cause of death is underway.

Larry Emmett, chairman of the World Boxing Federation made a public statement.

"The world has not only lost its greatest fighter, but its light. Bobby was undoubtedly skilled, but he was also an entertainer. He knew how to work the crowd. He was all personality, and it was one hundred percent him. Today I lost a friend. We all lost a friend."

Bobby Kade, real name Lash Greyson, is survived by Evie Greyson and four-year-old son Kade Lasher Greyson.

Oh, Kade. His father went to work one night and never came home. No time for goodbyes. My heart bleeds for him.

I sneak a look at him. He stares at the television without watching it, his thoughts trapped inside the clutter in his head, his jaw locked with the effort of fighting some internal battle he refuses to reveal. I ache to say something and touch him again, to somehow return all the stolen happiness to him and take his ghosts away.

When did I start feeling his pain? I wonder as I look at him. To glance at him sitting there, anyone would be forgiven for thinking he's relaxed. He's half reclined, his long arms draped over the back of the couch, one powerful leg stretched out before him, the other bent. But I know by the chords of his neck, the tightness radiating from his shoulders that he's consumed by tension. As if he's suddenly aware of being observed, his eyes flick to me.

Oh my god. My heart breaks when I see the anguish swirling in liquid pewter, so deep and full of blades.

Then he blinks it away, steel shutters slamming down as he lands a hard glare on me. Then he returns his attention to the television, leaving me lightheaded and gutted.

I turn my thoughts to Daryl, finding it odd that with every day that passes, he invades my thoughts less. In fact, the last time he came over irritated me. He just appeared, talking about divorce and the options I have before I'd fully opened the door to him. He didn't ask how I was, just launched into instructing me how to manage my future.

My phone pings.

Evie: *Can you and Kade come for dinner tomorrow night?*

"Kade, your mum just invited us for dinner tomorrow night."

He doesn't look at me. Just nods.

Me: *Yes, thanks. What time?*

Evie: *Come at six. We'll eat at seven.*

That night I send all the downloaded files of Kade's father to the printing company and pay the extra few dollars for express delivery.

I don't see Kade at all in the morning. He's gone before the sun breaks, and I don't see him again until we're due to leave for dinner. It's getting on my nerves the way we exist together but might as well be at opposite ends of the planet. Both of us stubbornly refusing to make the first move, although I'm alone when my morning sickness hits and he doesn't notice when I sleep past the alarm.

I select an elegant forest green dress that hugs my curves with the hope of catching my husband's attention. If I can switch off his brain for just one moment, perhaps it will open up an opportunity to talk. I find him in the kitchen, hands gripping the bench, head bent over the sink. Defeated. I pause at the doorway. His shoulders lift slowly as if filling his lungs is excruciating.

"Kade?" I whisper.

At the sound, Kade's head whips towards me, spine straightening and face hard as granite.

"Ready?" His voice is so strong and steady I wonder if I imagined the scene I walked into. I'm still lost in bewilderment when he snaps up the keys and walks out.

***

"I'm so glad you could make it, dear." Evie flashes a warm smile and lands a kiss on my cheek.

"Kade, how handsome you are. I trust you're well? You've been avoiding my calls, so now I have you here, your lovely wife can find her way to the den and I can chat with you."

I leave them to it, snatching a look over my shoulder at the two of them. Evie's eyes worship her son, and I imagine her standing beside an older version of Kade. It's so obvious I wonder why I never saw it before. The love she had for Lash still burns through her with more force than she lets on. With him gone, all that love is projected on to Kade. Tears sting my eyes. How painful to love like that and lose.

I find Daryl and Antony in the den, a whiskey glass in hand.

"Brynn, darling. It's so good to see you! How is married life treating you?" Antony asks, his smile wide.

The chill of rejection stabs at my spine and twists in my stomach, but I force a cold smile.

"Wonderful thank you Mr Walker, the season has been kind and the farm is doing well."

Antony laughs. "Just call me Antony, Brynn. It gets too confusing when there's three Mr Walker's here at once."

No, just two, I think.

Daryl steps forward uncertainly, brushing his lips over my cheek.

"Brynn. You look incredible."

"Good to see you, Daryl. How's the takeover going?"

Daryl's favourite subject is his company, so we make ourselves comfortable and I try and focus. Daryl details each project, throwing in the worth of each one so often I start tuning out. I glance at the clock and realise I've been listening to Daryl for over an hour, and Kade still hasn't rejoined us. The discomfort slides into anxiety until I wait for Daryl to pause, and excuse myself.

I know these halls from the years Daryl and I would run through them squealing, Kade standing in the shadows watching but never included. Always the same, it seems. He would continue to follow despite Daryl demanding that he go away, that he wasn't wanted there. He never fought back, never even responded. Just…remained.

Why, Kade? Were you so lonely that you hovered, hoping to be included all those years?

I slow my steps as I near the bathroom. Every door in this place holds memories. The laundry where Daryl and I hid when we'd filled the dishwasher with seashells and Antony was out for blood. I feel my mouth lift at the memory.

How did Daryl and I escape punishment for that? The memory expands. Kade's voice telling Antony it was him. Passing Kade as we ran down the driveway as he washed Antony's car as punishment.

I come to a stop before the office, and another memory invades me. Daryl and I were rifling through his desk, so sure we'd find a gun like they did in the movie we just watched. Kade telling us urgently that Antony was coming and we had to get out.

In every memory of Daryl, Kade was the quiet hero. Our guard, our rescuer. In the shadows of everything we did were a watchful set of silver eyes watching over us.

Even now, stepping in to save the day when Daryl and I found ourselves in trouble with the wedding. My chest burns.

Oh, Kade, how I love you.

The realisation smashes its way through my ribs, and I clutch the door frame for support.

I love him.

I love Daryl too, but there's no comparison anymore. Maybe there never was, and like Kade said, I'm just realising what's been under my nose this whole time. Daryl is a warm blanket on a cold night, but the love I feel for Kade is everything. He intoxicates me. He belongs to me. I belong to him. I feel him dwelling between the beats of my heart, just like he once described. *How did I manage to miss that?*

I recognise the feeling now, that warmth radiating from inside me. It unfolds into my awareness like my childhood memories. *Kade. Kade.*

Kade. Because this isn't a new sensation. This is something that has walked with me through the long corridors of childhood that I forced myself to suppress beneath the promise Daryl and I made.

And I remember. Silver eyes watching from the shadows, watching me dance. Watching the very moment he came to life inside my heart.

CHAPTER 31

BRYNN

I love Kade. I'm in love with my husband.

I shake as I find the bathroom and wet my face, filling my lungs and calming my pulse.

I just need to make it through the dinner and then Kade and I will talk. We'll talk the way we should have done as soon as this marriage began, how we should have communicated in the months that followed. How we should be talking now.

And it's my fault. From the very start I behaved like a spoiled brat, too distracted by Daryl to focus on our wedding, and the vows I'm sure now that he meant. I embarrassed him before all his friends and family at the first opportunity, behaved appallingly when he gave up his lifestyle to accommodate me, and betrayed him by allowing Daryl to stab him in the back in his own home.

But here we are, still together. *It's not too late.*

I feel something shift in me, become lighter.

Things are going to change.

I smile as I pass the office door, but a sound stops me.

"No, Mum. There's no other way. The decision is already made and there's nothing anyone can do to change it."

Kade. My heart skips and a smile plays on my face. I love his voice. I lean closer.

"But sweetheart, what if you just talk to her? Maybe-" Evie's usually calm voice is tight.

Kade's tone is one filled with bitterness. "I said no, Mum. There's no point. Our divorce is already being drawn up. The faster it's done the better in my opinion. It's neither logical nor fair to be trapped in a loveless marriage."

What?

"But it makes no sense. It's not supposed to be like this. What if-"

"Mum, just leave it alone. It doesn't matter how you think it was supposed to go. She married me to help her family, and you already know my reasons. But it's time to accept the truth and move on. And yes, I am positive. I assume the papers will arrive in the mail by the end of the week."

My heart bottoms out.

Kade has spoken to someone about a divorce? Of course he has. He has his farm to think of. He's the one set to lose everything, since I came to him with nothing. Nothing but my heart, and I have no choice but to leave that with him when I go.

I lean my weight against the door, hollow and cold.

I didn't stop to think what Kade's feelings were towards me. But now it's crystal clear. This was Kade being a hero again for poor Daryl and Brynn who keep messing up. Nothing more.

My throat burns. I never even had the chance to show him the kind of wife I could be. Too caught up in my own trivial dramas, I was too selfish to see what I had until it was too late.

Too late. The divorce papers are already on their way.

I manage to stagger back to the den, numb and shivering.

"Are you alright, dear?" Antony asks with a frown.

"I could use a drink." I manage. I might as well, since there's nothing left to enjoy anyway.

"Allow me." Kade appears on the threshold, an eyebrow lifted at me.

I lick my dry lips, and he watches. Always watching. A smirk slides over his face.

"I, uh, don't think my parents stock the drink you like, but I might find something almost as palatable."

I can't help but blanch. Kade's handsome face, shuttered and empty, reminds me that he doesn't want me.

He hands me a tiny glass with a splash of red in it. Piercing eyes watch as I bring it to my lips. Before I take a sip, I let it drop away. I can't drink this. I'm pregnant. The pain tumbles over me again. He's so tuned into me, intuitive and attentive, that I'm scared he already knows. He's shown me how well he knows me every day we've been together. Knows how I like my coffee, leaves the old quad bike because he knows I prefer its softer ride. Puts a chair on the verandah so we can watch the sun rise. Installs music in the tractor so I can sing. Knows the moment it's time to stop dancing, walking through the door to take me home the moment fatigue creeps in.

I gape at him, seeing him clearly for the first time. He knows more about me than anyone else, but he doesn't love me.

"Thank you." I whisper. He nods briefly and finds a seat.

I steal glances at Kade while Daryl continues his monologue.

***

"Dinner is served."

We all rise from the den. In the dining room, Evie gestures for us to sit. I shoot her a look of gratitude and see her eyes shimmering with sadness.

"How are you filling your days, Brynn? The odour of the cows doesn't put you off?" Antony asks and I see Kade's grip tighten on his knife.

"On the contrary, Antony, the air is sweet. Especially after the hay is first cut. It's such a crisp smell. I'm always a little disappointed when I put the last one in the shed."

"Kade makes you work? When did he teach you to drive a tractor? Isn't that Kade's job?" Daryl glares at his brother.

"No, Daryl. You forget I'd do it for my father when I was little." I remind him.

I feel Kade's pain at the digs from his family, and I don't bother hiding the edge in my tone.

"Anyway, Kade doesn't make me do anything I don't want to do."

I'm so agitated by their blatant attacks on Kade, consumed by the need to stop the injustice against him.

Daryl smirks. "I see he hasn't managed to rein in that temper of yours."

I place my knife and fork gently on my plate and stare hard at him.

"I'm just saying that Kade and I allow each other freedom in our marriage. I work on the farm because that's what I want to do. Not because it's expected or demanded."

Kade wings an eyebrow, watching with interest as I do what I should have done all along; defend him.

Daryl clears his throat. "Can I have a private word to you, Brynn?"

Inwardly I roll my eyes, but I fold my napkin on the table and excuse myself. The moment we're out of sight, Daryl rounds on me.

"What are you trying to do in there, Brynn? This is hard enough for me, but to have you shove your marriage in my face is just plain cruel. I thought we had an understanding."

"You don't know Kade like I do. He's a good man, and doesn't deserve to be belittled." The words are there before I think them, but as soon as they're out, I feel their honesty. I may not have Kade, but I can fight for him.

His blue eyes shutter. He clenches his teeth, barreling on. "Have you even *been* to see anyone to discuss a divorce yet?"

"The papers are on their way already." I choke out. In the next couple of weeks. Less than fourteen days left before our fate is sealed.

There's a gleam in his eye as he nods.

"I love you, Brynn. Trust that this will work out."

Without another word he turns, almost crashing into Kade. Kade's eyes are gray with the storm raging behind it, his muscles so hard they threaten to tear through his suit. He growls, acid over gravel.

"What do you think you're doing, Little Brother?"

Daryl shrinks. "Just talking with Brynn, you know?"

"Oh, I *do* know, Daryl. I heard it all. What are you going to do now. After the divorce is finalised, what is your next step because you seem to have forgotten that even if we're not married, *you can't marry Brynn.*

You know you can't change that. So…what do you intend to do?"

He's like a predator, moving forward slowly like a lion stalking his prey.

"That's your fault!" Daryl blusters. "You're the one who teased me and taunted me until I added that virginity clause in."

My lungs empty.

Why would Kade have done that? Why would Daryl have agreed?

Daryl continued. "You knew for years that I was to marry Brynn, but here we are with that ridiculous clause meaning she married *you*!"

There's genuine anguish in Daryl's expression when he turns to me.

"It was supposed to be simple. You were meant to save yourself for me."

I almost choke. More abrasive than I intended, I retort "I *did*, remember? I gave myself to you at the party that night, then *you* were the one that pretended it never happened!"

Kade stiffens. He'd never asked who it was I slept with. Probably because he didn't care.

But I don't expect the shock that whitens Daryl's skin.

"Brynn, I was talking with Alice all night."

My mouth dries and I shake my head. *That's not right.*

"No. I saw you go inside to meet her, and I took her place. You *knew* it was me. You said my name. I *know* your voice."

Daryl blinks, frowns. Drags a hand over his face.

"No. I saw you arrive, I saw you dance, then when you disappeared, I asked Bella if she'd seen you. She said-" He blanched, his eyes suddenly burning into Kade. Kade swallows loudly.

"Bella said she just saw *Kade* leaving the house, and that she'd ask him if *he'd* seen you."

Kade remains immobile and I press a hand over my mouth, clutching my stomach. If Daryl was with Alice, and Kade had been in the house...

Kade? I meet his eyes then, swirling depths of steel and calamity. I see the blade of truth.

I gave my virginity to Kade, thinking it was Daryl.

Let me make you feel good, Brynn.

"You...*knew* I thought you were Daryl, and you slept with me anyway." I whisper. The flash of guilt is all I need.

Daryl's voice is pure venom.

"You piece of *shit*, Kade. You slept with her and tricked me to adding in that damned clause so I couldn't have her. You manipulative arsehole. Well, you're not getting her either, are you? There's the real pisser in this psychotic mess. You're getting divorced."

I don't wait around to hear more. I run through the house without another word, jump in the car and peel out of the driveway.

CHAPTER 32

KADE

I see the second she breaks. I never knew the kind of consuming agony that would come with violet eyes flashing with betrayal. But the blades are many, and penetrate deeply. I clutch the wall for support as Brynn hurtles past me, trying to find a way to get air into my lungs again.

Oh, Christ it hurts so bad.

I gasp, falling to my knees, fighting off the darkness that threatens to envelop me. Little by agonising little, oxygen finds its way into my lungs again.

My little brother looks down at me, his features twisted in pain.

I caused that.

I hurt him when all I ever wanted to do was protect him. He'll never forgive me. Tears fill my vision and he blurs and turns away.

"Kade?" Mum's beside me, frantically tugging, trying to pull me to my feet.

"Mum?" I croak. "What have I done?"

I knew Daryl liked her, planned to marry her. But I also knew they weren't meant to be together. I knew it because she was mine. Through the centuries, events unravelled in carefully choreographed sequences, each with its own specific purpose to create a moment in time where Brynn and I would exist in the same place. But somehow I poisoned it.

Instead of trusting that fate would find a way, I intervened. I only meant to kiss her that night. I'd planned for Daryl to find us together and realise she wasn't the girl for him, or see that what I felt for her was stronger than anything he did and give up his pursuit. But she was so sweet, so perfect that I couldn't stop if I wanted to.

But my evil didn't stop there. I made Daryl add that single line into that document to eliminate him from the equation permanently.

Brynn and me, written in the stars, carved in stone millennia ago by my ancestors. And I broke it. Not only broke it, but shattered the fragments until even the shards had turned to dust.

She's divorcing me, and I don't know if my lungs will keep working if she's not beside me.

CHAPTER 33

BRYNN

*H*e doesn't even bother to chase me down to explain. Kade slept with me as a twisted revenge attempt on his brother. How heartless is that? If I'd detected any hint of affection for me, his actions made it clear how deluded I was.

A little way down the road I pull over and the deluge of sobs drag at my chest and soaks my face.

All this time, and I never really knew who you were.

But *he* knew *me*. Intimately, utterly.

I feel so dirty.

I don't pay attention to where I'm going until I pull up at our house. *Kade's* house. I entertain the thought of going home to my parents to lick my wounds, or Bella's. But of their own accord, my feet carry me up the verandah stairs. The postman has delivered my album of Kade's father, but I can't bring myself to open it. I pick it up and drop it on the kitchen table with numb fingers.

When I enter his room, the scent of him assaults my senses, is ingrained in my heart, because now I gave my heart a voice it won't stay silent.

How could you do this to me, Kade?

I sit on his bed, blood thundering through my veins. He's not even here and my body sings for him.

I slide open his bedside drawer. A pile of photographs sit on the top of his stack of socks. The stains of fingerprints layer on the back, the frayed edges brown and soft.

I curiously take them out and turn them over.

A young boy with dark hair and silver eyes smiles adoringly down at a plump toddler, the blond haired baby version of Daryl grins up at his big brother in pure delight.

The following one is of Daryl, a little older, tears swelling his huge eyes. His face is gentle, like whatever troubled him has been soothed away. His chubby cheek is pressed hard into the neck of Kade, fat little fingers wrapped around his big brother's shoulder, thumb lingering between slack lips.

There's more. Daryl and Kade. Kade and Daryl. Always, that strong emotion between the two brothers so evident I could touch it.

Kade never hated Daryl.

He never stopped loving him.

More photos. Daryl glowing in delight as Kade hands him a rope. The rope is connected to a cow, a bright blue bow on her halter.

That old, lame beast, eating the grass without a purpose. She belonged to Daryl.

The emotion in the images shifts as I flip through. Less of Kade and Daryl together. More of just Daryl. They're taken from further away. Me as a young girl catching a ball Daryl had thrown. The last image is of immediately after I secured the ball. Daryl scowls at the photographer, lip curled in irritation.

Kade loves his brother, but at some point, Daryl stopped loving him back.

What would change so much that Kade would go to such lengths to hurt the brother he loves?

Evie's words spring to mind.

"Gypsies fiercely protect the object in their hearts beyond every limit."

Is that it, Kade? Have I been wrong all this time? Are you trying to protect your brother from me? Am I so unworthy of your brother you would sabotage his wedding to keep him from making that mistake?

I can't begin to process. So much pain weighing me down. I need to clear my head, and to do that, I know the only thing that might help. I call a taxi and change as I wait. Thigh length skirt, simple tank top. They don't work together, but I don't care. I just need to dance.

CHAPTER 34

KADE

S he's home!

Mum brings the car alongside Brynn's, leaving the engine running as I throw the door open.

"Kade, dear. Just talk to her. Please."

I close the door, my lungs stinging and dread stabbing into my chest. I manage a nod, but something doesn't feel right.

I can't feel her in the house. I can't feel her near me at all, but the car's here. Perhaps when I broke us, it broke every connection we were meant to have. I need that, I have to find a way to rebuild it.

"Talk to her!" Mum reiterates and crunches the gravel on her way out.

***

There's so much I need to tell her. All those unspeakable, inhuman things that I did, I did them out of a selfish need to have her. I feel sick about the cruel tricks I played to get where we are.

Is there any point now?

I saw the expression on her face. I felt the sound of her heartbreak when she found the truth in my eyes. Does she know I did it all for her?

"Brynn?" I choke out with broken lungs.

The darkness answers back with heavy silence. She's not here.

The sky cracks open with the roar of thunder, the world breaking apart and dying along with me. The lightning illuminates the room, a snapshot of my greatest fears.

Sitting in the centre of the kitchen table is a thick document that can only be Brynn's divorce papers. I'm too late. A pain rips through my chest and steals my breath.

It's really happening. She's leaving me. My heart, my blood, my breath. Gone. I clasp my chest, but the pain just grows, tearing a cry of pain from my throat. Everything I am is smashing to pieces inside of me.

I crumple to the floor. Alone. In the dark. The barbed wire cutting into my lungs tightens, and drawing breath is an agony that only grows, my hand digging frantically into my chest to stop the damned pain.

But with every inhale, my breathing shallows, and an ancient understanding washes over me.

I know the answer, now. Without Brynn, I can't breathe.

"Brynn." I gasp, because that's the only thing left to say.

CHAPTER 35

BRYNN

*A*s soon as I arrive I know I shouldn't be here. I don't even make it inside. I just stand, numb, in the car park as the taxi pulls away and feel the rain bite into my clothes. I watch them all inside, drinking, dancing and laughing, carrying on like it's just another day for them. It is. It's just me that's changed.

Last time I was here, I was sleeping with my husband, I was so damned happy, and I hadn't learned I was pregnant. How much things had changed. Now I find Kade has been manipulating everyone. I once thought Kade married me to get some kind of sick revenge on Daryl, but now it appears he married me to stop me from ruining Daryl's life, although how I would have done so remains a mystery.

I shake my head, anaesthetised and empty. Why didn't Kade just tell Daryl he'd slept with me at the party? All these years could have been avoided. Daryl would have been furious at me. Kade could have put a stop to it years ago. What did he stand to gain by letting it go as far as it did?

I slip my shoes off, needing to feel the mud ooze between my toes. There is something about it that anchors me to the earth, stopping my thoughts from floating away and growing too big, but it can't take away the pain in my heart. Is this heartbreak? Is this how painful it is, because it fills every cell in my body and aches so badly its hard to breathe.

I walk through the night, along the quiet road, the steady pace of my feet the only thing that keeps my focus.

Images flash painfully through my mind. Something had transpired between us the day we'd come together at the lookout; what was that about? That moment when it felt like Kade was completely bare before me, and it was so incredibly breathtaking. He let me see him, and I was too scared to open myself to him. Would it have changed anything between us if I'd opened myself for him?

"What was that?" I'd whispered when the world tore apart and it was just Kade and me.

"It was *us*, *pakvora*." He'd murmured, wonder heavy in the rumble of his voice, and he'd held me so tight as if he didn't want to let me go.

And every time I lay in his arms, those ghosts of his came to play. *You will hate me too, pakvora, when you find out what I've done.*

But still, he'd held me close, and I could feel his fear grow. Why would he sleep with me and hold me like that if he just wanted to protect Daryl from me?

I'm so dazed, I don't notice the car lights shine on me until they pull up behind me.

"Brynn?" A shrill, familiar voice breaks into my thoughts. "You'll catch your death of cold, Brynn. Come on, I'll take you home."

The passenger door swings open and I blink when the interior light blinds me. The smell of expensive leather fills the darkness, cutting through the rain. Sophistication and class hangs in air that lands on me and struggles to warm my shivering body.

I blink to allow my eyes to adjust, gasping when I recognise my rescuer.

"Alice?" She nods, her mouth grim and flat. She doesn't want me in her car. I take note of her high heels, the stylish stockings, the pencil skirt that looked so classy on curves much more subtle than mine. The skirts Daryl wanted me to wear. Her red satin shirt tucked in, and a neat, carefully arranged bun made her look like she was ready to walk the red carpet. Just like Daryl needs.

The jealousy that was fueled by the easy friendship with Alice and Daryl had foundations I should have seen. Daryl was always subtly suggesting I dress like her, do my hair like she does. I could never put my finger on it, but it made me feel sick inside. Sick with…?

With clarity I seek the truth. I felt sick with *rejection*. Not jealousy. It was my ego reacting to the snub, not my heart, because Daryl and I had an agreement, and when Alice was around I was forced to see he wasn't fully committed anymore. I was so caught up in the promise we'd made to each other that I didn't think it through. I didn't need to. I know Daryl is a man of his word, and he would keep his promises. No matter the cost.

The sleepless nights after our wedding plans dissolved…Daryl only lost sleep over guilt. He was never heartbroken.

And neither was I.

The laughter bubbles up before I can suppress it, and Alice's eyes narrow.

"I'm doing you a favour, Brynn. You don't have to be like that. I was never a threat to you. Nothing ever happened between Daryl and me. We'd meet up at parties and just talk. He wouldn't do that to you. *I* wouldn't do that to you."

I slide my eyes over her. The regimented determination in the lines of Alice's jaw makes me think nothing ever happened between her with *any* man.

I glance down the road, the rain thick and persistent in the headlights, and sigh. I want more than anything to walk through the rain until it fills my lungs and takes away the pain, but I have other responsibilities now. My palm touches my belly, and I'm sure I'm just imagining the faintest sensation of a tiny heart beating alongside mine, the way only gypsy blood can. I lower hesitantly into the car, trying to position my feet just so to stop too much mud damaging her interior.

"I'm sorry, Alice. I don't intend to seem nasty, I just realised something that should have been obvious to me for years." There's no pain in my realisation, though, only a strange relief that lightens my shoulders. I look at her again. Her classic beauty, her bright blue eyes, the quiet gentleness that hangs around her like the expensive perfume she wears. The predictability that fits so well with Daryl.

"Why did you pick me up, Alice? You could have just driven past, after all, you and I both loved the same man for years, and you have every reason to dislike me."

She gasps, and even that's done with class. I watch her fingers jump as she looks at me sideways.

"I couldn't just let you catch a cold, Brynn. And why do you think I love Daryl?"

I smile, letting my head fall back into the soft leather.

"Because the only thing more obvious than you loving Daryl, Alice, is the fact that Daryl has been in love with you for years, and I've been the fool who failed to notice until now."

I watch shock widen on her face.

"You're wrong. I've spent my life listening to how one day you and Daryl would be married. I've held him while he told me how Kade stole you from him. And you can't tell me you don't love Daryl."

It's all so clear, listening to Alice, watching her struggle to understand what I'm saying. It's deeply scored into the subtle bitterness of her recalling Daryl's grief over a woman who wasn't her. Even when it stung, she took the high road.

The delirium of a heart set free makes my head so light, my epiphany has me grinning.

Wide. Honest. Liberating.

"I do love Daryl, Alice. I've spent the last few months wracking my brain, trying to work it out, and you've just shown it to me. He's been my best friend since we were kids. I've loved him for so long it's hard to know when it started. But I love him as a *friend*. As a brother. Nothing more. And if he stepped back for just one moment, he'd realise that he loves me the same way."

She doesn't say a word, but I see hope stir in her straightened spine.

As we near home, I break into her thoughts with genuine emotion.

"Alice, you're a good person. You really are perfect for Daryl. I hope, when the craziness passes, we can be friends. But right now, I need you to pull over. I need to speak to my husband, and you should be there for Daryl. He needs you."

On an impulse, I lean over and kiss her cheek. She stares at me, bewildered, as I climb out into the rain.

I pause before I close the door, and leave her with my blessings.

"When you tell him you love him, assure him that he's no longer held by his promise. Tell him I promised, too, but I'm the one breaking it. He's free to follow his heart, just like I am."

When I close the door, her car idles indecisively for a long time, but as I walk away I hear the engine rev, slowly making the turn towards Daryl's house. I smile.

As my feet finally land on the driveway, my tears begin again. I don't know what I will do, or say, but I mourn for the route of pain and regret we chose to get to this point.

The house is in darkness, and I frown, wondering if Kade is even here.

But I feel him, the echo in my heart that tells me he's inside. It's the first time I don't fight the pull. I climb the stairs to the veranda, knowing he's only a few strides away.

My fingers tremble on the door knob, a flood of trepidation almost overwhelming me. I know he wants to divorce me, but I can't go through life like Alice and Daryl, loving each other but never finding the courage to say it, letting life disrupt what's meant to happen naturally. I love Kade, and even if he doesn't want me, I need to say the words.

I swallow loudly, the door swinging open just as the lightning bites through the room. Kade sits in the corner of the kitchen, head buried in his arms.

"Kade?" I whisper, and his head jerks up.

His wet eyes carry a torment that fills his entire body. His slack mouth hangs on the pain. His skin burns and gleams with the effort of battling an invisible agony, his chest heaving too rapid and shallow. I feel it in my blood, his hurt, and everything I planned to say escapes in a whimper.

I drop to the floor before him, breathless from my heartache.

"Why are you here?" He grates out, his husky voice raw and broken from elusive oxygen.

I draw in a painful breath and stare into the silver pools that live in my soul. No matter what awful things happen after this, I still need to say it.

CHAPTER 36

KADE

Her eyes glow, more open and honest than I've ever seen them. But she'll never allow herself to find the truth that hovers forever out of my reach. Her heart. That's all I need, and she's too damned stubborn to see it. Now it's too late. How can she possibly find it inside her to look past the deception I've dragged her into. I've destroyed every hope I had of holding Brynn again, and with it, I've also dashed all hope of my brother forgiving me.

"Because I need to know why you did it." She whispers, her voice shaking.

Every cell in my body goes taut. I stab her with my scrutiny.

She stares at the floor, her heart slamming so hard against her skin that I can almost see it. I can feel it. It thunders in my own chest, my heart screaming around hers.

"I don't know if it will make any difference, Kade, but I need to find some kind of reason in this mess. I need you to talk to me, be honest.

And I need to be honest with you."

Honesty? The burn of truth scorches tracks through my already desecrated heart. Because truth is terrifying, and full of weakness and regret. My gaze lands on the parcel on the table, the first rays of sun like a spotlight of doom. The divorce papers are already here. She already knows most of it. There is no greater pain she can inflict upon me than the fate that already awaits me.

"I need to hold you, *pakvora*." I manage.

Her eyes shimmer, violet integrity stroking me.

"I…I need that, too, Kade."

And the truth sets us free. The moment it's past her lips, I drag her into me, wrap my arms around her and let my tears fall in her hair, my frame convulsing around hers in the darkness.

And ever so slowly, the air begins its burning return to my lungs.

***

I'm raw and carved out, the agony inside finally manageable. She came back to me. I loosen my grip on her as dawn creeps in but her hands still clutch at my back.

"Look at me, Brynn." I whisper into her hair.

Her head shakes. "If I do I'll have to let go, and I can't do that."

The ache that is Brynn throbs. "You don't have to let go, if you don't wish to, *pakvora*."

Her hands still hold tight, but she sits back, slowly lifting her swollen eyes to mine, fear I understand swirls behind them.

"Can I talk, *pakvora*? Can you allow me to explain all the bad things I've done, and give me a chance to fix this?"

She dips her head so slightly, but my exhale explodes.

She'll listen to me. I wet my dry lips, and pull her close.

"I knew you were mine the day I watched you dance in the rain. I can't even explain it, really. I know there is no sense in it, but it was like you suddenly came into focus, and from that moment on, you were the only clear image I could see. Then Daryl got it in his head you were supposed to be his around the same time, and after a few arguments, I stopped talking to Daryl about it. After all, we were all still kids, and I knew for him it was a phase that would pass.

"Only, as the years mounted, it didn't pass. I died a little inside watching something blossom between you, hoping you'd notice me, or that Daryl would find someone else and it would die a natural death.

"I never wanted to hurt either of you. But when I saw you at the party, I saw the way you looked at Daryl and knew I had to do something. Please believe me, *pakvora*, that it was my intention only to have Daryl catch you in my arms. I figured that would be enough to put an end to it. But one taste was all it took to be lost in you. I needed you more than I needed to breathe, and you were everything to me. Your surrender was so perfect, and you consumed every last shred of reason I had. I can't tell you how much it decimated me, knowing you were only there with me because you thought I was Daryl.

"And the guilt! I deceived you, and I should have come clean right then, but I was so scared you'd hate me, and I couldn't live with that. So I kept quiet. But the fire I planted in your heart burned stronger for Daryl because of my deception, and it almost broke me. That's when I tricked Daryl into that stupid stipulation in the papers that held the key to his future.

"That was when I knew he couldn't have you. But you still never noticed me. It was as if you never saw me, and every time I tried to approach you, something always intervened. I am not a man who can indulge in small talk, and I've been on the receiving end of enough strange looks to know I couldn't survive one from you. So there was nothing I could fall back on to bring your focus back to me.

"When the wedding was announced, I panicked. Antony discovered that you weren't able to fulfil your part in Daryl's contract, and I withdrew my own shares from your parent's farm to blackmail you to marry me, instead."

Her wide eyes stare, her lips slacken in shock, and it's my turn to stare at the ground. She wriggles in my arms, but I tighten my hold. I can't let her go, but it's all so futile. Admitting my deceit.

"I should have left it in the hands of fate, *pakvora*, and I held out as long as I could, but I've come to believe only in what the world has shown me. Everything that touches my heart slips through my fingers in time, no matter how tightly I hold it. Nothing good has come to me and stayed by my side, and I was too damned scared to trust that you and I would be any different. Everything I did was a selfish move to bring you closer to realising it was us that was always meant to be together.

"I did it knowing you'd hate me, and so would my little brother if it all came out, and every day I wrestled with myself, knowing that it was inevitable that it would. I can't even understand how I could do those things, but I know in my heart I'd do them all over if it meant I could hold you again."

She's so still in my arms that my skin hurts. Her voice is careful and low.

"I...don't understand. I *know* who you are. You are a man of scruples, Kade. Deception, corruption, manipulation...none of these are you, yet you've done them all. I mean, my parents? If I had declined to marry you, would you have ruined them?"

My heart stutters. I want to say no, but so many things I've already done were out of character.

"I don't know, Brynn." I murmur.

She falls silent. My little hellcat, full of fire and spark, is still. I hold her to me, my heartbeat reaching for hers, desperate to hold whatever I can of her for as long as I can.

Finally, with a deep breath, her sweet dulcet tone floats to my ears.

"I never asked who you were, Kade. The night I thought I was meeting Daryl...I went there knowing Daryl was waiting for Alice, and just assumed it was him. I can't put that on you. Maybe in some way I did know, because try as I might, I couldn't seem to picture Daryl making me feel what you did. I guess I ignored the signs, too. My parents, that was an awful thing to do. I...I don't know what to do with that right now. But that clause that Daryl added, he did that himself. I don't know how you managed to convince him to do that, but short of holding a gun to his head or physically threatening him-"

She looks to me, eyebrow arched. I shake my head. I didn't threaten Daryl.

"...Then that's his own stupid fault. Not yours."

Relief surges through me. I spent so much time beating myself up over it that it never occurred to me that Daryl could be responsible for his own actions. Daryl chose to go ahead with it, even though I planted the seed. Daryl.

My throat tightens, but I need to know.

"Daryl...you love him?"

A hint of a smile lifts her lips.

"Yeah." She sighs, and my lungs lock.

Reaching tentatively, her hands cup my face, the firm pressure on my jaw forcing me into her focus.

"I love my *friend*, Kade. It took me way too long to work it out, but I love him like a brother."

My blood hums. Her slender fingers drag slow circles on my forearm.

Do I dare take it as a sign?

"Brynn, can we talk this through some more before we commit to a divorce?"

My voice cracks open on my desperate hope and the caustic word that could destroy it.

Her breath rushes out. Her fingers stop circling so her nails could grip my arm.

"Yes." A broken whisper that sends my heart to the clouds.

"Let's get rid of it now. Please *pakvora*? I can't stand to have it near us."

Reluctantly, I climb to my feet, still holding tight to my girl, fighting to get feeling back into numb limbs. She frowns up at me, following my gaze to the table where the package sits like my last rights.

"Kade, those aren't divorce papers. You were the one who organised those. I heard you talking to your mum, telling her they were on their way."

Confused, I drag a hand down my face. "No, Brynn. I never even spoke to a solicitor. I heard you and Daryl discussing it, then the bank called to say you'd pulled enough cash out of our account to cover a high end solicitor. I was just waiting for the documents to arrive…"

We stared at each other like idiots in the morning light. Neither of us ever wanted a divorce.

"Then what was the money for? I don't understand."

She winds her arms around my waist and presses her head against my chest.

"It was for your birthday present, just like this package here is, too! I know it's early, but can I show you?"

She's buzzing, her body warm and vibrating with the return of her fire. But there is more I need to tell her. One more thing I need to reveal to her so I can be completely clean.

"Pakvora," I whisper into her ear, "There is one more thing I must tell you. I was crazy with my need to keep you with me. I was desperate to do anything to tie you to me. I'm so sorry, *pakvora,* but each time we made love, I hoped you would fall pregnant and you would be forced to stay with me."

I close my eyes, feeling her body tremble with quiet rage.

"Do you not think I could bring up a baby on my own, Kade? Do you think I wouldn't be able to do that without you?"

"No, Brynn. You don't need me. I know that, but I was clutching at straws. I intended to convince you to stay with me in the best interest of our baby."

She shoves me from her and my skin cries at the loss of her touch. Hands on hips, chin high and defiant she glares at me.

CHAPTER 37

BRYNN

*K*ade never wanted to divorce me?

He wanted me since we were kids. He waited for me for so long to come to him, and when I didn't he intervened.

He manipulated, he deceived, he sold his soul for me, and damn if that level of passion and dedication doesn't turn me on. Sure, we need to talk about how he caused my parents distress, but all I can think about now is Evie's words.

"Gypsy men love with their whole hearts. Unless you have experienced the love of a gypsy, you do not truly know love. Everything else is a poor substitute. They are consumed by it and they fiercely protect the object in their hearts beyond every limit. They are destined to love only one woman in their lifetime, and their need to fight for their relationship exists even if there is not a battle to begin with, because if they lose the one they love, their heart dies, and so do they."

Everything Kade did was driven by his need to have me. But I need to hear it.

"Tell me, Kade. I need to know if you love me."

His exhale explodes and he slams me into his chest.

"Christ Brynn, I love you completely with every part of me. My heart does not beat for you, *pakvora*. You are my heart. I always felt like I would die without you. Now I know it to be true."

He loves me.

"Then would you quit being so hard on yourself, Kade? You *do* understand that it takes *two* people to make love. Two people who are *both* responsible for contraception. Not just you. It was my decision as much as yours to use protection, and now it's *our* joint decision whether to have me bring our baby up, or if we want to do it together, as a family."

I feel the moment he freezes, that sweet moment when he registers what I've said.

His fingers bite into my arms. He drops so his silver orbs are level with mine, his gaze drilling into mine.

"*Pakvora.* Are you telling me..?" His swallow echoes and my lips answer him with an upward lilt.

His arms circle my waist and he spins me around in the kitchen, smiling so wide that sexy dimple doesn't end.

"Brynn, you've made me the happiest man alive." His eyes shimmer, and he's never looked as beautiful as he does right now, his heart open and full of me.

"Kade, I've loved you for longer than I realised. I'm so sorry it took so long to work out Daryl wasn't the one for me, but I never wanted to lead you on, either. I want to stay here, with you, and spend my life showing you how easy it is to love you."

"Say it again, Brynn." He pleads roughly, a stray tear sliding down his face.

"I love you, Kade." I smile, and his lips slam into mine. That passion, that hunger that saturates me. He was right. I crave it as much as he does. It draws us together. I burn as he rucks up my shirt, but he's caught fire. In a flurry of limbs and clothes, he pushes me into the wall, my legs wrapping around his hips to pull him closer.

"I love you, Brynn." He rasps, his eyes lock on mine.

My mouth drops as I feel that stretch and burn of my husband sliding inside me, until the pressure of him nudging the end of me causes me to buck.

"Look at me, Brynn. Watch. This is *us*." He whispers.

His eyes deepen into oceans of silver, and he shows me everything. He shows me what words are too weak to convey. His very soul shimmers and sparkles with ethereal perfection.

"Oh, Kade…" I gasp, in awe of the man inside me.

In every cell and nerve, something floats to the surface of me, and I surrender it to him. It unfurls, so much bigger than me. I feel him dip his heart into mine, his soul weaving through mine. I feel it all. Kade is my marrow. He's my blood and my air. We've been written in stone since the beginnings of time, and now we are together.

He moves inside me and I know he is everything. He growls at my nails, I moan as his teeth mark me. We move our hips, the ancient dance that sends us both to the stars.

Us.

***

"Are you going to show me this gift, or are you going to make me stare at it for another six weeks?" He grumbles, even as he dips his swollen lips for another taste.

"Hmmm…it might be a good idea to work on your patience…"

I giggle at his growl, handing the package to him as he places my coffee in front of me.

"Happy early birthday, Kade." I plant a kiss on his temple, inhaling his woody scent.

He tears the paper with a single swipe, shoving it out of the way urgently as he recognises the picture on the front cover.

"Dad?" He breathes in wonder.

He fingers the image, the cover photo where Lash stands with the belt above his head. I thread my hand through his hair as he turns the pages slowly.

He reads all the articles, though how he can distinguish words through his veil of tears baffles me.

"This means so much, Brynn. He was a fading memory, and you brought him back to me. I...thank you."

"It's all on the Internet, Kade, and I can find more. He looks so much like you."

"Maybe I shouldn't be so much of a dinosaur and learn how to use it."

I laugh. He is definitely his mother's son.

"There's a second part to your birthday present, but for this one, we need to take a walk. I found that on the Internet too."

He slides his fingers through mine. The simple act of walking hand in hand with Kade tugs so hard at my heart. He's mine. The grass has perked back up as if nobody entered the shed so long ago. I watch as Kade's muscles dance as he yanks open the doors, forcing them wide on stiff, rusted hinges.

I'd put a tarp over it, driving stakes in around it to keep the tarp from brushing against it, so all Kade can see is a huge, tarp coloured oblong. I quiver in excitement as he grabs hold of the tarp and rips it back. The midnight blue shines in the dull light, tail lights faded a little with age.

"Oh, *pakvora*!" His tone tight, his movements hasty in his hurry to reveal it.

"It's a Mustang. Same colour and year as Dad's. How did you even find this? These are so rare, and it's exactly like my old one."

He presses his head excitedly against the driver's side window, staring into the car. His hand slides over the panels with a reverence that makes me smile. I shiver in pleasure as I explain the transaction, watching his handsome features glow in awe.

"The man I bought it from never drove it. He was a sweet old guy. Told me how he'd been looking for one of these all his life. When this one came up for sale, he knew he had to buy it, but when he got there, he almost passed on the sale. He said he'd been haunted all these years by the shattered tears of the little boy who watched it go. He said he felt so guilty for taking it from the child that he parked it in his shed and couldn't bring himself to touch it."

Kade was only half listening, but he tore his gaze from the car long enough to settle a sharp flash of hope on me. He wastes no more time, stumbling to his knees at the front grill of the car.

There, just a little off centre was a small dent, one made by a distraught boy fighting to hold on to the last physical reminder of his father.

E P I L O G U E

KADE

*B*rynn is beginning to stir. She's curled into me, the way she does every night, her hand resting on the arm I drape over her waist. I inhale her.

If there's one thing I love more than my wife's scent, is the smell of me on her. She's mine. Heart, body and soul. Finally.

"Morning." She murmurs sleepily, her eyes still sealed.

"Mmmhmm." I smile.

I've been doing a lot of that lately. There's a lot to smile about. My wife loves me, I have a baby on the way, and the memories of my father, and a time where I was one man's entire world, have been sharpened by the pictures Brynn gave me.

I drag on my jeans, smirking as Brynn's eyes crack open and explore me with a hunger I understand. Her hand pokes out, and she presses an invisible button.

"Rewind!" She commands, hooded eyes waiting for me to undress.

"Coffee?" I grin, and she groans.

"Fine, but you owe me one." She mutters.

She staggers into the kitchen wearing short shorts and one of my shirts as I slide her mug across the bench at her.

"Oh, the sunrise is going to be incredible." She breathes, and I follow her outside. I'll always follow her.

I fill my lungs with the sweet air of our farm and sit beside my girl and watch the sun rise, her warm body curled against mine.

I'm in heaven.

***

Daryl arrives as I'm polishing the damaged bonnet of my Mustang. I tense up instinctively when Brynn walks over to him, bare feet on the gravel.

She kisses his lips and throws her arms around him, and I force myself to relax. He's not a threat any more, though why he's here is a mystery. We haven't spoken in months, the last time being when Daryl found out I'd slept with Brynn at the party all those years ago.

I polish the dent, teeth clenched and turn my back on them.

The crunch of gravel behind me has my heart sinking. I don't know what's coming, but I don't like it.

"Kade?" Daryl's voice, soft and hesitant.

I lock my jaw and glance up. His eyes flick between mine and the ground.

"Can I talk to you?"

My stomach churns. My baby brother, the missing piece of my heart. I can't say no to him. I never could.

"Sure." I huff, and feel that familiar guilt when he flinches.

I shake my head, angry at myself.

"There's a couple of chairs in the shed. We can talk there." I lower my voice to a less threatening tone.

The silence stretches awkwardly as I wipe off a chair and sit myself on the dusty one.

Daryl sits stiffly, lifting his face to mine.

My heart twists at the sadness shining from his blue eyes, and it's all I can do to refrain from pulling him into my arms and taking his sorrow away like I used to.

But that time is gone.

"Kade. I'm so sorry." He sighs, and my head rears back.

"What for, Daryl? What are you sorry for?"

Daryl's hand slides through his hair, sending his perfect style into disarray.

"After…after I found out what happened at the party, I was so angry at you. I wished you were dead, Kade, for ruining my life, for destroying my chance at being happy."

I feel his words like a blade. The remorse of hurting him is a pain that never heals. I clench my jaw against the sting, but Daryl keeps talking.

"I spent days cursing you, telling Dad just how cruel you were. But then I noticed the way he would bring it up again and again, just when I was beginning to calm down, he'd remind me how you hurt me. So I stopped talking to him about it. He became relentless, forcing me to revisit that anger. Then he tried to tell me that you'd been planning this for years with Brynn, and that you were laughing at me."

"That's not true! I would never-"

My little brother silences me with a wave.

"I *know* you didn't. And I know you *wouldn't*, Kade, but I saw in that moment what exactly went wrong between us. It was Dad. I remember sitting in his lap after we'd come home from that storm at Brynn's. I loved him, Kade. I worshipped him and told him everything.

"So I told him how my big brother shared a secret with me on the way home, how you looked at me with soul wide open and announced that one day you would marry Brynn. I was so excited for you. But Dad told me that I was the one who was meant to marry her, and over the weeks, months and years that followed, he convinced me that she was mine and that you wanted to steal her away from me, because you dedicated your life to making mine miserable."

Air hisses out from between my teeth and my fists curl.

"But I remember now, and I'm so damned sorry that I let him make me think so badly of you. It's I that have done you wrong, Kade, and I had to say it, even if you can't forgive me for putting you through that."

I'm off my chair in a second. Daryl springs to his feet and throws his arms over his head, his eyes squeezed closed, but I ignore it.

I throw my arms around my little brother's back and hold him so tight he struggles to breathe, my emotion causing my voice to falter.

"I never stopped loving you, Daryl, you're my little brother and I'd do anything for you. Anything except let go of Brynn. I couldn't do that. I'm so sorry, but I just couldn't."

I feel his hands on my back return my embrace and I keep holding, not wanting to let him go.

Finally, he pulls back, and I'm transported back to childhood. His blue eyes are shining and clear. The sadness is gone, the bitterness too, replaced by a light I haven't seen in them in years.

"You always knew how to make it better, Kade." He smiles, then takes a deep breath.

"You did me a favour, too. While I love Brynn as a sister-in-law, there's a woman who's been around almost as long. One who lives in my heart the way Brynn lives in yours."

I shift my attention to where my wife stands in a tight embrace with another woman I've known for years. Alice wipes her eyes and Brynn laughs, knitting the beginnings of a friendship that will bind our families back together. The way they were always supposed to be.

I can't help the shudder of emotion that catches me.

"Little Brother, you have no idea how pleased I am that you have found happiness with such a kind woman. She fits you well, Daryl."

He slaps me on the back and offers me a sly grin.

"...And she's a virgin."

ACKNOWLEDGMENTS

My husband is in every one of my books. He's the man I love with my whole heart, with the same dedication Archer showed Rain in Credence, and with the intensity of Kade's love for Brynn. He's my grounding, my muse and my greatest supporter. With a husband like him, how could I not write romance? As always, I thank him from the bottom of my soul for being exactly who he is. My greatest treasure.

Again. Still. Forever. Sharyn Constantine, Katie Dunn and Dora Kambouris - you are my past, my present and my future. My safe place to land and the solitary light in my darkest hours. I'm who I am today because of you.

To my invaluable beta readers, Sue Constantine, Christine Poulter and Emily Slade, I love how my story develops with your insights.

Oh, my esteemed editor, Shaz, how I adore your work, and the unwavering determination to push me to produce the best work I'm capable of. You help me grow. You are Rowena Spark as much as I am.

Never forgetting my readers, a very special thanks to you. I hope you loved Kade and Brynn as much as I do. They are both such strong, flawed characters, but they still got there in the end. I'd love to hear from you, so tell me what you think, ask a question, or send pictures of what inspires you.

Please visit me at www.rowenaspark.com and follow me on Facebook: RowenaSparkAuthor

ALSO BY ROWENA SPARK

STAND ALONE ROMANCE

Her Whole Heart

SCARS OF CREDENCE SERIES

Credence

Prudence (Release 2020)

Reticence (Release 2021)

CPSIA information can be obtained
at www.ICGtesting.com
Printed in the USA
LVHW051735021120
670484LV00006B/1566

9 780648 908920